Sex in the Office
A Wicked Words erotic short-story collection

Other Wicked Words erotic short-story collections

Wicked Words
More Wicked Words
Wicked Words 3–10

Sex in the Office
A Wicked Words short-story collection
Edited by Kerri Sharp

BLACK LACE

Wicked Words stories contain sexual fantasies.
In real life, always practise safe sex.

This edition published in 2005 by
Black Lace
Thames Wharf Studios
Rainville Road
London W6 9HA

Typeset by SetSystems Limited, Saffron Walden, Essex
Printed and bound by Mackays of Chatham PLC

ISBN 0 352 33944 6

Contents

Introduction

If this is your first *Wicked Words* book, then you are in for a real treat! We have published 10 *Wicked Words* anthologies so far, but this is our first themed collection – so it's just that little bit exciting. How much thinking about sex and flirting goes on in your office? Probably more than you think. Perhaps you are even in that racy 10 per cent of people who has actually made out in their place of work. It doesn't always go on at the office party while drunk. Under (or over) desks, behind filing cabinets, in stationary cupboards – or even in the boss's hallowed room – many of us manage to take time out of a hectic schedule to snatch a few moments' illicit pleasure with a colleague.

A wandering hand under the table during a meeting can certainly brighten up a post-mortem analysis of the year's financial report. And you'd never have thought it, looking at the quiet one from accounts ... it certainly cheers up the working day, although, if you do go all the way, you have to remember not to emerge giggling from the loos at the same time.

The characters in these stories go a good deal further than most of us would in real life, however. In Hannah Brophy's *Learning Procedures*, Miss Carlson, the foxy new temp, had got her boss's number. The officious and perfectionist Kevin soon gets his comeuppance good and proper. Ooh, and doesn't he deserve it!

It's not just temps, but lady bosses, cleaners and security guards who get real dirty in that familiar, anonymous environment of the over-heated, thickly carpeted, softly lit modern office block – stripping off and swivelling about in the boss's leather chair, or fantasising about some very naughty ways to reach a solution to a union dispute. There are also other places of work loosely based around 'the office' – such as Tulsa Brown's radio station in the *All Night*, and Angel Blake's customs search room in *Strip Search*. There is a rich diversity of tone and voice to the characters in this collection. I'm sure I've met Jan Bolton's filthy-minded Lord X of *The Tipping Point* somewhere before! And Hallie – perched on the edge of a Manhattan skyscaper in *Precipitous Passions* – is straight out of a ruder version of *Sex and the City*.

Who needs a bedroom, anyway?

Kerri Sharp (Ed.)

Want to write for Wicked Words?

We are publishing three more collections in 2005 – made in response to our readers' most popular fantasies. They are *Sex on Holiday*, *Sex at the Sports Club* and *Sex in Uniform*. The closing date for *Sex on Holiday* has passed now, but if you want to submit a sizzling, beautifully written story for the other two volumes, here are the criteria:

- Your short story should be 4,000-6,000 words long and not published anywhere in the world – websites excepted.
- Thematically, it shoud be written with the Black Lace guidelines in mind.
- Ideally there should be a 'sting in the tale' and an element of dramatic tension, with oodles of erotic build-up.
- The story should be about more than 'some people having sex' – we want great characterisation too.

We are obliged to select stories that are technically fault-less and vibrant and original – as well as fitting in with the tone of the series: upbeat, dynamic, accent on pleasure etc. Our anthologies are a flagship for the series. We pride ourselves on selecting only the best-written erotica from the UK and USA. The key words are: diversity, surprises and faultless writing.

Competition rules will apply to short stories: you will hear back from us about your story only if it has been successful. We cannot give individual feedback on short stories as we receive far too many for this to be possible.

Sex in the Sports Club – deadline for stories end Jan 05
Sex in Uniform – deadline for stories end April 05

If you want to find out more about Black Lace, check our website, where you will find our author guide-lines and more information about short stories. Its at www.blacklace-books.co.uk

Alternatively, send a large SAE with a first-class British stamp to:

Black Lace Guidelines
Virgin Books
Thames Wharf Studios
Rainville Road
London W6 9HA

Learning Procedures
Hannah Brophy

Kevin Stoddard fumed as the elevator jetted its way to the twenty-seventh floor. His secretary, Miss Darcy, had quit exactly four weeks ago. Since that time, HR had managed to find him three temporaries, each worse than the last. Salvation from the last empty-headed blonde had come from an unexpected out-of-town trip. He didn't have to see her or put up with her gum smacking for the last three days of last week.

So, what had HR done? Hired Miss Darcy's replacement the minute he was gone. And then let the incompetent temp train her. Last Thursday's email had informed him a new secretary would begin on Friday.

Of all the dunderhead moves: did HR understand nothing about hiring underlings? Starting a secretary on a day when the boss was out of town just set a bad example. The woman was here to work, but her first day had been spent goofing off, because he wasn't there to take charge and set the pace.

Also, and this really had him steamed, he was entitled to final approval of any new hires for him. Probably it hadn't helped that he had called the head of HR, Mrs Jacobs, a bumbling jackass to her face. But the giggling temp in week three had set his teeth on edge.

All this had rained down on his head simply because he refused to authorise a year-end bonus for Miss Darcy, to encourage her to work harder this year. Instead, the ingrate had found a better-paying job and quit with minimum notice.

Kevin scowled at his fellow workers as he made his way down the corridor to his large corner office. His colleagues scurried out of his way. He worked long and hard hours for that corner office; was it too much to expect that his staff would work hard, too?

As he rounded the corner, his pace slowed. Rising above a low file drawer were two very long, very shapely legs that ended at a charmingly curvy rear end. She wore a flared floral-print skirt, dark hose and three-inch heels. Very nice. Maybe HR had gotten something right.

He paused, momentarily enjoying the view, but then she straightened. Her back curved upwards until she reached her full height. Neon blue streaked her short dark hair. When she turned to face him, he noticed three earrings in her left eyebrow and at least six hoops in each ear plus a peacock feather that dropped from the lowest hole almost to her shoulders. The blue in the feather was an amazing match with the colour of her hair. Lord, have mercy.

This was a law office, not a strip club. What was HR thinking?

'Katie Carlson.' She offered her hand and automatically he shook it. 'Your new assistant.'

Blue hair? Facial piercing? Assistant?

'Miss Carlson, is it?' He hastily dropped her hand. 'I need to make a call, then we'll talk about what needs to be done.' What had those idiots in HR done to him this time?

Impatiently, he dialled Mrs Jacobs' extension.

'Hello, Kevin. I thought I'd be hearing from you this morning.' Mrs Jacobs' cheery voice greeted him. The fact that he hadn't had to introduce himself reminded him of how much he disliked caller-ID.

Each time Mrs Jacobs called him by his given name, his

stomach rolled. How many times had he told her he preferred to be called Mr Stoddard? Mrs Jacobs would nod and then answer with something like, 'Of course, Kevin.' And go on with whatever point she was attempting to make.

'I just met my new secretary,' Kevin announced, preparing to launch into his diatribe.

'It's the twenty-first century, Kevin. They are called assistants now.'

'Never mind that. Did you actually look at the girl before you hired her? She's fifteen and has blue hair!'

'Twenty-one, not fifteen, and the colour of her hair, I believe, is referred to as indigo.'

'I. Do. Not. Want. A. Secretary. With. Indigo. Hair. Do I make myself understood?'

'I'm not deaf and neither, I'm betting, is she. Miss Carlson has the best credentials I've ever seen. She should please even your impossible standards. Plus she already thinks of you as her grandfather.'

'Her grandfather? I'm forty-three, not eighty-three.'

'Really? Well, I mentioned that you preferred to have your *assistant* read her work to you when you were tired. Apparently, she did the same for her grandfather. If you run this one off, Kev, you're on your own.'

Kevin slammed down the phone and paced the area behind his desk trying to regain his equilibrium. His mind raced. This would make him the laughing stock of the office. But if he fired her, he would be stuck with incompetent temps who couldn't even file, much less type. No, he had to make the best of this, until he could find the secretary he wanted.

'Miss Carlson –' he spoke through the intercom '– please come in.'

Katie Carlson entered the office and placed a cup of hot coffee on his desk. She did not sit, but rather stood to the right of his desk in front of the floor-to-ceiling windows.

The daylight behind her highlighted her sheer skirt from the rear, allowing him to see the details of her slender thighs.

For a brief moment, he lost track of his train of thought. He took a sip of coffee to discover it was exactly as he liked it – one sugar, extra hot.

'You've come at a bad time. I've four weeks' worth of typing that hasn't been done, so we may have to work evenings to get caught up.'

Katie nodded and shifted her stance, but, as she did so, her pen dropped and she turned to pick it up. Kevin found himself mesmerised by the shadowy portrait of her round buttocks.

He realised she was speaking. 'What?'

'I asked, which files are most important?'

'That stack over there.' He gestured towards the empty credenza. 'Shit! Someone's reorganised my office; I'll never find anything.' But, as he looked around the room, he realised it was neater than he ever left it. This was a disaster in the making.

'Done.' She moved to the credenza, opened the doors, removed a large stack of files and placed them on his desk.

'Done? What do you mean done?' he asked, relieved that his work hadn't been lost, but near hysterical that someone had worked on his files without his supervision. 'No one is supposed to touch anything unless I tell them.'

The look she gave him strongly indicated what she thought of that. He scowled at her and flipped open the first file trying to ascertain how much work it would take to correct her mistakes.

Katie stood next to him, close enough for him to smell her sweetness. His lower body twitched. He must need a woman badly if a waif with blue hair could turn him on.

Katie removed each file as he finished. Unless asked directly, she said nothing. He flipped through the file and found neatly typed documents. Begrudgingly, he was impressed. He flipped to the front and noted that she had painstakingly detailed the work that had been done. Her clear notes enabled him to see what needed to happen next.

Stunned, he sifted through file after file. Of course, he hadn't read her work yet, and that would probably be disappointing. But she was amazingly bright and well organised. Maybe he could convince her to part with the blue hair and earrings, even if just the ones in her eyebrow.

'You've done this before, haven't you?' he finally asked.

'Yeah.'

Quite the little conversationalist. He watched her profile as she worked her way through the files. Her puffy scarlet lips and large blue eyes were really quite attractive.

Her skirt draped over his knee allowing his leg to touch hers. Even through his trousers, it aroused him. Carefully, his hand slipped under her skirt and hugged her knee closer to him as though she might try to escape otherwise.

He watched for a reaction in her face and was disappointed not to see her expression change. However, he felt her widen her stance. Was it for better balance or to give him better access?

'Tell me about yourself, Miss Carlson,' he invited when the stack was complete.

'What'd you wanna know?' she asked, briefly reminding him of her age and the gum-smacking temp. Automatically, he released her knee and sat back in his chair, attempting to put some space between them.

'What did you do before?'

She turned towards him and stepped over his legs so that she straddled him from above. Her cute little ass rested on his desk. Had any other person in his office tried this, he would have yelled at them. She acted like they were best buds rather than employer–employee. 'Best buds' was a status he sought with no one – and particularly not with one of his employees.

Instead of mentioning his objections, he remained silent, more fascinated with the way her skirt had stretched across her spread thighs and the hem had risen a few inches above her knees.

'I worked for another lawyer.'

'Here?' The conversation no longer held his interest. All he wanted was to place his hands under her skirt and push it up to her waist. He saw himself ripping off her pantyhose and panties and burying his head between her legs. He wanted to kiss her thighs and stomach and part the dark hair between her legs to delve deeply with his tongue . . .

'No,' she said.

'No what?'

'No, it wasn't here.'

'Where?' He prodded, trying to focus on her words. Getting information out of her was like pulling teeth, but he'd long stopped paying attention to her face; his attention was transfixed on her wide-spread legs.

'Why do you care as long as I do my job well?' she cheekily asked in a whisper. The atmosphere between them had changed so much that he didn't even bother to respond to her insubordination.

A bead of sweat had gathered across his upper lip. 'You have cute knees,' he said, as though that would justify his staring.

'Naw. They're too banged up from when I was a tomboy. The stockings hide it.'

So saying, she raised her leg high enough for him to catch a glimpse of white silk and she pulled an elastic-topped, thigh-high stocking down her leg to show him her scarred knees.

'Uh huh.' He studied her knees as she pointed out scars and then hopped off the desk to pull up her stocking.

'You don't wear pantyhose?'

'Too confining. My thighs like to breathe. It's late. Your mail from last week is in the right-hand drawer. I've typing to finish. If you need anything else, let me know.' Without another word, she disappeared through the doorway, carefully closing it behind her.

Kevin needed a cold shower. He needed not to think about her thigh-high stockings, her white underwear and her freedom-loving thighs. The little minx was trying to keep her job by seducing him.

Kevin's appointments kept him busy the rest of the day and well into the evening. Miss Carlson's efficiency put Miss Darcy to shame. He saw her briefly each time she popped unannounced into his office: with more coffee and a ham-and-cheese sandwich at lunchtime or returning finished files and picking up others that needed attention.

He worked late. By the time he was ready to leave, the office had been empty for hours.

Her workstation reflected her neatness and organisation. He stood at her chair for several moments secretly inhaling her lingering scent. It reminded him of the earthiness of a spring garden after a downpour.

He shook his head to clear it of unwanted thoughts. If this was the direction his mind was going, he needed to get laid tonight. Obviously, he couldn't work around her if he was just going to be horny all the time. Right now, his prick was hard enough to hammer nails.

The Beamer took corners easily as it slid into the late-evening traffic. He dialled as he drove.

'Hello,' a soft voice answered.

'Hi, sweet cheeks. How've you been?' he asked.

'Kevin, you bastard! I haven't heard from you in weeks.'

'Now, honey, I've been out of town a lot with work. Did you miss me?'

There was a brief hesitancy, before the soft voice responded, 'You know I did.'

He laughed silently to himself. Oh, yeah! She missed him. Ten to one she was seeing a dozen other guys.

'Listen, baby, I need to come by and see you. I can be there in ten minutes.'

'Kevin, I'm already dressed to go out. Tonight's the opening at La Carimba.'

'I heard about it. But nothing happens before ten o'clock at one of those places. I won't stay long. I just really need to see you. It's been too long, ya know?'

A long silence followed, before she finally spoke. 'Yeah, I know. Come on by. I'll leave the door unlocked.'

Kevin slipped into Julianne's apartment and was pleased to see that she had left the light on in the bedroom. Julianne was a woman who understood his needs.

She greeted him sitting in the middle of her bed, wearing a low-cut purple teddy.

'Wow! You look hot,' he said as he pulled off his jacket and tie.

'Thanks. Now, just what is it that you needed to see me about? Tell me, what couldn't wait even one more day?' she teased him. Raising herself to her knees, she lowered the straps of her teddy slowly to her waist.

'Oh, baby,' Kevin groaned as he discarded the last of his clothes. 'Suck me. My dick's thought about nothing but your luscious lips all day long.'

Julianne laughed and rolled to the edge of the bed. Her long tongue darted out of her mouth as she leaned over, and her hand closed around his painfully erect shaft and stroked up and down before she gently tasted the head.

Kevin moaned, braced his legs against the bed and arched his body towards her. Normally, he loved to watch, seeing soft, feminine pink lips cover his cock, enclosing it entirely as it slowly began to disappear from view. It was a sight he couldn't see often enough, particularly with a talented woman like Julianne, who would take him deep and hold him there while her tongue and tonsils did the work. Looking down on curly blonde hair bobbing over him made him hard. It made him hard just thinking about it.

But tonight, when he closed his eyes, the lips that covered him were the scarlet ones that had haunted him all day long, and the hair that bobbed was dark with bright-blue streaks.

Unable to stand it any longer, he called out, 'That's it, baby, take me deep. Oh, Jesus, that feels good.'

He felt like a machine gun firing rounds when he finally came, but it did nothing to bring him the sense of completion he needed. Nothing seemed to rid him of his pesky little fantasies about his new secretary.

Julianne languidly stretched back on the bed looking like a cat in the sun, supremely pleased with her performance. Her teddy still hung at her waist; her firm breasts and taut rosy nipples were bared for his view.

'Lift up,' he encouraged, as he pulled the teddy from her hips and down her legs.

'I thought you weren't staying long,' she chided.

'I'm not, but you didn't think I'd just leave and not tend to you, did you?'

Julianne giggled again.

'Turn over, baby. Put these under you.'

She rolled onto her stomach using the pillows he handed her to elevate her hips. His fingers trailed down her back, followed by his tongue. Her buttocks tightened as his hands and tongue continued their exploration. She squealed when he bit her fleshy cheek, but relaxed her muscles, giving him access to the area he sought.

Her little brown rosebud twinkled and teased him, sparkling in the light from his tongue's juices. Julianne moaned pitifully into the tangled covers of the duvet.

From the nightstand, Kevin grabbed a tube of lip balm and spread it on the shiny head of his erect penis, giving a final squirt to his thumb.

'We're not going to go there,' Julianne protested and squirmed as his thumb began to massage the lubricant into her reluctant opening.

'Yeah, we are.' Kevin's hand pressed against the small of her back, holding her firmly in place.

Julianne attempted to clutch her buttock cheeks together but, with his thighs wedged between hers, she was wide open.

'You can do this the hard way or the easy way, baby. It makes no difference to me. I like both,' he admonished.

'I hate you when you're like this,' she squealed, although her voice remained muffled in the covers.

'Sure you do.'

He removed his thumb and began to push and press his slick cock into her. Finally, her defences gave way and her body opened to him. The plump head caused her to thrash beneath him, but Kevin didn't hesitate. His hand snaked between her body and the pillows and pressed hard against her mons.

'C'mon, sweet cheeks, just a little more. That's it. Take me all. Oh, that's real good, baby.'

One of his fingers slipped further under her and began to stroke her clit. Without warning she went up like a flashpoint. The woman who had just complained about how much she hated it became a little firecracker in the bed. It was all he could do to hang on for the ride.

Kevin actually whistled in the elevator the next morning. It wasn't like he'd be heard; none of the rest of the staff would show up for at least another 45 minutes. The office was empty.

Today, the training of Miss Carlson would begin. It was time to take her through her paces. An image of a naked

Katie trotting around a corral, controlled by a bridle in her teeth and a whip in his hand made him smile. Today, her position in the firm would be made clear to her. She would learn to perform like the trained pony she would become. Keep those knees high, Miss Carlson.

Katie arrived precisely on time. His door remained open, giving him an unhindered view of her workstation. If she was aware of him, she gave no indication. He watched her struggle out of her lightweight coat and bend over to put her purse in her bottom desk drawer.

Today she wore a black suit with a short skirt and waist-length jacket. His phone rang as she momentarily disappeared from view. He was still talking when she returned with his coffee and papers, entering his office without his permission.

First things first – this girl needed discipline; she thought she could run all over him. He hung up the phone and barked at her, 'Don't come into my office without my sending for you.'

She set his coffee on the desk and continued just as if he hadn't spoken. 'Here's your schedule for today and yesterday's mail,' she said nonchalantly, placing them in front of him.

'What else?' he growled, realising her hands were still full.

'Stuff for your signature.' She stepped behind the desk and stood next to him, putting the stack of paperwork in front of him. 'Sign here.' She pointed a manicured nail at a line on the paper.

'Not without reading it.'

'Fine, read it. I'll come back.'

'No, if I have questions, I'll want you here to answer them.'

She sighed and shifted her weight on the balls of her feet – not once, but twice.

'What're you so fidgety about?' he enquired.

'It's so hot in here. The sunshine warms this room up first.'

'Take your jacket off, but you're staying till we're finished.'

'Whatever.' She removed her jacket. Her black blouse was completely sheer. Her translucent skin and every detail of her lacy, black bra, including the tiny pink bow that nestled between her 'C' cups, was readily apparent. The only thing that prohibited his view was the pattern of random white dots decorating the material. She tossed her jacket to a chair and bent over the paperwork.

Her scent was as he remembered – earthy, sultry and somewhat musky. He slid his chair back so he could once again look at her sweet ass. A vision of his cock being eaten up as it slid into her tight little bottom hole engulfed him.

'What're you doing?' She turned her head to look at him.

'Nothing,' he replied harshly, pushing his chair back under the desk.

He read the papers quickly. Her work was good, surprisingly so. Before he had finished signing, the phone rang. It was starting out to be one of those mornings.

Mr Lawrence, the senior partner, wished to see him. The meeting stretched into lunch and beyond, complicating his day. By the time he returned to his office, it was after five and everyone had left.

Between appointments and court appearances, he had very little free time. Training Miss Carlson was turning out to be a challenge – particularly since she appeared to be doing the superior job of keeping *him* tethered on the leash. He'd given up trying to get her to enter his office only at his specific instruction and to only do the work he authorised. In a week's time, she had not only caught up his work, she was also now helping other secretaries – making him look like he didn't generate enough work to merit having a secretary. If left alone, Miss Carlson would be running the entire law office within a week and the nation within the month.

On Monday, she wore a shirt with a top that didn't quite meet at the waist. Her belly-button ring caught the light as she put down his morning mail.

'Do you have any other locations pierced that we haven't seen yet?' he demanded, knowing full well it was none of his business.

'Yes.'

'Where?' He wasn't really sure he wanted to know. And yet he hated that he couldn't resist asking.

She just smiled, more of a smirk, really, as she left his office. She was killing him.

Tuesday afternoon was hell on earth. A run in Miss Carlson's stocking was detected shortly after lunch. Instead of using the ladies' room, she opted to change at her desk. Through the open door he watched the ruined stocking being rolled down her incredibly long leg at a leisurely pace then carefully removed from her foot.

Just before it hit the trash, she changed her mind. For several excruciating moments, she played around, using the stocking to bind her hands both in front of her body and behind, tempting him with visions of bondage. Lovers' games he wouldn't mind playing with her.

Finally, she became bored and disposed of the old stocking in favour of a new one. Her toes were pointed as she placed the new stocking over them, gradually covered the arched foot and pulled it agonisingly slowly up her long leg, higher and higher, until heaven was only a few scant inches away.

Her phone rang, interrupting her final adjustments. She spoke for a brief moment before hurrying off. Kevin sat back in his chair. Obviously, he wasn't going to get any work done this afternoon. Maybe he'd call Julianne again.

It was too early for her to be home. Conjuring up lurid images of Julianne wasn't working for him. No, it was time to put a stop to his lusting after Miss Carlson. But how to go about it?

Katie reappeared at her desk an hour later. He wanted to demand to know where she'd been, but he didn't really care. He called her into his office, and began: 'I want to drop some paperwork off at your house later tonight. I'll need it first thing in the morning and I won't get here until half-past nine.'

Katie blinked a couple of times before she nodded. Apparently, he had finally hit upon something that was new to her. Good.

'Write down your address,' he instructed.

As usual, she spoke very little but did as he requested.

'You live out pretty far,' he commented as he studied the card she'd handed him. 'Do you live alone?'

'Uh-huh. I like privacy.' She shrugged carelessly.

'Good, so do I,' he said, thinking, Yes, I do, sweet thing, and we're going to need it tonight.

At 7.30, he pulled up in front of the old farmhouse. The upkeep on an old place like this must be awful, but the well-tended yard gave the house a tidy appearance.

He threw his suit jacket and tie on to the back seat of his car and strolled to the porch. The front door was open and a disembodied voice greeted him. 'I'm here. C'mon back.'

Winding his way down the narrow hallway he passed a bathroom and two bedrooms to reach a room at the far rear of the house. Daylight outside was fading; the house lights had yet to be turned on. The gloom gave him a moment's pause, but he pushed forwards ignoring the warning bells in his head.

'Are you back here?' he asked at the closed door.

'Yeah. I've got a surprise for you.' Her young voice sounded happy, an emotion he hadn't really associated with her.

A cruel smile curved his lips as he pushed on the door. The room was completely dark. No lights, no windows. He stepped hesitantly into the interior.

'Hang on, I'll turn on the light,' her voice offered, giving him some relief.

A red light bathed the room like a photo lab, but, as his eyes adjusted, he realised photography was not the room's purpose.

Katie Carlson stepped out from behind a screen. Up until this moment, he had pegged her office appearance as relatively acceptable, even with the dreadful blue hair and assorted piercings. Now, he took a step back. Her wardrobe appeared to be cast-offs from the television show *Xena, Warrior Princess*.

Thick brown leather armbands, lace-up sandals and a sleeveless micro-mini leather dress gave her an Amazon-like appearance. Her height was not a factor, but her slicked-back hair and bizarre make-up enhanced her animal-like features. Dark lines resembling native tattoos swirled around her eyes. Jagged spikes radiated from the lines giving her a fierce, menacing appearance. The wicked, coiled whip attached to her waist implied she meant business.

He grinned. This was going to be even better than he'd anticipated. So, Miss Carlson had recognised his challenge and felt able to extend one of her own. As an unexplored fantasy unfolded in front of him, his cock jumped to attention.

What did she think she was? A little dominatrix in the making? Hardly. But he'd let her have her fun, and then they'd see who was the boss. For now he'd play along.

'Where do you want me, mistress?' he asked, struggling

to keep his sarcasm from being apparent. So sure was he of his status that he didn't even attempt to hide his rising erection.

'On your knees,' she commanded, pointing to a location in the centre of the room. Her voice surprised him with its authority.

From a far wall she detached a shiny metal chain. At the end of the heavy chain dangled fur-lined metal manacles, which dropped from the ceiling almost directly in front of him. She quickly secured his wrists, but the slack in the chain gave him complete access to every corner of the room. He snorted with derision. What good would chaining him do? He was still in control. Once he had her under his thumb, he would completely dominate her, both here and at work. Let her have her little fantasy.

But, before he was able to put his plan into action, Katie stepped away from his kneeling form and flipped a lever on the wall. The chain that secured Kevin slowly cranked upwards forcing him to rise to his feet to prevent his arms from being jerked out of their sockets. Soon he stood on his tiptoes, hanging by his hands from the ceiling.

Well, wasn't she just a little surprise. Her equipment was good, he'd give her that.

The door to the hallway opened behind him. Did she have company? Had he not been suspended so securely, he would have turned to see who had entered.

'I can't believe it took you ten days to get him here,' a strangely familiar female voice complained.

'Well, he was in court three days last week,' Katie responded tartly, defending herself.

Kevin swallowed hard as he realised why he knew the voice. Somehow this wasn't going quite the way he planned. But, despite his misgivings, his erection tightened painfully. Sweat beaded across his brow and under his arms.

Miss Carlson stepped behind him. Her voice purred

menacingly in his ear, 'You remember Miss Darcy, don't you? Miss Darcy, who worked sixty hours a week for you last year, but wasn't quite good enough for a year-end bonus? It seems she has some unfinished business with you. I know you'll want to give her your absolute, undivided attention.'

Kevin turned his head, attempting to evaluate the situation. Over his shoulder he could barely make out Miss Darcy in the red haze of the room. Her untended blonde hair fell about her shoulders in a way that used to irritate him, but now he found strangely erotic. As usual her attention was not focused on him at all, but somewhere on the ground.

'Step around here, Liz. Kevin wants to see,' Miss Carlson directed.

Liz Darcy moved to face him while continuing to fidget with a strap at her waistband. Kevin's knowledge of sex toys, he discovered at that moment, was severely limited, but it didn't require an instructional video to know that not only was Miss Darcy wearing a strap-on dildo, but it was also probably the largest one available.

'Girls, you're making a mistake,' he cajoled using his best courtroom tone but, before he could continue, a ball gag was slipped into his mouth from behind. Miss Carlson's usual efficiency was not working to his advantage this time.

'Liz and I can handle this without your interference or direction,' she spat, every bit as cold as the most accomplished dominatrix.

It was the longest sentence he had ever heard her utter and, to his amazement, she wasn't finished yet.

'Since you're so fond of fucking your employees we thought you would enjoy a turn-about. You know, goose, gander and all that?' She playfully patted his ass in a manner that left little doubt as to their intentions.

Kevin groaned.

Katie Carlson reached around his body and began unbuttoning his shirt, pulling it from the confines of his slacks. While Liz Darcy stepped closer to the front of his body, the obscene dildo curved upwards, bobbing between them.

Looking into his eyes, Liz gave him a shy, flirtatious smile. Aside from the dildo, she wore an open chain-mail vest which allowed her pert breasts to play a lewd game of hide and seek as she bent to unfasten his belt.

Jesus, he'd never been this excited. If she touched him at all he'd probably come in his pants. She was careful, he noted, as she eased his zipper over his protruding cock – even more so with the elastic band of his jockeys. His penis sprang free to dance in the cool evening air, vulnerable to whatever ministrations these two minxes chose to perform on him. Miss Carlson tied his shirt around his shoulders, leaving him naked to his knees where his pants pooled like a toddler's during potty training.

His penis looked tiny compared to the latex phallus, and Liz Darcy, seeing him make the comparison, stroked hers proudly, flashing him a gloating smirk before continuing with her tasks. Removing neither his shoes nor his pants she tightened the belt securely to his calves, immobilising him still further.

Small, cool slick fingers began to massage his buttocks – dipping between the crack to thoroughly lubricate him while Liz busied herself by leaning forwards and running her tongue around his navel. His nipples were drawn into hard points and, when her tongue moved over them, an electrical shock ran through his body.

He closed his eyes and didn't open them again until he felt fingers on his buttock cheeks prising them apart. He stared down into Katie Carlson's determined expression and felt the penetration begin. His tight muscles gave way most unwillingly.

'Smile for the camera,' she trilled, a most smug inflection in her voice, and jerked her head in the direction of a tiny red light he had failed to notice. She laughed as she moved away.

Slowly the dildo filled him, stretched him, and sweet agony tore through him. Smooth, long strokes enabled the pain and pleasure to swirl together. He wasn't able to stand much of this torture. Despite the horror of the situation – that he was being penetrated in the ass and enjoying it – he was unable to help himself. He came, spewing his milky white essence in a graceful arc to land harshly against the wooden floor.

But the movement behind him did not end. On and on Liz Darcy rode him. Amazingly, he hardened again almost immediately. Soft fingers clasped him. He opened his eyes to see Katie's dark hair descend over his cock as her lips took the turgid shaft into her mouth. Oh yeah, this was better than any fantasy he'd ever had. After the ignominy of being buggered, he was going to get a treat after all. Maybe Katie Carlson wasn't as cruel as she'd made out.

Liz Darcy cried out in pleasure behind him and her movement came to a halt just as Katie withdrew her lips from his penis. Not now. Not now. His pleading, muffled by the gag, sounded pathetic even to his own ears. When had he ever had to beg?

The door behind him opened and closed. Listening to the silence, he realised both girls had left the room, forgetting a major piece of equipment. The dildo was still firmly lodged deep within him. He strained to expel it without success. Minutes turned into hours and time folded in on itself. Exhausted beyond belief, he eventually collapsed, letting the manacles support the entire weight of his body.

Light filtered through the open door. Shit. What time was it? His clothes were tangled around him and he lay on the hard wood floor. Every muscle groaned in protest as he struggled to move his arms to see his watch. Eight o'clock. He was going to be late for work.

Above his head the manacles drooped, taunting him in remembrance of the previous evening. His belt had been loosened and a pillow and blanket had been provided, but the girls were long gone.

He wondered if Katie Carlson would show up at work today. Either way it occurred to him that he needed to send flowers to Mrs Jacobs, the head of HR.

Day Fourteen
Mathilde Madden

The phone rang and I picked it up and went, 'Finance, Jennifer Turner speaking.'

And I knew it was him straight away, of course, because he just went, 'Hello, Jennifer, you sexy little bitch.'

And I went, 'Duncan?'

And straight off, he said, 'I can't wait until you get home tonight, you dirty, dirty little slut. I am going to fuck you before you even get in the door. I am going to fuck you so hard you'll feel it for a week. But before I even start to do that I am going to get those knickers off you and press my tongue against your hot little cunt and lick you there until you scream. You're going to have a sore throat by the time I'm finished with you. A sore throat and a sore cunt – you dirty little bitch.'

And I just sort of went, 'Guh, wah,' because I was on the edge of my seat, listening to his torrent of filth, and that way I could get the corner of it between my legs and sort of rub, just so. And I was rubbing away, and he was talking away, and that's when I thought, Fuck! Because I remembered what a bad, bad idea such rubbing was, and so I stopped.

Now, if this seems a bit wanton on my part, remember it was day fourteen. It had been two weeks since I'd had an orgasm. Two bloody weeks! And for a one-a-day-minimum girl like me that's at least fourteen orgasms I

Anyway, that's when the phone rang again. And that's when I decided to go for lunch rather than hear what Duncan thought about being hung up on. But I'd just stood up and grabbed my bag when I spotted the sexy temp over at the water cooler. And he must have been out for a lunchtime jog or something, because he was all flushed and damp with sweat. He downed one paper cup of water and then another, greedy for it. I stared at him helplessly and dug my nails into my palm for the unfeasibly long minutes until he left.

Oh God.

Down in the sandwich shop below the office things were even worse. I felt like I was about to burst into flames, from the cunt outwards. As I'd left the office, my boss had even asked if I was feeling OK. I could see myself in the mirrored wall behind the shop's counter now and I did look rather flushed.

It was a tiny shop, and it was very crowded, this being the middle of the lunchtime sandwich-scramble. The queue was almost out of the door. There was this fat, suited man behind me and he was pressed quite close. I could feel his soft thigh right up against my arse. The blood in my clit was going pound-pound-pound and the whole of the deli counter seemed to be really erotic, from the luscious-looking cakes to the perky gherkins. When the busty assistant finally asked me for my order, I could barely squeak the words, 'Tuna baguette.' It was horrific.

And, as I said before, I'd already had a right day of it. Right from the way it had begun. I had been sitting up in bed, drinking my tea, putting off getting up by watching *GMTV*, when suddenly this boy band appeared looking all perky, bright-eyed and bushy-tailed and far too sparkly for 7.30 in the morning. Yeah, that was what Duncan had been going on about when he called me. What was the charming phrase he used – the boy toy bitches?

Now, the boy band sitting on the sofas chatting I could just about deal with, but then they played a clip from the video, and, oh my God, it was practically soft porn – five boys, shirtless in the pouring rain, practically fellating their bloody microphones in arty black and white. I felt my hips start to buck involuntarily in time with the grinding music; my lips parted a little and I rubbed myself gently against a fold in the duvet. My nipples were hard as anything, like little cherry stones, as my fingers glided down my body towards the waistband of my pyjama bottoms.

Of course, if it wasn't for the fact that I had been completely dry for fourteen whole days at this point I wouldn't be doing this. I wouldn't have been rendered a slavering animal by five nineteen-year-olds who had each been scrubbed, shaved and stuck into designer jeans. But this particular morning – my God – I couldn't even pretend to put up a fight.

And that was when Duncan came out of the bathroom, just before my fingertips reached their final destination, and I snapped to attention.

He smiled slyly. 'I saw you.'

'I was just scratching,' I lied back, rather unconvincingly.

'Oh sure. You're practically drooling.'

'I am not,' I said, unconsciously wiping away imaginary drool from the corners of my mouth.

And Duncan turned and headed out of the bedroom, chuckling to himself. 'I am so going to win,' he had said.

Bastard. Smug bastard.

Back in the shop, I grabbed my baguette and opened my wallet to pay, and that was when I noticed a piece of paper tucked inside where I keep my notes. And it had my name written on the front. I stared at it while I handed a fiver to the sandwich lady, unable to look away from Duncan's bouncy handwriting. Bastard.

So, because I was far too weak to chuck Duncan's missive in the nearest bin, I got out of the lift on the floor below the one where I worked, as that was where the ladies' loo was. And once I was locked inside a cubicle, all safe and cool, well, cool-ish, I unfolded the piece of paper.

Written on it was one sentence: 'You know you want to, baby', and below that was a photograph. A photograph that was about as pornographic as was possible with our cheap inkjet printer. And when I looked at it my cunt just went thump. It was of Duncan, lying on the bed with one hand wrapped around his hard cock. He was naked, looking sideways into the camera, with narrowed eyes, as he stroked himself. He looked beautiful. Bastard. Beautiful bastard.

I was so damn horny looking at this picture I was practically crying with frustration. And I would have stuck my hand into my knickers right there and then if it wasn't for the damn bet. The damn bet and the fact it was absolutely cheat proof. Because Duncan had made sure I wasn't going to be able to cheat from day one.

'What's that?' I'd asked.

'It's an integral part of our little game, baby. Absolutely integral.'

Duncan, in our bedroom, just before the two weeks began and just after I'd agreed to the bet, held up what looked like a pair of metal knickers.

And, of course, I was feigning ignorance. 'Yeah, but what is it?'

'It's a chastity belt, dummy, made to measure and one hundred per cent tamper-proof. After all, I can't watch you twenty-four-seven. What's to stop you cheating at work?'

Intrigued, I reached out and took the thing. It wasn't heavy. In fact, it seemed kind of flexible. It was metal outside, but lined with some kind of plasticky stuff inside and there were holes to allow for nature to take its course. But I didn't really see how it was going to work.

'OK,' I said, 'but isn't this going to make it kind of easy for me to win? If you put this thing on then I can't play with myself, ergo I win.'

'Heh, Jennifer, I'm not stupid.' And he did this slow smile thing that he does. It's kind of sexy if I'm in the mood. And I kind of was, because the chastity belt was kind of sexy. And the idea of being locked into it and not being able to come no matter how much I wanted to was kind of sexy too. And Duncan, well, he just is kind of sexy. In an obsessive kind of a way.

You know, that's the scary thing about Duncan – not the sexiness, the obsessiveness. He'd measured me for the chastity belt while I was asleep and sent off for it weeks ago (and they're not cheap – they're like hundreds of pounds) just to do this dumb bet. And I could have said no. Well, I suppose it wasn't very likely I'd say no, because I'm kind of keen on challenges but, even so, weeks of planning and loads of money and I still could have. And that's Duncan for you. He's a bloody weirdo. He's lucky he's so sexy, that's all I can say, because he'd be one miserable obsessive weirdo bugger if he wasn't.

Anyway, Duncan said, 'You don't wear it all the time, baby. Just when you're at work, and even then you have a key.'

'I do?'

'Why yes, so if you get all het up and decide to give in you can. Fair's fair. You'll have a key in an envelope like this.' And he held up this little envelope – like the kind of envelope you use for putting cash in, tiny and white. 'So, if you use the key, I'll know. And don't even think about replacing the envelope from your stationery cupboard, because I'm going to sign it, so you can't.'

See what I mean? Obsessive bastard thinks of everything.

So I was stood there in the loo and I'd screwed up the bloody picture Duncan had sent me and thrown it into the toilet pan, and I couldn't help looking at the key envelope in my purse. (Duncan even used to check that it was there, in case I tried to cheat by leaving it at home or something.) And that was probably the worst moment of the day so far, because I was feeling so desperate. I was going to have to sit through a three-hour meeting about some big event planned for that summer and I was in no mood for talking costings and projected income and expenditure. I was so tempted to say fuck it, to hell with the consequences, let's just get this bloody belt off and have a wank.

But that was when I heard a voice outside the cubicle. It was my boss, talking to someone else. And that basically saved the day, because nothing else on earth could kill a desperate urge for an orgasm like the sound of my boss's voice.

So I snapped my purse shut – tempting little key and all – and breezed out of the cubicle.

But before I could so much as give my boss a nod of greeting her eyes were lighting up and she was smiling a relieved smile, bearing down on me in a big scary manner that made me crush myself up against the sinks.

'Jennifer! Oh, thank God you're back from lunch. Listen, the chief exec's got to do some big TV interview this afternoon, so they've moved the meeting forwards half an hour.'

'Half an hour, so that means it's starting –'

'Right now, yes. So we need to hurry. Hold my bag, will you.'

And with that she shoved a heavy brown shoulder bag

into my hands and whisked herself into the nearest loo. Which just happened to be the one I had just shoved a nude picture of Duncan down. Trapped, all I could do was hope she didn't look down.

Anyway, I scooted off to the boardroom with my boss in tow and found what I hoped was a secluded seat at the far end of the table, where I could slyly eat my lunch.

At first, the meeting was boring. This was a good thing. I wanted the meeting to bore me into a light coma where I was not thinking about anything sexy. But then the head of celebrity liaison stood up and took command of the overhead projector, and I was done for.

He started running through the bands he had booked for the charity pop concert under discussion. And he had a swishy Power-Point presentation with video clips in it to illustrate each one.

And, yes, I might have guessed, the boys from *GMTV* were back. How come I'd never noticed before today how pornographic all pop videos are? I squirmed in my seat as yet another sequence featured them getting their kit off and writhing around. I thought I might die.

My hands shook as I picked up my camomile tea and took a long frustrated sip.

And that just made things worse, because it wasn't long before I felt the pressure start to build in my bladder, and that always makes me feel really horny. I looked around the room, trying to gauge how inappropriate it would seem if I excused myself to the loo, and then I saw my boss looking at me with a rather weird expression on her face, and I put both my wandering hands on the table sharpish.

My boss's face had the effect of a cold shower. Which was brilliant. So I kept right on looking at it – feeling calmer every minute. I imagined my boss having sex. And that worked pretty well. Then I imagined her on the toilet. And that worked even better.

Three hours and some rather repulsive fantasising later, I emerged and headed for my workstation and relative safety in numbers. I couldn't quite believe it when I picked up my voicemail and had five messages. Five!

Message one began with a too-familiar gravelly growl. 'Hey, baby, I can't believe you hung up on me. Is the pace getting a bit much to bear, huh? Sounds like I'm going to win this one, doesn't it? And you know what happens then. I get you for the whole weekend. My bitch. My little sex slave. I haven't even decided what I'm going to do with you. Maybe I'll tie your hands behind your back and have you suck my cock, all evening, while I watch TV. I think I'd like that.'

I flicked the delete button as fast as I could. Bastard. But here's the thing, his message, which I guess was supposed to get me in even more of a lather, actually worked the other way. It calmed me down a little bit. Arrogant sod.

I took a deep breath and gritted my teeth, praying the next message was work related and preferably involved some urgent reason for me to stare at columns of numbers for the rest of the day.

But message two, while at least work related, was just a boring drone from reception saying that the petty cash books I had ordered had arrived.

Message three was him again. 'Oh, so you're not picking up the phone now. Is that how you think you can hold out? I know you want to win. I know you want to have me as your personal weekend slave. Have you thought about what you're going to do to me yet, when you win? Which you won't, by the way, but you can dream, baby. Have you been thinking about me with a collar round my neck? You want to tug on my lead? Drag me around the flat?'

Yes I do! And yes I will! I thought decisively as I hit delete again and clamped my thighs together, feeling ever more confident as Duncan's underhand tactics seemed to be backfiring again.

And he was bloody well back again with message four: 'Course I'm not going to lose, am I, baby? Oh no. You are. I saw how hot and squirmy you were this morning and I thought, No way is she going to last another twelve hours. You just like your little pussy far too much, don't you? So why don't you toddle off to the loo and unlock yourself with that handy key. You know it's going to be mind-blowing after all this time, don't you? And, as for a weekend as my sex slave, a weekend of bondage and subjugation, well, don't tell me a tiny little part of Jennifer Turner isn't getting even wetter at the thought of calling me master.'

And that was when my heart sank into my shoes, because that's the way it goes with Duncan: every time you think you've got him he finds a whole new level to crank it up to. Because, you know what, he had a point. The idea of being his sex slave did kind of turn me on. (Even taking account of the fact that at this particular moment wallpaper paste would have turned me on.) When it came down to the question of whether I cared if it was me or Duncan who spent the weekend chained to the bed, I really had to admit that both were equally sexy. The only reason I was so keen on winning this damn bet was because: (1) I enjoyed winning and (2) I enjoyed Duncan losing.

But then, just as all looked lost, came message five: 'Jennifer, can you call me as soon as you get this; there's been a problem with the wages payment for this month and if it doesn't go through today there will be hell to pay. I need you to sort it out.' And, oh double fuck, I was back into the reality so fast it almost made me nauseous.

And so, despite everything else that was happening, for the next two hours I was helplessly embroiled in matters financial. By the time I'd sweet-talked and bullied my way out of the impending no-wages-paid crisis, I was exhausted, late and feeling about as unsexy as I ever had. So, result: that slave was mine.

Then, finally, I was staggering out of the office and down the crowded street. I'd made it. I practically drifted into the station on autopilot and began the crawl home.

The train arrived about five minutes late, which wasn't all that unusual. No word as to why, which was even less unusual. But I so didn't care. I was in heaven. Not only was I about to get one hell of a shag after two weeks of being all pent up, but I also had a whole weekend with gorgeous Duncan as my personal sex slave. And I was close enough, so I let myself think about the thing I hadn't let myself think about all day for fear of getting overcome. I thought about what I was going to do with Duncan when I won.

See, for all Duncan might have been a clever boy with his chastity belt and his key in his special signed envelope, he didn't quite think of everything. For example, there were my little oases where I was stuck on the train to and from work and there was just no way I could take the belt off, even if I was desperate, and so I could fantasise to my heart's content in relative safety.

I wanted to see that big bastard on his knees. I wanted him on his knees, with his wrists strapped behind him and a blindfold over his eyes. I wanted to see him opening up his mouth to take a cock right down his throat while he gagged and begged and spluttered and squirmed. Maybe it'd be a great big strap-on (because Duncan isn't the only one who knows how to flex his credit card on the net) or maybe it'd be a real-life cock – I was sure I could find one that was willing. Either way, it was going to be Duncan, on his knees, choking and gagging.

And then I was rubbing my legs together so rudely on the train that the stuffed suit opposite me was looking and I had to stop.

Half an hour later I banged in through the door waving my signed and sealed envelope and Duncan turned and smiled. Anyone would think he was happy to lose from the big grin he'd got pasted on his handsome face because, thanks to my late-running train, it had just gone seven. I'd won.

Still smiling, Duncan said, 'How about I relieve all that pent-up frustration, before punishment commences?' And he garnished this offer with a little tongue flick.

Too pent up to speak, I just nodded once and practically sprinted for the bedroom.

And, oh God, it was so good. I wouldn't actually recommend fourteen days' enforced abstinence or anything, but, shit, the minute the tip of his tongue touched my clit I was screaming. So fucking good.

And it didn't take long. Duncan tried to do right by me, I could tell; tried to tease it out a little when he could feel me start to buck wildly after two or three tongue flicks. But it was a losing battle, because my body just wasn't going to wait another second. So, in less than two minutes, I was flying high, just inches from coming and then, with one more long lick, the pressure was just perfect and I was off, soaring into space as fourteen days' worth of tension left my body through the nearest available exit. Bliss.

And then, before I was even aware of where I was, something was being pressed against my ear. Something hard and small. And it was talking. I could hear a strangely familiar voice, which was saying, 'At the third stroke the time will be six, fifty-nine precisely, bip bip bip.'

What the fuck?

I sat up, so confused. And then after a long moment of horrible realisation and staring at Duncan's big, big grin, I said, not really believing it, 'You changed my watch?'

'Er, yeah,' said Duncan.

'You bastard.'

And he was holding a pair of handcuffs and, as he began to snap them on my wrists, he said very softly, 'Well, you didn't actually think I was going to lose, did you?'

Bastard.

Coffee Break Alison Tyler

Café Americano.

Espresso.

Cappuccino.

A shot in the dark.

That last one sounded perfect, because that's what I was doing. Taking a shot in the dark by even being here, standing before the black-and-white marble counter at the upscale café in my office building, staring at the delicately curvy handwritten menu on the chalkboard rather than staring at the gorgeous man less than one foot away. I knew his name by now – Declan. I had picked that up after two weeks of ever so casually hanging around the café far more than I had any business doing. Christ, I'd drunk more cups of coffee than a long-distance trucker during those two weeks, and I was jittery as all hell to prove it. But Declan was worth drinking too much coffee for, worth staying up all night for, worth taking a shot in the dark for.

He had longish blond hair that fell in front of his clear green eyes and a smile that made women – and many men in the equal-opportunities world of Tinseltown – do a double take. He was 22, exactly my age, and he dressed in classic 1950s Hollywood cool: black jeans, black T-shirt, heavily battered motorcycle boots. A wallet chain dangled from his back pocket, and a colourful pin-up girl tattoo peeked out from under his right sleeve.

I didn't think I had a chance with him, and it didn't matter anyway, because I was already taken. Seriously taken. Two years into a relationship taken. Yet that fact didn't stop me from ordering my coffee, from taking too much time to fish out the crisp bills from my red leather wallet just so that I could stand close by him, from holding on to Declan's hand a beat too long when receiving my change.

Being taken didn't keep me from spending all those extra caffeinated-awake hours fantasising about him. I lost my nights to thinking about what it would be like to kiss him, and then moved quickly on to what it might be like to fuck him. Unreal. That was my sense. Simply from the way his mesmerising green eyes watched me when I entered the café, I knew how it would feel to be locked in his embrace. Or better yet, bent over the cool stone coun- tertop waiting for him to slowly lift my pleated skirt, then to gingerly lower my pale-blue panties down my thighs until I was totally exposed. I stroked myself on my old leather sofa while I pictured him fucking me, working his cock between my legs at just the right speed, thrusting inside me while gripping a handful of my long black hair. He would call out my name as he did me. I could hear his voice, memorised now, echoing in my head as my finger- tips played over my clit. 'Danielle,' he'd say, 'oh God, Danielle, you feel so good.' I would try to respond, but fail, my voice gone, my face pressed against the cold stone, body held rigid as the climax built inside me. A long line of coffee drinkers would wait for us to be finished so they could grab their morning espressos and be on their way.

Coffee became my number-one aphrodisiac, and in weeks I was an addict. Not just to the coffee bean, but to being near Declan.

'You're back again?' he'd tease when he saw me enter- ing the café each day with my white mug in hand.

'Just can't get enough,' I'd confess, tilting my head as I smiled at him, playing coy as the bitter-strong aroma of coffee hit my nostrils and the sight of him working the machines made me wet. The scent of the coffee bean wasn't supposed to excite me. But it did. Even watching a percolating coffee maker on a TV ad now got me all turned on.

'Well, you always know where to find me ...'

Sure, I did. He was merely an elevator ride away. I worked in an office upstairs for Jenna Malone, a rich Beverly Hills matron who wrote romance novels in between her various cosmetic procedures. One novel, then an eyelift. A second novel, then lip implants. After her next publication, she was planning a full-body overhaul, one to keep her looking as sexy as the wayward co-eds she wrote into her stories. My job was to run errands in her white convertible BMW and keep her day-planner up to the millisecond.

Oh, yeah, and I also had to pretend to like her books.

Jenna had a philosophy about romance versus reality. In her world, romance could only take place in distant locations: faraway islands or mountain getaways. To her, reality was stark and bland, as unsexy as the thick cigarette-smoke-like smog that hung over Burbank. Maybe this was why she constantly worked to change her appearance, hoping forever to transform herself from reality into something new and sleek. And maybe it was why she never took my opinions seriously. Because, even before I met Declan, it was my belief that romance could happen anywhere. Even in an upscale office building on Doheny Boulevard.

Even in a coffee shop.

In Jenna's office I answered her phone with the same smile as always, but now my smile was all for Declan. During those first few weeks I developed an addict's need. I no longer cared that I couldn't fall asleep before three a.m. The insistent pull within my veins kept me draining my coffee cup just so I had a reason to go downstairs to the café and see him.

Turns out I didn't need a reason. Because soon enough

he began coming upstairs to my floor several times a day on the pretence of delivering coffee to other customers in other offices, then dropping a free cup off for me (and one for Jenna, as a cover). There were others in the café who could have done the deliveries; but Declan did it just so he had a reason to come upstairs and see me.

When we realised we both had the same reason for going upstairs and downstairs, we started meeting in the middle, on an empty floor that offered plenty of places to hide. A mega-record company had recently vacated the space in favour of brand-new digs up on the Sunset Strip. Until a new business moved in, the floor was ours, for ten minutes at a time. Declan would push me up against a cool plaster wall and kiss me, and I'd wriggle one hand between our bodies and stroke his hard-on through his chic faded black jeans. I'd work my hand along his shaft, and cup the head in my fist. Then I'd give him a firm squeeze, as if showing him who was boss. As if. By that point I was all his. But I liked to play tough girl.

'God, Danielle,' he'd murmur as I played him through the denim, 'you're going to make me come.'

'That's the idea,' I'd whisper.

'You tease,' he'd say, grabbing me tightly against him, crushing me to him. I could feel his hard, lean body, the muscles in his flat stomach, the strength in his arms. I could feel his cock aligning perfectly with me, so ready, so hard, and that would make me moan.

'Jesus, Danielle,' he'd say, face pressed to my hair, 'you're just a little slut.'

'I'm your coffee slut,' I'd correct him with a laugh, ending our conversation. We had to make the most of every minute, which meant more kissing and fewer words. If Jenna had written our story, she'd have said that our bodies spoke their own language. But that was bullshit. We were simply too busy to talk, lips pressed together, hearts racing. He'd groan when my fingers undid his button-fly so that I could stroke his naked cock, and I'd lean my head back, giving him perfect access to the tender skin at the base of my throat. He'd kiss me there, gently at first, then harder as I pumped him with greater force.

When we parted, I'd return to my office looking as flushed and feverish as the pretty but dim heroine in my boss's latest novel. The girl's name was Jacqueline and, of course, she found love in a distant island paradise. But we had similarities nonetheless. I didn't make much of the comparison at the time but, looking back, I definitely fitted the genre. She was young and curious and careless. I was young and curious and careless, as well. I paid attention only to my own desires, and I didn't bother myself with any impending consequences. And there *were* impending consequences.

Plenty of them.

You see, my boyfriend worked in the office, too. Did I mention that? I suppose it's important. In Jenna's novel, Marlon would have been the antagonist – and he definitely did his job at antagonising me, although his presence didn't stop me from roaming, didn't make me hesitate for a moment. In fact, I'll admit that I might have been spurred on a bit by my proximity to danger. Marlon worked at the kidney-shaped white desk across from mine, and he never appeared to be suspicious about my lengthy sojourns downstairs. I may sound proud of the fact, but in reality I'm simply amazed that Declan and I pulled it off for as long as we did.

Marlon was the novelist's assistant, her right-hand man, and he spent hours listening to her read her work aloud, always listening for word repetitions, his greatest pet peeve. Sometimes I would eavesdrop outside the door to Jenna's inner sanctum. I'd hear the two of them debating a word choice, replacing 'caress' with 'stroke' or 'driving' with 'thrusting' or 'petting' with 'rubbing'. Then I'd return to sit breathless at my desk, imagining Declan doing the things to me that the novelist's characters were doing to each other in their sandy island getaways. Caressing. Stroking. Thrusting. When I could handle it no longer, I'd grab my cup and head downstairs again.

You know. For coffee.

Declan was always ready. Within days of the start of our affair, he'd worked out a deal with his Goth-inspired co-worker. She'd cover his disappearances for him, and he'd let her sneak out early in the evening, or show up late in the morning. She gave me suspicious sidelong glances from under her black-tipped bangs whenever I came in. Or she'd roll her kohl-rimmed eyes and sigh sorrowfully, as if she had all the sadness of a Cure album bottled up inside of her. But she never said a word to me. As soon as I walked through the door, Declan would slide out from behind the counter and head after me to one of our rendezvous spots. Once a new modelling agency took over 'our floor', we retreated to a variety of different locations. Our favourite was a secluded spot behind the building, by the loading docks which were never used. We couldn't have actual sex there, not out in the open, but we made out like high-school kids, which was just as good – at least, for a while.

Declan seemed to know everything I wanted. He'd hold me in place with his hand in my long hair. He'd kiss me until my lips would be bruised when we parted. He'd make me so wet that I took to carrying a spare pair of panties with me in my handbag, knowing that, at some point during the day, I'd need to make a quick change. As soon as he was aware I had extras, Declan began confiscating my dampened pair, promising me that, when he got home that night, he'd come in them. 'Thinking of you,' he told me. 'I wrap those panties around my cock and come so hard, thinking only of fucking you.' That vision made me even wetter than I had been. Would I need to start carrying whole sets of lingerie in my bag, doing multiple changes throughout the day? I sort of liked the idea, emptying my lingerie drawer panty by panty until I had no choice but to go stark naked under my clothes.

'Where were you?' my boyfriend finally asked one afternoon when I returned from an overly long illicit encounter.

'Getting coffee,' I said quickly, before running my tongue along my bottom lip, remembering how it felt to be crushed in Declan's embrace.

Of course, the 'getting coffee' excuse meant that I always had to remember to bring my chipped white porcelain mug with me. To have it filled to the brim before returning to the third-floor office. 'Getting coffee' meant that Declan and I only had about ten minutes to ravish each other, but, as any real romance novelist knows, lovers can do plenty of damage in ten minutes, fantasy island paradise or no. I grew adept at dropping to my knees and undoing his button-fly with my teeth; of drawing out his cock and sucking it with the hungry force of a woman on a mission. And my mission was simple: to make him come. He became knowledgeable at opening my bra with one quick flick of his thumb, of stroking my breasts while telling me exactly what he wanted to do with me when we finally were truly alone. And it didn't take long for us to need to be alone. We moved quickly from foreplay to fucking, and we fucked everywhere we could – in the underground garage, in my car, in the men's room.

While my boyfriend and my boss discussed whether 'sofa' was sexier than 'lounge' and whether 'taunt' was a true synonym for 'tease', Declan and I explored the possibilities of oral sex in an elevator, of putting out in a parking lot, of canoodling in the kitchen. I'd return to the office flushed and damp, but with my full cup of coffee, adrenaline rushing like caffeine through my veins.

Usually, I was the one to head downstairs for a cup of joe. But, when Declan wanted to see me, he still dropped off extra cups of java for us. Jenna thought he had a crush on *her*. 'That coffee boy', she called him. 'He's always bringing me free drinks,' she would say.

Marlon thought it was cute in a pathetic sort of way. 'He must be half your –' he started, then stopped, biting his tongue. Sometimes he wasn't quite as smart as he thought he was or as he pretended to be. 'I mean,' he continued, 'he's just some pretty boy, I'm sure. All fluff and no brains. Nobody who could entertain you.'

But what did Marlon know? His idea of entertaining was spending the afternoon searching for word reps. And he took no notice of my growing addiction. I quickly upped my coffee intake to a record high, explaining my longer absences from the office by a new fascination with the specialty coffees, ones that took slightly longer to prepare. Double espressos and fancy mochas. Anything with whipped cream topping and sprinkles.

'It's good today,' I'd tell Marlon. 'Columbian. Rich and dark. Should I get you a cup?' My hands would be shaking from all the coffee, my heart racing at triple speed, but Marlon never seemed to see. Besides, he liked tea. He even liked to discuss the different types of teas. One for morning, one for mid-afternoon. One as a late-night pick-up. Teas were for the intellectual set, he felt, and Marlon tended to preen about his intellect. He had a Masters, for God's sake, while I was nothing more than a college drop-out. He could give our boss sixteen words for 'sparkling' without resorting to a thesaurus. He made fun of my *Cosmo* subscription, of my occasional California-girl use of 'like' in a sentence, of the fact that I thought making out in a drive-in was hot.

I couldn't give anyone sixteen words for 'sparkling'. After glittering, dazzling and spellbinding, I have to admit that I'm lost. Truthfully, I probably couldn't give anyone sixteen words for *anything*. But I could have told Marlon how Declan had put me up on the cool porcelain edge of the sink in the men's room, of how he'd taken away my panties and spread my thighs so that he could reach my freshly shaved pussy without any barrier. Of how his sweet tongue traced perfect pictures up and over my clit, making ovals and diamonds and figures of eight until my legs shook uncontrollably and I could no longer speak or breathe or think.

Or I could have told Marlon how I'd learned in *Cosmo* the perfect way to go down on a man, fist wrapped tight around the shaft, mouth a magical sucking machine. I could have explained in great detail how I liked to lick my fingertips slowly, while Declan watched, then trick them along his balls, tickling him gently as I sucked him so hard. I could have described how my lipstick smeared all over his skin, leaving rose-pink streaks on his body and my cheeks, and that I was starting to only wear a nude gloss to minimise the retouch factor.

At the very least, I could have told him about how Declan was, like, totally cool, and that the thought of making out with him in a drive-in made my knees weak, while the thought of fucking him in the same drive-in was what made me come each night long after Marlon had gone to sleep. Drinking coffee versus tea started to feel like a reason to fight. What was macho about tea? How could anyone find interest in discussing the merits of oolong over white jasmine? Maybe that was the lack of sleep talking – but even the smell of tea began to repulse me, while I found the very grinds of coffee left in the bottom of my mug to be fascinating remnants destined to turn me on.

Of course, I didn't bother trying to explain any of this to either Marlon or Jenna. They never took my opinions seriously, anyway, even if I was the model reader, exactly the type of chicklet Jenna's publisher catered to. I was the type of girl supposed to dog-ear the pages of her latest tome, living my romantic life vicariously through the escapades of Jacqueline, Jenna's favourite heroine. In reality, it was Jenna who lived her life on the pages. While I lived mine minute by coffee-flavoured minute.

After listening to Jenna and Marlon explain in grave detail that fantasies could only happen in faraway places, with half-dressed native girls and horny sailor boys, I learned about romance versus reality. I learned that fantasies could come true on the vacant second floor of an office building, with a handsome blond man who served coffee and a sultry dark-haired girl who kept having to buy yet another set of pretty panties. The closest *we* got to a sand dune was the gravel in the abandoned dock. The nearest we made it to half-dressed native girls were the models who preened in the atrium between shoots, downing their Diet Cokes and smoking Marlboro Lights.

Declan was everything Marlon was not. My boyfriend, lost in his head, intellectualised everything. Including our sex life. Or lack thereof. And, while Declan might not have possessed a Masters, he had what every romance novel hero has: passion. Electricity. A spark of danger. In fact, the only thing he couldn't offer me was true privacy. All of our meetings were on the sly. Until my boss went away to a writers' conference and Marlon chose to take that same week off to head to the mountains to work on his own writing, an assortment of flavoured teas at his side. This left me and Declan with a room of our own. Or an office, really. A whole office, with a front lobby and two private rooms. Although, truthfully, we didn't really need the whole office. We only needed the rug.

On that very first day, we fucked hard on the floor of the lobby, right in front of my desk. My pink sundress was hiked up to my hips, and my panties were lost somewhere in the corner of the room below the framed covers of the novelist's three books. There were more covers than books because her work had been translated into a variety of languages. So underneath the Dutch version of *Does He Love Me?* lay my twisted pair of petal-pink panties.

Declan kept on his black jeans, and the feel of that faded denim against my naked skin as he ground his body into mine was almost too good to believe. He held me down, held my face in his hands, looked at me with an expression that must have mirrored my own. One that said exactly what I was thinking:

God this is good.

Better than good. It was necessary. We had waited too long for this. We had fucked in every corner of the building, without ever being free to make noise. We had come close to being caught so many times that I'd lost count. Now, we were ready. So ready. His cock was rock hard, and he plunged inside of me with a rhythm that I felt in my own racing heartbeat. He stared into my eyes the whole time, making me tremble with the look on his face. Making me realise how much I wanted to be with him. Not to be with someone who made me feel second best in intelligence and class.

He rotated his hips in small circles as he fucked me, and I reached down between our bodies and slid my fingertips against my clit, pressing hard, gaining the friction I needed to come while he filled me up inside. The climax beat through me, making me beg him for more, for anything, for everything until the waves of pleasure slowly started to subside.

Declan flipped me over and fucked me from behind. I stared at the desk where I worked, at my chipped coffee cup, empty finally since I had no need to keep running downstairs and having it refilled. Then I closed my eyes and let myself feel every sensation. Declan's hands on my waist, holding me steady, his body slamming into mine, slowly and forcefully, rocking me powerfully with every movement. I cried out as he pounded into me, and then I bit into my lip, startled by how loud I'd been. Yet I wanted to be loud. I wanted to make noise. I wanted to be heard.

This was such a long time coming. We'd had to hide for so long. Now, we had room. We had space. We had time. As Declan rocked me, he slid one hand along my waist and then brought his own fingertips between my legs, playing over my still-throbbing clit while continuing to fuck me with that powerhouse force. I groaned and shifted my body, arching back on him. Melding myself to him.

'You like that, don't you?'

Yeah, I liked it. I liked the fact that we weren't pushed up against some wall, or bent over some executive's expensive convertible, or riding up and down in some freight elevator, hoping against hope that the UPS driver wasn't about to make an unexpected delivery. I liked that we were in a large room, with more than enough space around us. And I liked that he didn't have to put his hand over my mouth to muffle the sound of my pleasure, my teeth biting into his fingers to let him know how desperate I was to scream. But all I managed to say was, 'Yes, oh, fuck, yes.'

He understood, and he touched me harder, grazing his short nails against my clit before pinching it between forefinger and thumb. I felt as if I were melting, falling, dissolving into pure pleasure. My body responded to his touch by contracting on his cock tightly, fiercely. We were so in tune, playing off each other, working each other in perfect rhythm.

'Oh yes, you like that,' Declan muttered, his voice low and raw.

He kept touching me, kept fucking me, and I hissed something, some string of nonsense words as I started to come for the second time.

That's precisely when I heard the key in the lock. *Oh,*

God, I thought. *Oh, God. Oh, God. Oh, God.* This wasn't a compromising position. There was no compromise involved. This was a flat-out confession.

Jenna, home early for no explainable reason, pushed open the door and strode into the room while Declan and I flew apart from each other in super-speed and tried our best to look as if we hadn't just been fucking doggy-style. Try this yourself sometime. It's not possible. Especially when your dress is hiked up around your hips and your panties are on the floor half the room away from you. It's just not possible to act innocent when your lover's cock is still hard and glistening from your own liquid sex juices and his jeans are open in the centre, as if he's chosen to put himself on display. Yes, his cock was worthy of its own pedestal, but now wasn't the time to unveil the majestic towering force.

My boss stopped, clearly startled to find me away from my desk. And then just as startled to find the coffee-delivery boy in the room with me. She looked at me, looked at Declan, looked at me again, and then headed directly to her office without speaking a word. Yet I thought I caught an expression in her icy-blue eyes as she strode by me. Not one of understanding, though. One of out-and-out jealousy, although her Botox-enhanced brow couldn't furrow to show her displeasure. I was living her words, while all she could do was write them. And have them translated into seventeen languages, including Dutch.

'Oh, God,' Declan said, his thoughts echoing my own from a moment before. 'We're fucked.'

'No –' I couldn't help but smile, because I felt a wave of relief at no longer having to hide '– *I'm* fucked. God, Declan, you fucked me so good.'

Now he grinned too. Marlon would have used a different word there. I knew it. He would have gotten out his red pen, insisting that there was a jarring repetition on the word 'fuck', one that would pull the readers right out of the story. 'You're *screwed*,' he might have said. 'You're *finished*. You're *done*.'

But none of those words rang true to me. And I supposed that was something I'd have to discuss with him when he returned – at least I would right after my next coffee break.

The Tipping Point Jan Bolton

I must have been about six months into my position
working as a research assistant for Lord X when he let it
be known that he had an enthusiasm for 'uncustomary
caprices'. Given that this information was imparted with
a large leathery hand on my bottom, there could be little
doubt that he was referring to whims of a sexual nature.
But quite how 'uncustomary' Lord X's fancies would turn
out to be was something of a shock, even to a young
woman with a fair degree of intimate experience under
her belt. I'd heard that the upper echelons of older-gener-
ation male politicians were prone to enjoying curious
pastimes now and then, and, when such proclivities made
their way into the tabloids, I must confess that I always
tittered at the salacious details. Despite my prurient
interest in scandal in high places, I never expected to be a
party to kinky behaviour at first hand, although, looking
back, I guess I almost willed my involvement in it to
happen.

I've always found secret societies and covert clubs so
thrilling. As a child I delighted in making up passwords
and creating mock official documents out of old bills and
photo-booth pictures, swearing my friends to secrecy and
hiding packets of cigarettes in old hardback books that I'd
cut the guts from. The hidden and the encoded; the
clandestine and the curious – these are the things to
which I am drawn.

I also like prising secrets out of people about their sex
lives. During tipsy conversations at university girls' nights
in, I'd always steer the topic to erotic matters, trying to

coerce my colleagues into saucy confessions. They never admitted to anything particularly memorable: a bit of light bondage, a few sex toys, some dressing up. Of course, no one in my circle of bright young things would go into details more scandalous than elliptical chat about silk scarves and ice cubes; the sort of thing women's magazines recommend to spice up your love life. None of them spoke about the emotions and thoughts they'd had while intimately engaged with their Jessica Rabbit, or fastened to a bed post with handcuffs. It was all very 'what I did in my bedroom' – the almost-to-be-expected behaviour of young lovers. I'll bet that few of them had indulged in what I found myself doing over the course of that dull damp winter of 1999.

It is fair to mention at this point that my behaviour during the weeks leading up to Lord X's announcement had been somewhat flirtatious. I was trying to wheedle myself into his good books for a recommendation that would better my chances of an increase in salary. I'd heard that a number of senior research positions were due to become available, some with postings abroad, and, if I could secure a place on one of them, I would be looking at having a very handsome CV by the time I was 25 and possibly a civil service post that would set me up for many career years to come. So my reaction was not entirely one of surprise when he rose to my teasing bait, and it took considerable effort not to betray how pleased I was with myself for having had this effect on him so easily. Of course, one must never reveal a trace of triumph to Alpha types like Lord X that you have manipulated them, or that you can read them like an open book – for that would ruin their own sense of achievement in the sport, and sport is, after all, a pastime in which Alpha types love to excel. So I engineered my expression into one of feminine fluster on that cloudy Wednesday in November and waited for him to elaborate. Before I tell you what that was, I think I'd better recap, to describe exactly what was happening to prompt such an unprofessional detour from political matters in hand.

For months I had been assisting Lord X in the preparation of a counterpoint paper concerning the extension of bus lanes and road tolls to peripheral areas of London. The whole business was becoming so deathly dull that I began to wish I had opted for my second career choice in the Royal Navy. Yet here I was in the chambers of Parliament itself, with my foot on the first rung of a career in politics. I couldn't give up because of some tiresome rigmarole for the Transport Committee. I was, for the most part, delighted to be there; there were fewer buildings in the world more esteemed than the Houses of Parliament.

I'll always remember, setting foot into the Lords' chamber for the first time, how the weight of English history and tradition, with all its trappings of pomp and privilege, and ermine-cloaked authority, had struck me in the gut as something of a pleasant surprise. I had feared I would find the sombre ceremonies moribund and irrelevant in a London that pulsed to a sound more evocative of South Central Los Angeles than Westminster, but, in fact, the reverse was true. Witnessing a debate on my first day in the House, I felt a sense of pride – to be British and to be part of a majestic continuum. Here was something not dowdy, but mighty; for goodness sake, I walked past a document no less profound than the Magna Carta on my way to the canteen every day.

Every part of the building was steeped in tradition. Not for me a staff room of table football and plasma screens tuned to MTV. The décor of the office in which we worked could not have changed much from the 1940s. With heavy wooden-panelling on the walls, solid oak desks, thick Turkish carpet and book shelves lining one complete side of this vast room, it had an air of constitutional propriety about it. One couldn't imagine anything more frivolous occurring in this environment than perhaps taking a nip from the odd bottle of single malt that was locked in one of the desk drawers. And yet, paradoxically, it was this stifling ambiance, I'm sure, that was conducive to the extremities that Lord X – and those like him – went in finding pleasure through very private means out of Parliament hours.

It was about 4.30 in the afternoon; almost dark outside with the central heating turned up far too high for my liking – a time when drowsiness can set in and the listlessness that questions the point of analysing yet another focus-group report.

I became aware that Lord X had been watching me at particular points during my trips up and down the bookshelves, ascending and descending the step-ladder to retrieve any number of lever-arch files dedicated to 1997's research findings.

It was my ascents that seemed to catch his eye the most, however; I spotted him looking at me through discreet glances over my shoulder. It was true that I'd begun to wear increasingly flattering outfits to work. Of course I wasn't sporting anything too dressy or showy, and certainly not revealing, but I selected garments that showed my firm rounded figure to its best advantage: plunging V-shaped necklines, wide-hemmed, tailored trousers and, on this occasion, a crisp cotton white shirt and a satin-lined, very formal-looking navy-blue skirt with a vent cut into the back and a column of 2″ wide buckles that formed a vertical line from the waistband to the base of my spine.

I made my way backwards and forwards, selecting files and photocopying them before carefully replacing them and scaling the ladder, which was fixed into the floor on smooth runners, to put them back in order.

It transpired that the vision of my bottom, flaring under my waistline into two perfect globes, clad tightly in my business skirt, reached what Cartier-Bresson coined the 'decisive moment' at about 4.33p.m., just after the huge clang of Big Ben, when the silence of the room was broken by Lord X's rejoinder, 'I love it when your skirt raises just a little. It does brighten up a dull afternoon.'

He then immediately coughed and croaked – a nervous reaction to the suddenness of his inappropriate outburst, as if it had issued forth of its own volition and he was fighting to prevent further unconscious desires bursting through. He sounded as if his arousal was choking him and had to be outed lest he would strangle.

I froze on the ladder, considering the magnitude of repercussions that could ensue as a result of such a proclamation. For a few torturous seconds he must have anticipated a torrent of feminist fury, a raft of disciplinary procedures and claims of sexual harassment appearing on House of Commons internal memos ... the unspeakable procedure that these days is so likely to spiral out from an older gentleman's more sporting observations.

Any fears he may have had were dispatched as swiftly to the wastebin as an email request for charity sponsorship as I turned 45 degrees to the left and regarded him from my lofty position. Despite his being so much older, at least 50, and being my employer, I just couldn't resist a tease. I patently avoided referring to his announcement and asked him instead, 'Would you want me to look in the older files, sir, like those positioned on the top shelf just a row along from your desk? I would have to reach up even higher to get at them.'

'Oh, yes,' he stammered. 'Yes, that's a very good idea.'

I slowly descended the ladder, swaying my hips and presumably whetting his appetite even more. I pushed the ladder along, looking him in the eye as he settled in for the display. When I got to the perfect point in the tracks I once again ascended the metal steps. The old goat was now shamelessly craning his neck, looking right up my skirt as I bent one knee to lean onto the flat level top of the ladder. In this position he was getting a shadowy view of my crotch and the swollen pouch of my sex pressed tight and plump against the cotton of my knickers, just visible to him as a flash of white.

His eyes darted about, shining as he became playful, to settle on some long-filed tome. 'Townsend, I need you to reach for Policy and Practice in Highway Reform,' he said.

This old, brown-leather book was just possible to reach from where I had placed the ladder but it would require a stretch long enough to send my skirt riding up to at least the bottom of my knickers. Still, there was little point being genuinely coy at this stage, and I swallowed my pride and went for it, wriggling slightly as the skirt lifted to show the tops of my hold-ups and two slivers of flesh at the base of my meaty bottom.

He let out a groan of appreciation.

Before I treated him to too much excitement, I kneeled up straight, pulled my skirt back down as if nothing had happened and began flicking through the onion-skin pages, resting the base of the heavy book on my pubic bone as I looked for mind-numbing facts and figures that I could recite about transport reform, prolonging the sweet agony, imagining what lusty desires were coursing through his imagination, and how hard he would be in his trousers.

'Did you know, sir,' I began, 'that they drove sheep through Chalk Farm until war broke out in 1939?' I feigned an engrossed interest in the weighty file. 'And tram lines ran all the way to Primrose Hill, right up until 1952.'

'Well, I think I had better see that for myself,' said Lord X, obviously suffering exquisite torment at my stringing out this curious seduction. He surely could not have expected a reaction more animated at best than a flush of girly giggles, and now I was showing him my knickers and teasing him mercilessly.

'Bring it to me without delay,' he boomed.

I knew he was excited beyond measure that I hadn't scolded him for taking our working relationship into this potentially dangerous new zone of mixing pleasure with business. A sense of relief and of pure devilment must have been running around his veins, his pulse racing with lewd anticipation at the thought of getting his hands on me. I dragged it out even more.

'Lord X,' I began, beginning to introduce a girly inflection to my intonation, 'if I bring it right over to you and lay it on your desk, would we be able to look at it together?

'Of course, my dear,' he said, his voice tight with lust. 'But, before you do, I think I'd like to test the safety levels of that ladder, what with you balancing those heavy files. I wouldn't want you to fall or have an accident due to my negligence.'

He pushed his chair away from the desk – enough to show that my assumptions were spot on; his crotch was straining with tension due to an almighty tumescence. He adjusted himself and walked over to where the ladder was positioned and stood beneath it. I knew what was coming – and what he wanted. Call it sexual intuition, but I knew he didn't want me to descend just yet. I placed the book on the top platform and slowly began to lift my skirt once more. I could feel the tension in my calves; my heart beating in reaction to my daring display, and a slick warmth beginning to pool between my legs. My sex lips were swollen and moist; it felt as if they were blooming to full shape – into the ripe pouch that looks so inviting to men and yet is, for the most part, a sight not experienced by the female – unless she has a habit of studying herself in the mirror from behind.

Lord X was about three or four feet beneath me. Somehow the distance added to the spectacle, as he kept telling me to stay where I was so he could 'admire the view from on high'. I leaned forwards once more and this time added to the display by sliding my right hand between my legs and rubbing the tight cotton that covered the pouch.

'You dirty girl,' said Lord X. 'Playing with yourself in my office. It's a disgrace. I think you should show me exactly what you would do left to your own devices.'

'Well, that would mean I would have to take my knickers down,' I said, affecting a voice not entirely commensurate with one who has an MSc in Political Sciences.

'Oh no you don't,' said Lord X. 'I'll be the judge of that.'

And then the ladder wobbled slightly as he stepped up two levels, within touching distance of my arse.

'Feel how tight they are, sir,' I complained. 'I can't possibly do what I want to do with knickers this tight around me.'

'I suppose you want to play with yourself, eh? Want to make yourself orgasm in my office.'

I nodded my head. And then it came – a firm and gentle caress of my bottom cheeks with the heel of his hand and slowly, slowly, a thick curled finger slipped under the gusset and into my hot juicy centre.

'Oh, Townsend,' he croaked, 'I think we've got a situation here.'

He levered his arm to a position that gave him maximum potential for manipulation, and began to go at fingering me with the enthusiasm of a teenaged boy getting his first feel of a girl, but tempered with the experience of remembering to rub over my button with each alternate stroke

'Do you like that?' he whispered into my ear. 'Do you like me touching your dirty little cunt like this?'

'I think it's disgusting, sir,' I replied. 'You should know better, a man of your position. What will the Transport Committee say when you tell them your report was postponed because you had to rub your young assistant between the legs and make her climax.'

'I'll tell them it was your fault, you little minx,' he said, entering into my fantasy of inappropriate honesty. 'I'll tell them I had a hard-on so big that neither of us could concentrate on Highway Reform Policy. And, speaking of which, Townsend, you're going to make me do something I might regret if you don't get down off the ladder now. I'm about to shoot in my pants when I'd rather be doing it all over your sweet little face with my hands on your arse.'

He was now shamelessly masturbating. He'd freed himself from his trousers while he'd been fingering me, and I could now snatch glimpses of his penis shining like a rude beacon in the almost hallowed room. I was imagining what it would feel like to descend the ladder and sit right on it, or take it into my mouth and suck on it as I squatted under his desk. More pertinently, I wondered what it would be like to have it thrust into me from behind. It was, I suppose, what one would call the tipping point.

I descended the ladder with his hands on my backside and the air thick with tension and the scent of our combined arousal. I then hurried to lock the door so that we wouldn't be interrupted. In the meantime, he tucked himself away for a moment while he reached into his drawer and produced two glasses and a bottle of vintage red wine. His restraint impressed me; I was so hot and moist in my sex that it was literally aching for attention, yet he seemed calm and able to control his lusts, despite what he had said.

'Look, you won't think badly of me if we have a little recreation time, will you, Townsend?' he began, suddenly businesslike and observing me over the top of his varifocals.

'I wouldn't be here now if that were likely,' I said, still the coquette. 'I don't want to cause any trouble . . . I just, well, I think you would probably appreciate me more than men my own age, and I would like to give you an afternoon to remember.'

I meant the flattery, too. I was bored with vain go-getters that were my contemporaries; the City boys and snooty girls who bullied their way up the career ladder without a trace of humility. For all his power and standing in society, Lord X had old-fashioned Class with a capital C and an education that had taught him manners and good grace, even in the most compromising of moments – such as adjusting one's genitals in female company.

I touched his arm very lightly with one finger, looked into his eyes with a cheeky expression and bit my bottom lip. It was then that the brown leathery hand made its way to my bottom, and he leaned in closer to me so that I could smell his lemony cologne and a whiff of quality leather. Despite the fact we were alone, and no one could hear, he whispered into my ear – a gesture so discreet and understated that a thrill of illicit pleasure ran through me like a dart of sexual energy. It was then that I was informed of the 'uncustomary caprices'.

I giggled softly into my hand and wriggled myself against him.

'I do like a game girl,' he said. 'I like to be able to see things and say things.'

I could feel his erection poking into the top of my hip as I took my first sip of the fruity red wine and kept looking straight ahead. I wondered what it was he liked to see and say but I made a bet with myself at very short odds that it would involve my bottom and his verbal appreciation of it.

I began to question him about what exactly it was he liked to see and say as we clinked glasses and settled into stringing out our arousal until it reached bursting point.

'How about two girls together, rubbing each other between the legs?' I ventured.

'Well, that would be pretty, but they would have to be

absolutely filthy with each other, and very natural ... not like those silicone monstrosities from California.'

'Is it to watch a live sex show or lap-dancer?'

'Christ, no!' he thundered, then laughed. 'Watch some bored tart fold her drug-ravaged body around a greasy pole ... no thanks.'

They're not all like that,' I countered, realising swiftly that I had neither met nor ever spoken to such a person. 'What about those "gentlemen's clubs"?' I offered.

'They're all right, I suppose, but it's all too Americanised for my liking. Too much toothpaste and hairspray. None of them has that, that ...'

'Understated Englishness?' I ventured.

'Exactly!' he said, as if I had hit on something quintessential. 'I don't want some brassy scrubber writhing around all over the place. I don't see the point. Some of them are quite pretty, I suppose, but they all seem too experienced. None of them has the right air of naughtiness about them. No, I want a dirty English girl with a good education and an adventurous spirit.'

He sat back on his chair and patted his knees, so I sat down sideways on top of him. He snuck a hand round me and into my shirt, and then whispered in my ear in a mock-admonishing voice, 'Oh Townsend, I'm disappointed that you didn't know what I wanted.'

I swivelled my head towards him, getting the chance to study him at close range. His hair was thick, grey and wavy. His eyes were clear blue and his skin well cared for.

'You were supposed to go over my knees, not down on top of them,' he exclaimed.

The thought hadn't occurred to me, and I chided myself for not being more intuitive to his predilections.

'Does that mean, that ... that ...' I began fearfully.

'Oh yes. It means exactly what you are thinking, my girl. You are going to get some old-fashioned discipline meted out on your sweet, darling little bottom. But don't think I will spare you just because you are pretty,' he said. 'In fact, it'll be extra hard because of it!'

With one fluid movement he stood up, making me slide off his lap to my feet. Before I had the chance to decide for myself whether or not this was a good idea, he flipped me onto his lap and had pulled me over his thighs. I suddenly found myself in an ignominious position, blood rushing to my head, staring at the carpet.

And then came the moments he relished. The large leathery hand caressed flat circles over my cheeks. The curling meaty finger snaked into my crevice. The practised touch of decades of pleasing wives and mistresses played under my knickers and over my clit. It was the ecstasy before the punishment.

After such tender ministrations he pulled my white cotton knickers down over my globes and laid me bare. Then came the action. The flat palm came whacking down onto my flesh in ten rapid smarting strokes.

'You dirty girl. You've been asking for it for so long. Since your first day, in fact,' he growled.

I yelped in indignation.

'What! Why?' I sobbed, as the next ten whacks landed onto my increasingly hot arse.

I wriggled and struggled, trying to free myself from his enthusiastic spanking.

'You have been trying to distract me since the very day I interviewed you,' he said, now pinching my reddened cheeks. 'Don't think you can get one over on me; I full well know the wiles of females.'

How could he have known? I had not given anything away. His pinching was an insult to my injured bottom and I began to wriggle fervently as his left hand pressed down more firmly on my back.

To temper his cruelty, an occasional tender caress was applied, and I realised that I had fallen into the hands of a master spanker and expert in female strategy. Despite the smarting sensation in my bottom, my sex was wetter than ever, and what I needed and craved was for him to give me the pounding I so rightly deserved. I could feel his hard prick pressing into me through his trousers and after another ten strokes of his hand he released me to fall like a rag doll onto the carpet. It felt natural to effect a sulky expression to add to my naughty girl persona and, when I looked up at him through tear-stained eyes, I looked right into the fleshy column that protruded from between his legs and was being pumped by his right hand.

'I've got something girls like you can't wait to get inside them,' he teased, luring me to wrap my mouth around it. 'I bet you want this, don't you?'

I crawled up his legs and laid my head in his lap. He stroked my hair tenderly, yet this was accompanied by a very stern announcement.

'I'm going to do it all over your face in a second. And I want you to love it. You're going to get my spunk in your mouth and love it.'

'But, Lord X,' I protested. 'You just said I was going to get it inside me. Properly, I mean.'

'Oh you will,' he promised, 'but all in good time.'

And with that he cupped one hand around the back of my head and brought me into close quarter with the right honourable member. It was a clean and musky column of handsome gristle and I set about it with relish. He liked to manipulate it, and took delight in rubbing it across my face, prodding it into my neck and nose and making sure I was fully acquainted with it before ordering me to open wide and take it fully into my mouth. He groaned, gasped and laughed a satisfied chuckle of a man who had got himself an unexpected treat.

I licked and sucked and pressed a hand against his balls, still snug in their pinstripe home. I was, by now, creaming into my swollen sex and completely desperate to come. I knew there would be no chance of his seeing to my needs once he'd had his fun, so I had to take matters into my own hand. With one hand skilfully playing with his cock as I took it into my mouth, I reached down and felt the pool of oozing warmth between my thighs. I pressed two fingers against my clit, not moving my hand frantically but allowing my hips to do the work, thrusting back and forth across my hand as if I were a man fucking a woman.

The sight of my abandoned display was all it took for Lord X to reach his ultimate moment. He pulled out of my mouth and told me to look up at him. The very next second he shouted out my name, shot a jet of milky fluid onto my face; then another and yet more, until my face and neck were liberally splattered.

I couldn't hold back. The combination of the sound spanking and my own teasing of him had conspired to make me more turned on than I had ever been in my life. It was the first time I'd been spanked, and the firm mastery he had inflicted on my bottom had brought out the bad girl in me – which, in turn, brought out the pretend stern taskmaster in him. It was a perfect match. It gave me an illicit thrill of confidence, and I knew the sight of me enjoying my own orgasm would be something he'd want more of.

'Watch me, sir,' I cooed. 'I'm going to come for you. You've made me have such dirty thoughts about you.'

And with that I let go – and felt myself spasm into the delicious abyss, as Lord X stroked my hair with a tender touch.

We relaxed with the wine for a while, stunned into silence at first but soon exchanging glances that glittered with the promise of future erotic fun.

It wasn't long before I was accepting lifts home, and days out to country pubs and walks in the woods under the guise of research into rural transport initiatives. The more outrageous and exhibitionist my behaviour became, the more I found myself being treated to wonderful lunches and special favours. Increasingly I allowed him to indulge his ever-more outrageous kinks.

I bared my bottom over a farmer's gate and was treated to a hearty hand-spanking with the threat of dog-walkers surprising us at any minute. He didn't care who caught us, and I admired his gusto. Once, while caught short in the New Forest after we'd polished off two bottles of wine, he begged me to let him watch as I relieved myself – except he wouldn't let me take my knickers off. He made me pee onto the ground through my knickers, which he loved. He masturbated over me as I humiliated myself before him. It was so very, very wrong, and it felt so very, very good, and my drunken laughter rang out in the autumn air as I wet myself for his amusement. And he thrashed me afterwards, too – but not very hard – with a handful of birch twigs as we made a pact to be as naughty as possible, as often as possible. I remember being driven home that day, knickerless and glowing with the delicious thrill of having behaved so impeccably filthily for my Lord.

There are so many naughty things we did, Lord X and I. We were a perfect complement to each other, despite the gap in ages between us. Those winter nights that led up to the new millennium whizzed by in a blur of tempered ribaldry. I accompanied him to soirées on the Parliament terrace, brandishing files and policy reports and being every inch the serious-minded assistant, while, barely an hour beforehand, I would have been on all fours in a Knightsbridge dungeon.

These days I head up my own research team. In summer 2000 I got my foreign posting, out to Belize where giant lizards bake in the afternoon sun and a trip to the coral reefs costs a fraction of a weekend in a New Forest hotel.

Lord X and I occasionally bump into each other at London gatherings. Why, only last month we were at a directors' convention in Pall Mall. I was entertaining some clients in a rather grand reception room lined with books. I heard a familiar voice behind me, addressing one of the young, attractive silver service staff in the most beguiling tone: 'Oh look, there's the book on social policy that I edited back in 1976. Would you mind reaching up there, my dear, seeing as you are so much younger than I?'

He watched in subtle appreciation as she scaled the ladder fixed in runners and stretched to reach the book as she teetered on the platform.

I smelt a tang of lemony cologne, and a whiff of leather as a whisper came in my ear. 'Happy days, Townsend. Happy days.'

The All Night Tulsa Brown

Radio is a glamorous business – for about fifteen minutes. After that you realise it's low-paying, hierarchical and – in my small Midwestern city at least – sexist. The day shifts went to the men, the resonant bass-throated devils whose voices had been shaped by whiskey and cigarettes.

I got the city when it was asleep. I was Sherry Sharone, the velvet vixen on CHQT from midnight to six a.m, the shift we simply called the All Night. In some places that would have been fun; there's hot radio after the sun goes down. But my station was a paragon of easy listening, also known as Death by Syrup. If my audience wasn't already comatose, I was supposed to lull them into it.

'Glide, Sherry,' the programme director admonished me. 'You've got a good voice but you have to mellow your delivery. Pull up over them like a blanket, and quit being such a –'

'Live wire?' I said.

'Bitch.'

It was hard. I was frustrated. By two a.m. of my working night, my fantasies swung between riding a big cock against the wall of a thumping, throbbing dance club, and doing something unspeakable to every copy of 'My Heart Will Go On'.

The All Night didn't lend itself to a social life. What opportunities weren't squashed by my strange hours were ground under the station's 'rules of decorum'. At 27, I remembered my club days like a distant dream: a copper-coloured wash in my short, sandy hair and the twenty – or so – extra pounds swaying on my breasts and hips. On a dance floor I bounced, the distinctive female jiggle that swivelled men on their bar stools. I missed that, but even more I missed the thrill of a needy groan against my ear, desire on the verge of agony. 'Please, Sherry' always sent a stripe of lightning through my jeans.

My friends couldn't understand my current 'date difficulty'. 'Men phone you all the time. Well, at least on the request line.'

It made me sigh. There's a cardinal rule in radio: the listener is king – unless he wants to meet you. Then you have to assume he's a nut. It was a safety issue. We weren't allowed to respond to fan mail, and we had a video security system on the door. I even had a 'panic button' in the control booth, a silent alarm that would get the police over in two minutes, thirty-five seconds.

I appreciated that. Some of my fans were no-frills suitors whose calls never made it to air.

'Ah, c'mon, Sherry. I've got eight hard inches.'

'And it's attached to six feet of loser. Bad ratio, fella.'
Click.

The 'Romeos' were even worse, perhaps because they were so devoted. Carl was indefatigable.

'I know how to treat a lady like you, Sherry.'

'I eat balls for breakfast, Carl.'

'I'm a great cook!'
Click.

In truth, I loved being on air. There's a heady magic in getting paid to talk, like spinning straw into gold. To look out the big plate-glass window in the control booth at the twinkling city ignited something ravenous in me. I wanted to bewitch every listener, reel them in and hold them like stars in my hands.

And I discovered something: you can sail away on the stream of your own voice. It's like daydreaming while you drive. The words pour out in a smooth, effortless flow and your mind skips ahead, a flat stone over water. After eight months, my fantasies had pooled deep, fed by two springs, hunger and boredom.

But that wasn't like sex. One night in the middle of August the velvet vixen was feeling ragged, and getting punchy on the phone-line buttons.

'Hi, can I request a song?'

'No.'

'Hi, can I –'

'Nope.'

'Hey, could you play a song for me?'

I spun around in my chair. The man leaned in the doorway of the control booth, holding my garbage can and grinning. At the edge of my consciousness I registered his uniform: short-sleeved work shirt and canvas pants in denim blue. Cleaning company. I even remembered that I'd seen his wide back earlier, bent into the staff-room sink.

That hadn't prepared me for his front. He had a strong neck and square jaw, features that were more pronounced thanks to a marine-recruit haircut. This man looked *shorn*. He wasn't muscle bound, but broad shouldered and tight hipped, the devastating V of a fine male body that spoke to my female parts in basic English, especially the part tucked high under my summer skirt.

His whole body tilted in a deferential way, like a ranch hand at the back door of the Big House, yet he gazed at me with bold familiarity. Had I met him somewhere? No, I wouldn't have forgotten this barroom buck.

My professional training had vanished. For long seconds I was speechless in the flush of heat and high-school goofiness. Damn, he was cute.

'No. No requests,' I blurted at last. In the corner of my eye, I noticed my digital countdown clock – this song was ending in eight seconds, and then I had concert tickets to give away. 'Get out.'

He lifted an eyebrow, and touched his forehead in a

mock salute. 'Yes, *ma'am*.' He took my garbage can with him when he left.

Thank God I could have punched those buttons in my sleep and talked my way through an earthquake. The tickets went to caller number eight – other than that, I had only a vague idea what planet I was on.

Oh, that was classy, Sherry. A man walks through the door and you revert to monosyllables?

I felt the sting of a different regret, too. I'd been outright rude. Had I been doing the All Night so long I didn't know how to communicate with people, only talk *at* them? As soon as my next song set was in progress, I slipped out of the booth and went to find him.

He was vacuuming a hallway, intent on his work, strong shoulders and forearms swaying with easy grace as he manoeuvred the industrial-sized unit. Yet there was still something precise in his movements. Military? I thought of the salute, sarcasm to be sure, yet so deft it made me think he'd practised.

I waved to get his attention. The vacuum's engine gargled to a stop.

'Look, I didn't mean to bark at you. It's just that we're in ratings right now. I have to stick to the Play List.'

'That's OK. I was just hoping for something with a *beat*.' He gave the hose a little back-and-forth shimmy, as if dancing with it. 'Besides, I've listened to your show a lot. I already knew you were –'

'A bitch?'

'Nobody's fool.' His smile was strangely shy, glimmering with a secret. 'Sherry Sharone *owns* the night.'

Bald flattery, and I didn't care. I tingled in the wash of the accolade.

'Well, drop by the booth when you have a minute. I'll see what I can do.'

Guests were absolutely forbidden in the control room. There was only one place he could stand upright and not be seen through the big window: the narrow space between two high bookshelves, directly across from the control board. His shoulders touched wood on either side and he had to flatten himself to the wall, a handsome, straight-armed toy soldier.

And soldier he was, part-time at least. Jeff was 24, a final-year engineering student who was a weekend reservist. That haircut was army, not marines. And he worked nights, too? It made me laugh and shake my head.

'Is there a single minute of your day that isn't planned out for you?' I asked.

'I like to push myself, see how much I can take.' That smile again, the private one.

I glanced at the clock. 'Well, push yourself to hold still for thirty seconds. I'm going to turn on the microphone and you can't breathe, blink or fart until I say so.'

'Yes, ma'am.' Jeff's eyes twinkled. He seemed to take pleasure in saying it and, to be honest, so did I. This time the words stroked me like a warm hand.

Very few commercials are read 'live' on radio any more – it's too dangerous. A squeaky chair or rattling script can ruin it, even if you don't flub your lines. Still, some clients liked the spontaneous flavour, and I knew I was good at it. With Jeff as an audience I was *great*.

He was rapt, enthralled. I felt his gaze as if it was a tangible heat source, the steady, bone-warming glow of a radiator. My eyes stole away from the script to savour him: his square-shouldered stance pulled his shirt tight across his chest, nipples raising the fabric like kernels of corn; the solid jut in his work pants wasn't a hard-on but a healthy animal readiness.

And he waited against the wall because I'd told him to. The idea was slick and wanton, and sent curls of excitement into my thighs.

'. . . So settle back and relax in the luxury of fine furniture from Hanson's. You deserve it.'

Even when I'd turned off the mike and punched in the next pre-recorded ad, Jeff waited, obediently still.

I finally laughed. 'At ease, soldier.'

'That was amazing.' The words were hushed with awe. 'You sound like smoke and steel.'

'Oh, it's a little genetics and a whole lot of training.'

He shook his head. 'Maybe for the others, but you're different. That ballsy voice is *you*. The first time I heard it, I thought, that's one hard, hot lady. It's a dream come true to meet you. I've waited so long.'

He'd waited? My skin prickled, thin fingers of uneasiness crawling over my bare shoulders.

'How ... did you get this job?'

'I applied for it.' He grinned. 'Three times.'

Revelation smacked me awake. 'Are you a star fucker, Jeff?'

His smirk spread wide. 'Not yet. But the night isn't over, is it?'

Alarm ran from my heart to my hands, burst painfully in my fingertips. A fan or a stalker? I was alone in the station with God-knew-what. My thoughts whirled: push the panic button – no! Get him out of here – no! Get yourself out of this booth ...

Then fear ignited into something else. *How dare he.*

'You punk. You snot-nosed son of a bitch! Who the hell do you think you are?' A burning wave pushed me to my feet. 'I get cheap come-ons ten times a night from celebrity sluts like you. Yet you march in here with a vacuum cleaner and expect to be something different? Did you think I'd fall at your feet?'

Surprise had wiped the insolence off his face. He took a step. 'Sherry, I –'

'Back against the wall!'

He obeyed abruptly, shoulders hitting the wood with a satisfying thump. I glared at him, my heart pounding. But damn – this commercial break was ending. I felt a spasm of deep, ingrained reflex: keep the show on schedule.

My finger flew up, an order, a threat. 'Stay.'

I dropped into my chair and took a breath. I flicked the mike. Three, two and . . .

'Welcome back, night people. I'm Sherry Sharone on CHQT. It's two thirty-four, a long way to dawn, but I have mellow favourites from yesterday and today to get you there. And, hey! Didn't get your tickets for the Amanda Marshall concert? Well, you and five friends . . .'

I slid into the contest promo, the words flowing in a professional purr. The rush of adrenaline was still galloping through my body but I was riding it now, and it veered off suddenly.

So he wants you, I told myself. What are you so upset about? It's not like he's one of those nuts on the phone. If you'd met in a bar you would have danced a jig out the door with him.

Jeff hadn't moved. He remained at attention between the shelves, lips parted, breathing lightly. And something extraordinary was happening. I watched in fascination as his fly swelled into a pronounced bulge. I'd just yelled at him and he was getting a hard-on? My clit pulsed in sweet surprise.

He had to be uncomfortable, yet he still didn't stir. There was something about that – his arousal, discomfort and obedience – that stroked me. It plumbed the deep, silent fantasies that had pooled in my empty hours alone with the microphone.

For a brief moment, common sense raised its yappy head. It didn't stand a chance.

If he was dangerous he would have done something already, or threatened to. He had a chance to jump me in the hallway, when my back was turned. He's followed every order I've given – so far.

'. . . your choice for smooth radio, QT One-oh-three.'

Music up, mike off. For a moment there was only the low simpering of the love-struck singer.

'You were right, Jeff. I *do* own the night – or I own this one. And I don't like to be surprised by sudden moves from mouthy pick-up artists. But that doesn't mean I can't be impressed.'

His gaze crept over, hesitant, hopeful.

'Now, if you made a mistake you can walk out of this station. I'll see that you get a referral for your next job. Or – you can keep me company. Show me that you know how to behave with a hard, hot lady. You want to be a star fucker? Persuade me.'

I felt a thrilling tremor, the power of the spoken word. I'd never said that to anyone, not even in my fantasies, yet it rolled off my tongue as easily as my own call letters.

'Here's the rule: nothing interferes with my show. And no surprises, nothing that might *alarm* me. There are two magic buttons in this room, Jeff. One is a direct line to the cop shop – I don't even have to talk. They'll be here before you can get out the front door.'

'And the other one?'

'Use your imagination.'

He paused, then smiled as he began to unbutton his shirt. 'I have plenty of that, ma'am.'

I stared, mesmerised. With the buttons free, he simply shrugged the shirt off and it melted to the floor. His chest was breathtaking. Naked, he looked larger, his broad pectoral muscles stretching out in smooth, hard undulations, divided down the centre by a line of flat brown hair. It thickened on its way into his pants: a bristly, animal promise over his abdomen.

'Give me your belt.' The coolness of my voice astonished me. Where had those words come from?

The colour of his eyes deepened to hard hazelnut. He

unhooked the buckle then pulled it out of the loops, a brown snake gleaming dully.

He faltered and I saw his predicament – how was he going to get it to me without throwing it? Suddenly he folded the belt into an elongated figure of eight, and clamped it between his teeth. It looped on either side of his face like a bow, and spread his mouth in a grimace: a bridle or a gag. The sight seared me. My pussy lips throbbed, wet and engorged, pushing against the cotton centre of my panties.

With the belt still in his mouth, Jeff slid down the wall, then scooted across the floor on his ass and hands, beneath the level of the window. He slipped under the control board, next to my bare legs.

It happened so swiftly I almost shrieked. Instead, I wheeled my chair back and glared down at him. He was crouched in the opening like an oversized dog in a kennel.

'What the hell are you doing?'

He offered the belt to me. 'I thought I could massage your feet.'

The folded leather was stiff, resilient in my grasp. I felt the wet spot where his tongue had touched and it sent an illicit tingle through me, as if he'd licked my hand.

'All right. As long as you're quiet.' I slipped my feet out of my sandals.

Jeff's hands were hot, strong and experienced. He rubbed slow, delicious circles around my ankles, drew long lines of pressure with his thumbs. Every digit was patiently caressed. Adored. Molten pleasure flowed through my legs like lava, straight into the waiting portal of my cunt.

The tart scent rose from under my loose summer skirt. I was sure he could smell me; I could smell myself. Leaning back in my chair, I watched him through heavy eyes, relished the big, half-naked body crouched at my feet. I felt like a sultana: powerful and decadent. My free foot rested on one of his thighs, and I slid it over to his crotch, letting the prodigious bulge fill the curve of my arch. Granite. I ached for it.

But this sultana still had a show to do. I forced myself upright to reach the microphone.

'Not a peep,' I ordered, and underscored the command with light but distinct pressure on his crotch, the way you accelerate a car over a rise. I heard a low, ragged breath beneath the control board – pain or pleasure? My pussy swam. It was all pleasure to me.

Mike on. Music fade. 'Ooh, that lady's voice is something else, isn't it? Melissa Etheridge, and before that . . .'

Movement beneath the desk: I felt Jeff lift my foot higher. Before I could register surprise, wet heat sizzled in a white line up my leg. My God, he was sucking my toes! For a second I was speechless, the most dreaded offence: dead air. Then my survival instinct kicked in and I heard my own voice as if from a distance, a liquid growl.

'. . . smooth favourites to sail you away – QT One-oh-three.'

Jeff began to lick his way up the inside of my left leg.

I leaned back and pushed my ass to the front of the chair, hiking my skirt high over my thighs. Jeff's free hand teased me through my panties, thick fingers stroking the soaked fabric. When I stretched the cotton panel over to one side, the heat of my sex must have hit him like a furnace. Jeff moaned in his throat and moved up eagerly, straining to reach me with his mouth, his head squeezed into the tight opening between my legs and the top of the control board. But I couldn't move back to give him room – we would have been in full view of the window. His tongue just managed to reach me and darted at my sex in dainty, maddening little flickers, a snake tasting the air.

Oh, God, I had to ride this man.

I pushed his face away. His brown eyes were ethereal; his exquisite mouth smeared.

'Yes, Sherry?'

'Go to the women's washroom and wait on the couch. Be ready. We won't have much time.'

About twelve minutes, actually. I could programme the computer to automatically play four songs in a row, no more. It was the station's way of making sure none of us slipped out for a beer.

Jeff left the control room in a bent-over crouch, a contortion that sent a welt of delight through me. I programed the queue of songs one-handed, pressing my sex with the other. It was another insipid line-up dictated by my Play List, but I could have fucked that man to the soundtrack of *Mary Poppins*.

I rummaged in my purse for a condom, then, as a last thought, I grabbed Jeff's abandoned shirt – he'd need it later. A laminated card fell from the pocket and I bent to retrieve it. It was his cleaning company photo-ID tag: Carl Weaver.

My eyes zigzagged between the photo and the name. Why the hell hadn't he given me his right one? Then revelation thumped me in the chest. Carl! It was the same Romeo who phoned me all the time on the request line, I was sure of it. But why hadn't I recognised his voice?

Because I'd been too busy ogling his body. He'd known I would, that sneaky, lying son of a bitch!

He's also hot, Sherry. He almost set your panties on fire. You want him – why the hell are you so upset?

Because the prick tried to put one over on me. I remembered his flattery in the hallway: Sherry Sharone was nobody's fool.

Damn right. The Princess of Pop kicked off the set and I charged out of the control room – I had eleven minutes, twenty-four seconds. I was halfway down the hall before

I realised I still had his belt, folded over in my clenched hand.

The ladies' room was feminine but spare: in addition to the sinks and stalls there were cheap silk flowers, a full-length mirror and a red faux-leather couch. He was sitting on it in his underwear, but when I opened the door he got to his feet, a painful rip of hot skin separating from vinyl.

Good. Suffer a little, I thought.

Then my gaze dropped; I couldn't help it. His underwear was a cross between briefs and boxers, clingy, white, thigh-hugging shorts that pushed out in a thick, delectable swell. *Cock.* The knowledge seared me, an electric V surged beneath by navel. I almost swayed, but caught myself.

'Do you think you're clever?' I demanded.

If he'd planned to sweep me into his arms, he changed his mind. 'Sherry . . .?'

'Answer me! Do you think you're a smart ass, *Carl*?'

Now he knew. He assessed me for a moment; his eyes touched on the belt. Then he fell into a new stance, feet spaced in line with his shoulders, hands clasped dutifully behind his back. He stared over my shoulder at the far wall, the distant, respectful gaze of a private getting court-martialled.

'No, ma'am. I was just willing to do anything to meet you.'

His obedient military pose was intoxicating. I tried to shake it off. 'Did you think I was stupid, that I wouldn't find out?'

'No, ma'am, I assumed you would.'

'Then why? What the hell did you expect me to do?'

The words were low, thick, a hungry secret. 'Punish me, ma'am. Good and hard.'

The wallop of desire made me drunk. The room seemed to waver with sex. Surreal. Over the loudspeaker, the

Princess was winding down to a syrupy finish; Bette Midler's oldie was up next. Because of the mirror I could see both Carl's front and back, his hands clenched over his white ass and the hard-on that threatened to break through his fly. My whole body simmered with immanent heat, cunt and heart throbbing in rhythm.

'Then pull off your shorts and show me how you want it.'

He was breathing rapidly through parted lips, eyes half-closed in a dream. But the rest of him moved with deft precision. When he flipped down his underwear, his cock bobbed, a meaty shock of male colour. His nest of dark, wild hair flattened into an intricate swirl on its way down his athletic legs. In that girlie room he looked like a beast.

But a well-trained one. Carl turned to the stalls and reached above his head, gripped the metal beam over a door. He shifted to find his footing, bracing himself. The bridge of naked skin was an alluring shock against the grey metal backdrop, his vulnerability stretched out and waiting for me.

I'd never done this – and yet I had. Hand between my legs, pictures flashing against my eyelids. Or mouth to the microphone, swept away in the throaty stream of my own voice while my mind skimmed across a vast, bottomless sea.

I wrapped one end of the belt around my hand, buckle in my palm. Bette was crooning above us, her voice like polished brass.

'*It must have been cold there in my shadow...*'

Crack! The sound reverberated through the bathroom, sharper and wetter than it really was. God, I loved an echo. Crack! The contact of the leather on his skin went through my whole body; my pussy clutched hungrily.

'*...I could fly higher than an eagle...*'

Pink stripes were rising on his ass and legs. I felt the

glow radiating from my own centre, as if I was beaming the colour onto him. A beacon.

'Harder, Sherry. I can take it.'

Crack! Carl's skin gleamed; the dark hair up the cleft of his buttocks was flattened by sweat. Every blow forced a grunt from him now, a guttural breath of endurance. I drank the sound like champagne.

When I glanced at the mirror I caught a sliver of raw wickedness: the brown leather snake licking at Carl's hard, muscle-knotted body and the ruddy cock that leaped beneath. Behind him my own curvy female form was swaying in a dance, skirt swinging, heavy breasts in a tube top shuddering along with the lash.

I knew if I touched myself I would come.

'*. . . thank God for you, the wind beneath my wings.*'

Bette's big finish. Two songs left, I had just over six minutes. 'All right. That's enough.'

Carl's arms dropped from his handhold. He turned, panting, eyes a liquid plea. A gleaming dribble leaked from the swollen mushroom head of his cock. I wondered if a whipping alone could make him shoot.

Well, we weren't going to find out tonight. I tossed him the condom packet, then reached under my skirt to yank off my panties.

'Let's go, boy.'

I let him take me from on top. I welcomed his sweaty weight, and was surprised by the care he took in entering me; I truly felt the rigid, luxuriant shape of his cock, every firm curve as he opened me. My breath escaped in a long rasp of fulfilment. I was finally plugged into the Earth's current and yet I was that power, too. It flowed from me.

Carl began to buck, the ancient, lawless drive of thunder. He burned me against the carpet with instinctive, animal thrusts. I loved the sensation, pushed up to meet it, yet I revelled in the look of him: face contorted, eyes squeezed shut, a low desperate song rising up from his balls. I dug my heels into the small of his back to spur him and he twisted with a fresh moan, his pleasure shot through by the renewed stings. I was certain I could feel the heat of his stripes on my ankles.

It ignited me. In my mind's eye I saw it all again: his mouth spread by the folded leather, his muscular nakedness clinging to the beam. I felt the shock of contact that sizzled into my body through the belt. Lightning rod.

Bright, twitching loveliness. My pussy muscles squeezed and released, to clutch again in sweetness. Ecstasy sparkled on my surface, sunlight on waves, but far below I felt the movement of stronger currents, water bending.

'Coming!' Carl barked. I had the gratification of watching him from a point of silky serenity, riding his pulses while I still rode my own, enjoying him writhe and smooth out again, gasping. It stirred me with a nameless satisfaction. Triumph.

We gazed at each other for a moment, hearts thumping. Then the silence drove into me like a needle: dead air.

'Get off, get off!'

Can you float at a run? I hurried down the hall, tugging up my skirt, air cooling my sweat-sticky skin. My whole body was heavy with ebbing bliss, but my mind sprinted. How long had we been off the air – twenty seconds, thirty? I burst into the control room.

'Woo ... Andre Bocelli on QT One-hundred-and-three. That man's so hot I actually melted.'

Somehow I kept going, a languorous chatter that rose from a secret place, my own creamy centre. My voice was caramel. I knew I'd be in shit over the blank air, and I didn't care. They wanted me to glide? Hell, I was soaring.

And thinking. In my mind's eye I saw Carl getting dressed down the hall, imagined him pulling up his shorts over the pink stripes on his backside. I wondered how long the colour would last and felt a strange gust, both hard and tender. Possessive.

I glanced out of the window at the familiar city lights, still spread like a scattering of stars. I didn't need to gather them all in my hands. It was enough to hold just the one.

My impulse was naughty, definitely *not* on my Play List, but I was in trouble already. And I wanted to give him something. The All Night was no longer a shift, it had become an adventure.

'We'll start off our next set with a song for a very special guy. Carl, this one's for you, some old gold from John Mellencamp.'

I cranked my monitor. The brazen, ballsy guitar seemed to shake the whole sleepy building and seconds later the control room door opened. My toy soldier was grinning from ear to ear.

I'd chosen, of course, 'Hurts So Good'.

Union Blues Monica Belle

Outside my window it was a perfect spring day, warm and sunny, with just the faintest breeze rustling the leaves of the plane trees along the Marylebone Road. Even the traffic seemed less urgent than usual, and above it the blue of the sky was marked only by twin vapour trails. One of the jets was still visible, a tiny arrow far above me. It was headed south and west, somewhere hot, maybe Florida, or Rio.

The buzz of the intercom on my desk brought me sharply down to earth, and the offices of West Central Railways. Mr Hawkridge's voice sounded from the tiny plastic grille, as if he had somehow been miniaturised and trapped within the office intranet, something I had fantasised over more than once.

'Frances? Come up to the boardroom, please.'

'Yes, Mr Hawkridge.'

I hadn't expected the call for a good five minutes, with the union meeting scheduled for eleven a.m., and he was normally punctual to the point of obsession. As the youngest man on our management team he seemed to feel he had a lot to prove. He also seemed to feel the need to exert his authority, calling me Frances while he insisted on Mr Hawkridge. It was annoying, and all the more so because the way he behaved towards me put an all too familiar tingling sensation between my legs.

The boardroom seemed an odd choice for the meeting, with just a single representative from each of the three main unions in attendance. I'd expected it to be in Mr Hawkridge's office, but possibly he was hoping to overawe them with the formal, affluent atmosphere, or make them feel important, or whatever, but there would be a reason. Mr Hawkridge liked mind games.

One floor up, across the open floor of the main office, the low, constant hum of PCs and the air conditioning cut through with the gentle babble of voices gave way to the hush of the boardroom as I entered. Mr Hawkridge was already seated, in the high-backed leather chair normally reserved for the chairman. He waited until I'd closed the door before speaking, and I noticed that the slats on the internal windows were closed, cutting off the view of the main office.

'Frances, good. I wanted to speak to you before the meeting.'

His tone was clipped, precise, exactly as he was, with his tailored suit of fine, light-grey wool, his dove-grey silk shirt and perfectly knotted tie. There was just a touch of grey in his hair, but his strong, clean-shaven face was full of youthful confidence, also a hint of amusement, as if everything was no more than a game. He gestured to a seat, a plain black swivel chair placed unobtrusively in one corner.

'Do sit down. Now, as you know, I have a meeting scheduled with representatives from the three principal railway unions. At this stage, the negotiations are strictly off the record and, frankly, I think they're testing the water, this being only the second year of our franchise.'

He went on for a while, explaining that he wanted me to observe the meeting but deliberately not record what was said, my true function being to support him if the reps claimed that anything had been agreed when it hadn't, or presumably if he wanted to backtrack on something he really had said. I took it all in, nodding at the appropriate junctures while wondering if the meeting would drag on into lunch and spoil my chances of getting down to Hell on Heels during my break. There was a pair of zebra-patterned boots I just had to have and, with any luck, they'd be reduced to something approaching a sensible price.

Five minutes must have passed, because the intercom went to say the reps were coming up from reception. Two minutes later they filed in, by which time I had my laptop open on the desk, looking efficient and feeling slightly too hot. Company policy demanded smart dress, and I might have been Mr Hawkridge's little sister, style-wise, in my blue-grey two-piece, white blouse, stay-ups and sensible heels. With my hair up and my glasses on, I was everything they expected, my sole rebellion a pair of scarlet knickers in a heavy, luxurious silk – not something I intended to show.

I'd met all three reps before, men united only in their politics, and in being as out of place in the walnut veneer-tinged light of the boardroom as Hell's Angels at a scooter exhibition.

In they filed. There was big and brash Larry Ryan, B.U.R.W., part Irish, part Caribbean and part bastard – big, crude and forthright. I knew he fancied me; he took every opportunity he got to ogle my legs and chest whenever he popped into the offices. I wouldn't have minded, looks-wise, but he was always cutting me short, being condescending or patronising, presumably in an effort to get over his own feelings.

There was Jim Levens, U.W.R., young and keen and determinedly working class. I was sure his thick Manchester accent was put on, or at least exaggerated, and his principles more acquired than instinctive. He was lean, tall, with piercing eyes and an earnest manner, also the most intellectually aggressive of them, something which, like Mr Hawkridge's attitude, touched that politically incorrect spark of desire within me to submit and call him 'sir'.

Then there was Reg Davies, T.S.W.U., who acted as if

he'd been around since the railways were nationalised, and looked it too. He was huge, over six foot, but square in bulk and with an enormous belly hanging out over the waistband of blue polyester trousers that had been developed over years of pie-and-a-pint meetings. I actually liked him for his down-to-earth cheeriness, although physically he was by far the least attractive. But at least he was friendly.

Each of them had brought his own particular, very masculine, scent into the room, and there was soon a heady collision of aromas: of smoky clothes and aftershave and testosterone. I was one girlie in the midst of a bunch of hulking, macho blokes, even if they did behave themselves these days. Since the introduction of politically correct working practices and a non-sexist working environment, I could tell that each one of them was bursting to be able to swagger and bellow, and fart and openly share their porn mags if someone gave them the liberty to do so. This tension made for a peculiar, and almost sexually charged, atmosphere.

'Good morning, gentlemen,' Mr Hawkridge greeted them. 'Do sit down. As you know, this is a purely informal, preliminary meeting, also confidential.'

'What about your secretary, then?' Larry Ryan asked, jerking a contemptuous thumb in my direction.

'Ms Tisbury Jones is my PA. Her discretion is absolute. As I was saying, this is an informal preliminary meeting, at which I hope to –'

'Make us back down,' Jim Levens interrupted. 'We won't.'

Mr Hawkridge raised an eyebrow.

'Should we not at least assess each other's positions?'

'The position is simple,' Levens answered him. 'The U.W.R. wants pay parity between drivers on driver-only trains and guards on dual-staff trains.'

'The position of the B.U.R.W. is also simple,' Ryan put

in. 'We demand that the pay differential between guards on dual-staff trains and drivers on driver-only trains be maintained.'

'Then the issue would seem to be between your two unions?' Mr Hawkridge suggested.

'No,' both men answered as one, before Levens then carried on.

'We fully support our brothers in the B.U.R.W.'

Both Ryan and Reg Davies nodded their agreement.

'Mr Levens, Mr Ryan,' Mr Hawkridge said, sighing, 'that sort of bargaining strategy went out with the Callaghan government. You know as well as I do that what you're asking for is an impossibility. So, let's cut to the chase here. What is it you actually want?'

I began to let my mind wander, looking at Jim Levens's lean, strong hands, powerful yet sensitive, the hands of a working man turned to less physical employment. It was a shame we had to meet in the way we did, because it was not at all difficult to imagine those same strong hands on my body, being very tender, very careful, as if he was handling cut glass, his brilliant eyes full of worship and desire as he undressed me, garment by single garment.

Larry Ryan would be different. I knew what he wanted to do: to take out all his anger and inferiority on me, maybe throw me down on the desk, tear my blouse open, pull off my bra, wrench my skirt up around my hips, rip my knickers off and . . .

Only Reg Davies would pull him off, take me in his arms, comforting me, stroking my hair, at least until he lost control and pulled out his cock to make me take him in my mouth.

They were talking, an ultimately pointless discussion as they manoeuvred for advantage. Before long it had begun to get detailed, the provision of staff restrooms at stations, the company's new disciplinary procedure,

'Don't sweat it, Jim,' Larry Ryan cut in, and casually pushed down the front of his trousers to pull out a truly monstrous package.

I swallowed, staring at the huge, dark shaft lying on his thigh, a good eight inches long, and as thick as my arm. He grinned. I could only stare at it, wondering how it would feel in my mouth, wondering if I could actually get my jaws open wide enough to do it. Mr Hawkridge gave a gentle cough, then spoke.

'Come along, Ms Tisbury Jones. As you know, I have another meeting scheduled for two o'clock.'

I nodded mechanically, and rose, unable to stop myself.

'Under the table, I think, Ms Tisbury Jones,' Mr Hawkridge stated. 'After all, we wouldn't wish to lay ourselves open to charges of impropriety, would we?'

'Under the table, yes. Impropriety, no,' I managed weakly.

I moved a chair. I got down on all fours and crawled in under the table. I found myself faced with Larry Ryan's open thighs, his monstrous cock in his hand, ready for my mouth. His chair was a little back, and I knew the others would be able to see, whatever Mr Hawkridge had said. I shuffled forwards, swallowing hard as I caught the thick, male scent of his cock. He looked down, grinning.

'Out with your knockers then, love, and get sucking.'

'No!' I protested, looking around at Mr Hawkridge in appeal.

'Having Ms Tisbury Jones expose herself is not part of the deal,' Mr Hawkridge pointed out.

'Bare knockers are a standard part of blow-job procedure,' Jim Levens insisted, wagging his finger at Mr Hawkridge. 'Ask anyone.'

'True,' Reg Davies agreed, nodding his head earnestly. 'It was always done tits out in my day.'

Mr Hawkridge glanced between the faces of the three

reps, all of whom bore expressions of obstinate determination. He drew a sigh.

'If you could expose your breasts, please, Ms Tisbury Jones.'

I opened my mouth to speak, but shut it again. Five quick, angry motions and my blouse was open. Another and my bra catch was undone. One last and my breasts were bare. I took them in my hands, holding them up to show the men in the hope that I could instil into them at least a little of the shame they should have felt.

'There, is that what you wanted?' I demanded.

Larry Ryan nodded. 'Nice, nice ... not too big, not too small, very firm.'

'I like 'em small myself,' Reg Davies remarked. 'Nice and pert.'

'Nah, nah,' Jim Levens disagreed. 'Big is best, a working woman's breasts, full and heavy, good for child rearing.'

'That's bollocks,' Reg interrupted. 'Four kids my Linda's brought up, and her with a pair of fried eggs.'

'Do you mind!' I cut in. 'I am supposed to be performing fellatio.'

They went quiet. Jim Levens gave me a surprised look. Reg Davies shrugged. Larry Ryan lifted his cock up a little higher, offering it to my mouth. It truly was impressive, so thick his hand hardly closed around it. The head was big and solid and glossy; so suckable and, after all, it had to be done.

I took him in, my jaws gaping as wide as they'd go as my mouth filled with solid, meaty cock, right to the back, and not even half of it in. The others were watching and, as I began to suck, Reg Davies tucked his thumbs into his trousers, nodding thoughtfully as he spoke.

'I feel I must point out at this juncture that the restrooms under discussion are for the use of the T.S.W.U. and U.W.R. in addition to the B.U.R.W.'

'Perhaps we should allow Ms Tisbury Jones to deal with the matter in hand before moving on to further discussion?' Mr Hawkridge suggested, then gave a light laugh. 'Or perhaps that should be "the matter in mouth".'

I'd have given him a dirty look, but I was too busy performing my magic on the wonder tool of Larry Ryan. I was beginning to feel in need of some attention downstairs myself, and I was wondering if I'd have the time to fit Mr Hawkridge in before lunch. On the desk would be good, the way I always imagined it, with me on my back and my legs rolled up to let him in, nice and deep.

'As it goes, I'm not sure I can wait,' Jim Levens said suddenly.

'You'll just bloody have to,' Larry Ryan answered him with a grunt. 'I ain't rushing this.' Then he turned to me and said, 'Having a good suck down there, love? I'd love to do it all over your face. Ooh, you're going to make me come any second.'

I nodded on my mouthful of cock, took him as deep as I could one more time and moved down to lick at his sac and gently fondle his balls, rolling them over my tongue to make him gasp and shiver. Jim Levens gave a low groan.

'I've got to fuck her or I'm going to come in my pants. Be a mate, Larry, and move your chair back. I need some room.'

'Yeah, all right, but you'd better be quick.'

I was separated from Larry Ryan's equipment for a couple of seconds as he pushed his chair back on its rollers.

'Hey, no,' I protested, but Jim Levens was already pulling down his fly, to extract a long, pale cock, already erect.

'Skirt up, ducks,' he ordered, 'and don't worry, it won't take a minute.'

Mr Hawkridge coughed.

'I think not, gentlemen, at least, not without further concessions.'

'Fuck that!' Jim swore. 'Equal rights, that's what I want, and that's what I'm having.'

'No argument there, Mr Levens,' Mr Hawkridge said coolly. 'Once Mr Ryan has taken his pleasure with Ms Tisbury Jones, you may take yours, in her mouth, as previously agreed.'

Jim Levens's mouth came open, shut again, opened again, like a goldfish. Then he spoke. 'OK, you corporate running dog, what do you want?'

'This year's pay linked to inflation?'

'No way!'

'Frances, would you be good enough to lift your skirt?'

'But Mr Hawkridge ...'

'Your skirt, please, Frances. I wish to demonstrate to Mr Levens precisely what he is missing.'

'But Mr Hawkridge ...'

'Frances,' he said patiently, 'I really do think matters would be a great deal easier if you simply did as you were told, don't you?'

'But Mr Hawkridge ...'

'Frances?'

I threw him a last, desperate look, but my hands were already on my skirt. All four of them were staring at me as I tugged it up, to show off my expensive scarlet silk knickers, and my bottom, most of which was spilling from the sides. I was already kneeling, which showed plenty, but pulled my back in a little to make the best of myself. I know how much men like to see that in-bending curve twixt breasts and hips.

'Fucking gorgeous,' Reg Davies breathed. 'Now that is an arse!'

Larry Ryan was leaning sideways out of his chair to get a better view, erect cock in his hand. He blew his breath out.

'What a peach!'

'Red knickers,' Jim Levens drawled. 'I love red knickers.'

'Stockings too,' Larry Ryan added. 'Real class. Stick it out a bit more, love.'

I threw him a resentful look but did as I was told, pulling my back in as tight as it would go.

'Fucking gorgeous,' Reg Davies repeated. 'There used to be this bird worked in the union president's office, back in the sixties it was. She used to wear red knickers and a skirt so short you could see 'em when she bent down. The Red Flag, the lads used to call her, and –'

'Mr Davies, perhaps if we could proceed?' Mr Hawkridge broke in politely.

Jim Levens stood up, rubbing his hands.

'The pay–inflation linkage, Mr Levens?' Mr Hawkridge enquired.

Jim nodded, his eyes never leaving my out-thrust bottom.

'For a period of five years?' Mr Hawkridge added.

'Five years? Fuck that!'

'No, Mr Levens, fuck that,' Mr Hawkridge responded, pointing to where my knickers were pulled tight over my pussy.

Jim Levens swallowed. His cock looked as if it was about to explode.

'OK, OK, five years,' he panted.

'Hold on just a minute, you're forgetting something here,' Reg Davies put in. 'What about the T.S.W.U.?'

'What about them?' Jim Levens demanded impatiently.

'Well, I want mine, that's what,' Reg answered him. 'And I'm not having your sloppy seconds, Jim Levens. Come on, love, pop your knicks down; you need a man for this job, not a boy.'

'Just one moment,' Jim snapped. 'May I remind you who has seniority here? Three times your members, I've got, Brother Davies, so I reckon that gives me the right to go first.'

'Seniority?' Reg Davies demanded. 'The U.W.R. may be

the bigger union, but that does not mean you have seniority, my lad, not by a very long way indeed. Founded in eighteen-sixty-four, we were, eighteen-sixty-four.'

'By you?' Jim Levens enquired.

'I'm not that bloody old, you young pup,' Reg answered him. 'But, if you're to make an issue of it, I'll remind you that I was holding picket lines when you were in nappies, and before, so how about a bit of respect for your elders, eh?'

'Maybe you were,' Jim Levens retorted, 'but where were you boys the year before last when four of our boys were accused of kipping on the job, eh? That's what I'd like to know.'

'Secondary action, secondary action,' Reg Davies interrupted. 'And the lazy buggers were asleep, and all –'

'Are you saying my members sleep on the job?'

'I'm saying what I know, plain and straight.'

'Oh, you are, are you, well, just you –'

'Oh for goodness sake!' I yelled. 'One of you can sodomise me if you really have to, but please stop arguing!'

All three men went quiet.

Reg Davies nodded. 'Seems fair.'

'Seems fair, brother,' Jim Levens agreed. 'Er . . . who goes where then?'

'I'm in the fanny, you're up the bum,' Reg answered. 'Stands to reason, that.'

'Why?'

'I need to go underneath, I do,' Reg asserted. 'On account of my weight and my age, you see. I haven't the puff I had when I was a young man. You, though, you look like you've the right equipment for the back door, so Fanny here, she climbs on top of me, like, and you slip it in up the back way, see?'

'Oh, right,' Jim answered, glancing down at his old chap. 'Come on then, Fanny, get 'em down.'

I nodded, feeling slightly weak, and reached back to

pull down my knickers. They were going to get in the way so I took them right off and crawled forwards, to take Larry's cock in my mouth again as Reg lay down. I was watching him from the corner of my eye as I resumed sucking. Reg pulled his cock out, already hard for me, thick and stubby, maybe even thicker than Larry's, but not nearly as long.

He gave me a happy nod as he saw I was looking. I came off Larry and mounted up, straddling his huge hips to ease myself down on his erection. He fitted me beautifully, and I couldn't help but sigh as my pussy filled, right up, bringing me that wonderful, glorious, incomparable sensation of being really open around a big man's cock. He was so comfy too, like being mounted on a well-stuffed sofa, only a sofa I could fuck and fuck and fuck.

I'd begun to bounce up and down, I couldn't help myself. His huge tummy was right on my pussy, which was very rude, but it was going to make me come, and soon. Larry wheeled his chair in closer, beside me, and I opened wide to take him in, sucking happily as I rode Reg's cock. I could see Mr Hawkridge, sat back with a satisfied smile, steepling his fingers over his stomach, his eyes firmly on the junction between my mouth and Larry Ryan's cock.

'Hold it still a minute, ducks,' Jim said, as his long, strong hands closed on my hips.

He gripped tight, holding my bottom for penetration. I felt his cock touch me between my cheeks. I felt myself open. I felt myself fill, and all three of them were in me – three rough, tough, working men, sharing me, their lovely hard cocks in my body, my mouth, my bum and pussy, all at the same time. It was so good, perfect, and, as they began to get their rhythm inside me, I knew I'd be coming in just seconds. They'd taken over: Larry's hands in my hair as he slid his huge cock in and out between my lips; Jim in my bottom so deep I could feel his hair tickling between my cheeks; Reg filling me completely, pussy stretched so wide and pressed hard to his flesh, so good ... so good I was already coming, and, if I hadn't had a good six inches of thick brown cock in my mouth, I'd have screamed the building down.

As it was, I gave a little muffled gasp as, through the angle of my skirt, I discreetly pulled the ridge of my panties tightly over my clit for about the hundredth time for the past fifteen minutes. I was actually coming, licking my lips as I did so, revelling in the delicious explosion in my knickers.

'I beg your pardon, Frances, did you say something?' Mr Hawkridge asked.

I looked him in the eyes, my cunt still pulsing between my legs. 'No, no, nothing at all, Mr Hawkridge,' I replied as I snapped out of my daydream and back to the mundane reality of the union meeting. 'I was just thinking how we might resolve this issue.'

What She Really Wants
Sage Vivant

Appalled, Etang watched Sarah apply yet another unnecessary layer of eyeliner. Despite the concentration required for careful application, Sarah chattered blithely on.

'His boss is a total bastard,' she said. 'I don't know how he worked for him even for three months. So I think it's good that he's looking for a new job.'

'Except that this is the third time he's been out of work in the past year,' Etang reminded her, running a hand through her maintenance-free locks because the mirror compelled her. Sarah needed an enormous amount of boyfriend counselling, yet she never heeded Etang's advice. It was hard to stay patient with someone so determined to ruin her life.

'It's not like he's a loser who's always getting fired,' Sarah said defensively. 'He just recognises when a situation doesn't suit him.'

Or when it looks like he may have to work harder than he thought he would, thought Etang. 'Lofty principles won't keep the money coming in,' Etang said instead. 'Suppose you marry this guy. Do you want to support him every time he's between jobs?'

The bathroom attendant, a large Bahamian woman with a sweet smile, wiped the counter near where Sarah had splashed a small amount of water moments before. Etang made eye contact with her and nodded her thanks in that noblesse oblige kind of way she'd always admired in movies. Being gracious to support staff cost nothing and often ensured creature comforts later.

'Etang, honestly.' Sarah turned to her, exasperated. 'It's not always about money. I love Michael and I love how he always tries to stay true to himself. He may go through difficult periods financially, but he'll always have his dignity.'

'And, when his landlord accepts dignity in lieu of money, he'll have nothing to worry about. I just don't understand why you'd want to put yourself in a position where you know money is going to be a constant battle. You've got a great job and a good future, but Michael could drain you in a matter of months. Who needs that?'

'He's not draining me.'

'Well, he will.'

'How do you know that?'

'Look around, Sarah. There are financially stable men and then there are those who haven't a clue about how to get money and what to do with it when they have it. You can actually *choose* which kind you want to be with, in case you haven't noticed.'

Sarah closed her cosmetics bag and looked directly at her friend. Her blonde lashes were thick with black mascara and the eyeliner she'd just applied would have been perfect for a music video. Nobody would mistake her for the investment banker she was.

'I think that, until you fall in love, you have no idea what I'm talking about,' Sarah said with exaggerated kindness in her voice.

'And, until you understand that love is a decision and not an avalanche that leaves you debilitated and helpless, you will continue to date men who bring less than you do to the relationship.'

Sarah laughed. 'Touché,' she said, shrugging. 'I've got to get back to work. I am a breadwinner, you know.'

Etang groaned and followed her out of the ladies' room, tipping the attendant as she passed.

As Etang left the office that night, she made a point to wish a fond goodnight to both the janitor and the front-door guard. Those who were the little people today could end up in a position to be useful later, so she made it a point to be nice to them. She learned the names of the ones who were mildly useful now, such as Thomas at the front gate, because, if she ever came to work without her identification badge, Thomas would be more inclined to admit her because she'd smiled and addressed him by name. She was less eager to learn the names of the janitorial staff, as their immediate benefits were not as obvious. She prided herself on knowing how the world functioned and didn't hesitate to put that knowledge to work.

She didn't exchange any pleasantries with the front guard that night, though. Two thoughts troubled her: the job interview she was to have tomorrow and the note she'd found on her desk when she returned from the ladies' room with Sarah.

She waited until she was on the train heading home before removing the crumpled note from her coat pocket and rereading it. 'You looked very pretty today,' it said.

What a ridiculous grade-school prank, she thought, exasperated by the mysteriousness of it. What manner of grown-up passed notes to people they found attractive? How could she be working with such immature individuals?

This is why I don't date.

She thought about the men in Sarah's life and how none of them knew the first thing about the importance of money. Now this note – sent by some idiot who thought it would be fun for her to figure out who sent it.

She didn't recognise the handwriting, nor did she have

any idea who might have written it. Or why. She made it a rule to maintain a fairly professional demeanour with her male co-workers. She'd been at Silverman–Hart since graduate school ten years earlier and had dedicated too much time and energy to her career to have it obliterated or even compromised by some office romance. She'd seen Sarah get passed over for a promotion because of her involvement with one of the brokers in the arbitrage department. Etang refused to let anything but her work be the basis on which she was judged at Silverman–Hart.

As the train sped by the steady stream of suburban homes, she grew more irritated. She'd wanted to use this train ride as an opportunity to perfect her responses to her boss's anticipated interview questions tomorrow. Now this silly note consumed her thoughts instead. Who would have sent her such a thing?

Ninety per cent of her co-workers were male, so the elimination process could be lengthy. These things surely didn't come from out of the blue, so the best strategy was to think about who had ever leered or flirted or stared or otherwise indicated an interest in her. She sighed. The process would not be easy – most men had shown interest in her at some point. Etang had no illusions about her looks. Taller than most women, and many men, her slim but strong figure attracted stares wherever she went. Her mocha colouring, too, was strikingly different than most of the decidedly Caucasian people she worked among. She'd never developed the ability to discern whether those stares were looks of longing or merely curiosity, a fact that wouldn't help her now in the least.

Yet, there was no question that Fletcher had more to say to her than most of the people in the office. He'd complimented her outfits on more than one occasion and had even teased her about her love life.

'You need a cruise, Etang,' he'd said one day when she was buried in buy and sell orders. 'After a couple of weeks on a ship, you're bound to relax. And I hear lots of rich guys look for women on the high seas!' Everybody in earshot had tittered. What he knew about her love life could have been scrawled on a thumbnail, but he'd not let that stop him from making jokes at her expense. She'd decided not to take offence, however, because she didn't think his intent was malicious. But, as she reviewed other incidents in her memory, she began to question whether his teasing was innocent ribbing or a calculated effort to make her feel just a little less confident about herself because there was no man in her life.

Fletcher was her age (early thirties) and no stranger to luxury. He was handsome, which fuelled his arrogance, but he was also conversant in the nuances of affluence. He spoke to clients as if he'd just had cocktails with them (and maybe he had) and carried himself with an ease she envied – the kind of confidence one had when in one's element. He exuded power, in spite of the fact that he had none. Or did he?

He was being considered for the same promotion to senior account executive she was and would be interviewed tomorrow, as she would. Her rise to stardom, as it were, had been faster than his but she'd worked so hard that Silverman–Hart had virtually no choice but to move her along from entry-level brokerage clerk to account manager to account executive quickly. Fletcher brought in the same kind of six-figure deals but he didn't make the same show of diligence that she did. The next promotional step for both of them, though, would not be based on sheer hours and energy but rather certain managerial skills and talents, even indicators of visionary ability. They were equally matched but, with his connections and easy, confident style, he might be deemed better suited to the new position.

What would sex with Fletcher be like, she wondered

idly. She closed her eyes to the passing landscape and allowed herself to imagine his well-moisturised skin against hers, her breasts in his finely manicured hands, the weight of his toned, muscled body on top of hers. He'd undoubtedly had many women in his time and would know how to read her body. He'd employ that uncanny erogenous-zone radar that especially gifted lovers had and zero in on every vulnerable pink and precious spot she had. She squirmed in her seat as she considered the possibilities.

He wasn't unattractive. And this wasn't the first time she'd fantasised about him. When he'd first joined Silverman–Hart, she had found him more than a little distracting. His nipples were often outlined against his crisp Oxford shirts, which were tapered to the lines of his admittedly Adonis-like physique. He was every woman's dream, truth be told, and that was precisely why she hadn't allowed herself to fall for him.

As she'd told Sarah just hours before, love was a decision. And she'd decided not to spend any time loving Fletcher, either with her heart or with her body.

But dammit, he smelled divine, too. She could always tell if he'd just been in the elevator or at the copy machine because the lingering scent of whatever he wore – something with lavender but with a hint of musky citrus, as well.

Fletcher wanted the job as much as she did. Why would he be romancing her suddenly the day before they were both to be evaluated for the same position? He was up to something. Had to be.

She winced as she realised the nature of his devious plan. Clearly, he was trying to undermine her self-confidence by distracting her with something unexpected. If she thought too hard about her unknown suitor, she wouldn't adequately prepare for her interview. And then he'd trump her for the position, the son of a bitch. She smiled wryly as she concocted a new fantasy involving Fletcher:

In response to her return note – I look even prettier naked – he emails her with a request for a date that evening. As he hits the send button, he winks at her from his desk across the hall. She agrees but, when they get to the restaurant, she unbuttons her coat just enough for him to get a sense of the corset she's wearing underneath. She runs a finger along her cleavage and shoots him the most penetrating gaze she can muster.

'I don't really need any food,' she says. 'Do you?'

When his eyes gleam with sexual expectation, she hails a cab that whisks them off to a majestic but eerie old house. She leads him to a dungeon, where his horny leer mixes with uncertainty, especially when she tells him to strip – and then proceeds to shackle his hands and feet to a horizontal board where he has been instructed to lie.

His cock is exceptionally long and surprisingly thick. If he weren't such an asshole, she'd consider sucking it, but, as things are, the evening is not about his pleasure so she restrains herself from that particular primal urge. Instead, she calls in an equally handsome man with a fondness for cock equal to her own.

'Alistair, massage Fletcher's hard-on with this oil, would you?'

The oil is the sort that heats up under friction. The combination of Alistair's unwelcome enthusiasm and the oil's chemical properties results in a gloriously confusing time for poor Fletcher. He is disgusted by being jerked off by another man and aroused by the manipulation of his engorged cock.

Etang watches, strutting around the board where he lies, making him watch her ass as she passes. She bends over to play with herself and exposes her slippery pussy to him as Alistair vigorously pumps the very organ Fletcher wants to wield for himself. Though she had intended to wait a while longer, the whimpers coming from the table speak of her impending victory – her power – and she fingers herself to a monumental climax, denying him the satisfaction of having any physical role in her pleasure.

When she recovers from her tremendously satisfying come, she wipes her pussy with her hand and passes that hand under Fletcher's nose. His eyes, normally sparkling with mischief and confidence, look up pleadingly at her and she laughs from deep in her throat. Throwing her coat on, she turns to leave.

'Make sure you milk every drop out of him before you leave tonight, Alistair,' she says before emerging into the dark night and hailing a cab to take her home.

Fletcher wished her good luck the next morning, to which she mumbled a half-hearted expression of similar wishes. What gall, she thought. Slipping me a note like that and then being duplicitous enough to wish me well.

'I see you're wearing your power suit,' he commented affably enough. In her crimson Anne Klein wool crepe jacket and skirt, she knew she was an especially commanding presence. His compliment might have been an attempt to belittle her choice. She recalled him bound in chains and felt a little better.

At four o'clock, she entered Aaron Thompson's office for her interview. Fletcher had been in for his an hour earlier and she'd purposely avoided looking at him so she wouldn't make any assumptions about how it went. All that mattered was how she performed for hers. His had to be irrelevant to her or she'd choke on her own. He *would not* win.

'I won't waste too much time on the formal questions,

Etang,' Thompson said, smiling affectionately at her. 'I know how you work and the value you've already brought to this organisation. I also know that most clients would probably be grateful for the privilege of looking at you.'

She stiffened but fought against showing it. He'd never made any reference to her appearance and, as her boss, surely understood that to do so exposed him to harassment charges. Not that she would file any, but his disregard for propriety discomfited her. She thanked him and smiled politely.

'That suit is stunning,' he continued, lingering too long on his visual sweep of her body. 'My wife used to have your panache.'

What was she supposed to say? 'I'm sure she still does only you haven't noticed'? 'That's what happens when people age and get bored with their partners'? 'I thought you'd never notice how breathtaking I am'? Instead, she smiled effetely.

Thompson had been making a lot of money for a very long time. His wardrobe was impeccable, from his designer shoes to his cufflinks. His hair, full and always styled with classic flair à la *Gentlemen's Quarterly*, was permanently sunkissed, probably the result of all those hours on his yacht. His wife, a bored but pretty woman, always wore enough jewellery to dazzle and then some (money was obviously still a novelty to her, Etang assumed). She was undeniably well kept. Thompson was rumoured to have had various affairs during Etang's tenure at Silverman–Hart, and Mrs Thompson probably turned a blind eye to keep herself in the comfortable style to which she had become accustomed.

'You're a rare breed, Etang. A powerhouse of a broker and an incredibly beautiful woman.'

How long was this flattery going to continue? Should she change the subject or would he soon get back to the interview questions? She didn't want to risk offending

Thompson but neither did she want to keep the conversation focused on her physical qualities.

But there, in that instant, she saw the twinkle in his dilated pupils, and understood that it might very well be in her best interests to string him along just enough to create a little sexual tension. She wouldn't compromise her no-fraternisation rule, of course, but she could probably create the illusion of the promise of sex with this man. Perhaps if he thought he'd be getting some, she'd stand a better chance of claiming the senior account executive position.

'I'm flattered that you pay such close attention to detail,' she purred. 'You know I pride myself on that same quality, as well. I've always been glad that we're in sync on that – and so many other things.'

Thompson surely had more viable sexual prospects than one of his own employees, thought Etang. At least, that's what she was banking on.

'I think we'd discover a great deal more shared interests if we worked more closely together,' he said.

Oh shit.

'I'd like that,' she replied, desperately wishing he'd ask her about commissions and loads.

Eventually, discussion did turn to more work-related issues but the tone had been set by his initial line of questioning. When Etang headed right for the ladies' room upon leaving his office, Sarah followed her in.

'Damn! You look like hell. Didn't it go well?'

Etang checked for feet under the stalls before she continued. When she was satisfied they were alone, she confided how the interview went.

'So, I just don't know. He's never been so lecherous towards me in the past. I can't understand it. I didn't know what to say.'

'Men,' Sarah spat. 'Total pigs. When is he going to make a decision?'

'Friday.' Three more days.

'Good luck, honey.' Sarah hugged her friend.

Once back at her desk, Etang found another note. 'You are radiant in red.'

A tactic that once reeked of Fletcher now suggested Thompson. After all, what would be the point of Fletcher continuing with his mysterious missives now that the interview had passed? He no longer had any vested interest in seeing her discombobulated.

But Thompson had just gone on at length about her appearance, particularly commenting on her suit. Had he delivered the note while she was in the ladies' room? Wouldn't someone have seen him? Even if they had, they probably would have assumed the paper had something to do with work and nobody would have been impertinent enough to sneak a peek at it.

Damn it. She wanted that job. Thompson's attentions were not only ill timed but completely out of line. He was placing her in an exceptionally awkward position and she resented him deeply for it. She hadn't spent ten years of her life in this place to rely on her feminine charms to get promoted.

As she pondered her predicament, she felt Fletcher watching her surreptitiously from his office. Gathering her composure, she took a deep breath and pretended to collect some papers to take home with her. The janitor excused himself to reach under her desk to get her waste basket, and she nodded a polite greeting as she got up from her chair not only to give him access but also to catch her train. She didn't know this janitor's name and wasn't in the mood to enquire after it – she quickly departed with her randomly selected papers and the day's note, sick to her stomach with confusion.

Thompson, were he not married, was precisely the sort of man she imagined herself with. As comfortable with money as Fletcher, he had an added measure of grace and style that came with maturity. Rather than engage in childish teasing, Thompson came right to the point, unconcerned with being labelled a provocateur, perhaps even secretly pleased about it. People with money and power often bandied about those privileges without thinking about it. Etang put Thompson in that category.

Sex with Thompson would be like one long, skilful massage. Because few things had true urgency to someone who'd achieved what he had, he would approach lovemaking with a conscious appreciation that most men couldn't manage.

On the broad veranda of a bungalow atop a hill overlooking the most scenic view on Bali, Thompson dribbles a fragrant oil down the length of her torso. Amidst languorous swirls of Pacific breeze, he uses his fingertips to cover every inch of her skin from her neck to her pubic bone. He caresses her curves so slowly she wants to scream – he seems to want to memorise every slope on her waiting body so that he can recall it later. Though her breasts are small, he kneads them as if there is much to savour about the feel of them in his hands. He saves her nipples for last, first licking them to absolute attention, then sucking them until they ache, and then finally massaging the oil around her areolae and pinching her nipples gently between his fingers.

He presses his rigid cock against her thigh, as if she needed to be reminded that he not only had the most perfectly shaped specimen of manhood but also that it was hard and ready for her. She starts to spread her legs but he stops her.

'Would you like some champagne before I eat you?'

She agrees, mostly because she wants to show him that she can control her passions, too. That she understands how prolonging lust intensifies it. That she doesn't want the night to end.

As she drinks, he parts her thighs and the scent of her pussy, strong but sweet, betrays her reserve. With butterfly kisses strategically scattered to elicit the strongest response from her, he makes his way from the inside of her ankle up the length of her calf. He dallies at her knee, finding the most sensitive spot – one she didn't know she had – to spend an eternity teasing before he inches up the inside of her thigh, leaving tingling sensations as punctuation to his kisses. Finally, after what seems days, he is dangerously close to her mons, breathing warmth on her clit, threatening to give her what she most wants. When his experienced tongue circles her swollen clit, she arches her back in anticipation and spreads her legs in wanton invitation. His face, finally buried in her steamy cunt, consumes her, licking and sucking and lavishing speed and pressure where it is most needed.

He engages his fingers as well, slowly spreading her juices back behind her pussy, tickling her asshole with the prospect of entry. She doesn't care any more how cool, calm, collected or worldly she appears to him – she wants to come hollering. She wants to hear her come echoing in the pristine tropical mountains, disturbing everything from the tides to the sleepy vegetation.

And, he wants to hear it, too, because he wants to know that he's responsible for the kind of noisy, wild abandonment he's witnessing. While she's still calling out her release, he slips his perfect meat inside her and pumps her in tandem with the spasms in her cunt. Her orgasm is endless and her juices never stop.

And, when she begins to recognise reality again, she realises he has clasped a flawless diamond necklace around her throat.

* * *

The notes continued to arrive. Wednesday's said, 'Your beauty leaves me speechless' and Thursday's asked, 'Why did heaven let you escape?' Thompson conducted himself with the height of professionalism. To the untrained eye, he behaved towards her as he always had, but she had the notes and the memories of the interview to show that his intentions were not wholly professional. She played along, neither mentioning the notes nor commenting on the inappropriateness of his interview comments. Her fantasies had grown to nearly unmanageable proportions, making work-day interactions with him difficult. When he spoke to her, she saw lips moving that had feasted on the flesh between her legs.

By Friday, she fought against trembling in his presence. After all her hard work, this was not the time to fold or crumble, she chastised herself. Do your work, ignore the heat in your panties, and stop imagining his head in your cleavage. She dedicated herself to fine-tuning a report she'd been working on for weeks, but, to her astonishment, he stopped by her desk to tell her to stop.

'From what I've seen, Etang, I think the report is as close to perfect as you're going to get. Any additional work is only gilding the lily at this point.'

She quietly agreed and sat strangely still for a few moments after he walked away. Did he think she was wasting her time on the report? Was she postponing delivery, and maybe disappointment, by continuing to work on it when it was actually quite ready for submission? Worse still, would any of this hurt her chances at the promotion? Her ringing phone jarred her from her reverie.

'Hey. Let's have lunch,' Sarah's voice said on the other end of the receiver.

The diversion would do her good. She picked up her purse and headed out.

* * *

'Well, you'll be happy to know I dumped him,' Sarah announced, grinning widely at her friend.

'I'm proud of you. You won't regret it.'

'I found somebody new.'

Etang sighed. 'Oh, Lord. And what kind of financial straits is this one in?'

'He's gainfully employed and seems quite good natured.'

'Seems?'

'Yes, well, we haven't actually been out yet. I'm going to ask him later today.'

'Sarah. How many times have I told you that, when you make the first move, you surrender the upper hand? The man then has all the power – he knows you want him and he gets too cocky for his own good. Wait for him to ask you.'

'He's not like that. He's kind of Zen. Very balanced.'

'Do I know him?'

'Don't laugh.'

'I promise,' Etang said warily.

'It's Benicio. You know, the janitor.'

'The one on our floor? I didn't know that was his name.' She tried to recall what he looked like, but realised she'd never really paid attention. It didn't matter, though. A janitor couldn't possibly be viable dating material.

'He's gorgeous. Kind of shy, though. That's why I have to make the first move.'

'But Sarah – he's a janitor. What kind of dates do you think you're going to have? What on earth will you talk about? How to get your sinks clean?'

'Do you ever stop being a snob, Etang? I wonder why I tell you anything. Unless I date a Rockefeller, you're just going to play disapproving mother, aren't you? And what right do you have to give *me* any advice on dating? When was the last time *you* had a fucking date?'

Her blood slowed, then drained from her face and

appendages. Sarah's words left her cold. She got to her feet and said in a low voice, 'I'll see you back at the office. I hope you don't mind if I don't eat with you today.' And she strode out of the restaurant, grateful for the sunshine and cacophony of life that drowned out her thoughts.

At four o'clock that afternoon, Thompson called Fletcher in to his office to deliver the news regarding the promotion. As she applied a quick coat of lipstick, Etang tried desperately to read his expression when he emerged from the office, but he showed nothing. The janitor excused himself once again as he reached for her waste basket. This time, she made eye contact with him and smiled at him. Anybody functioning on a level of purely adolescent lust would have been taken aback by his dark, Latin looks – he was incredibly handsome. But he was a janitor, nonetheless. She was called in to Thompson's office less than a minute later.

'Have a seat, Etang. I wanted you to know I've reached a decision about the senior account executive position.'

An awkward silence hovered in the room while she waited with raised eyebrows to hear the news.

'Both you and Fletcher were very strong candidates. I really struggled to decide which of you would outperform the other. But, as you may know, I also interviewed a few candidates from outside the company, and it turns out that one of them fits the bill perfectly. He'll be starting in two weeks.'

The news made the appearance of the day's note even more mystifying: 'For you, lipstick only gilds the lily.'

'Ugh!' she muttered with an exasperated huff, crumpling the note in her fist. From across the hall, the janitor was watching her, so she was careful to avert her eyes and give the impression that some deal had gone awry and that she was angry about it.

How dare Thompson continue to send her these notes when he had no intention of giving her the job she wanted? Were the notes supposed to soften the blow? She sat on her hands to keep from flinging something across the room.

How could it be Thompson? She'd worked with him long enough to know that love notes were not his style. And the flirting that had characterised her interview was nowhere to be found in the rendering of his decision. Had he written the notes or not? He'd used the expression 'gild the lily' earlier that day; and it wasn't a common expression. It had to be him and yet it made no sense for it to be him.

Her hand clutched a handful of her dark hair as she rested her head in her palm.

'Is everything all right?'

She looked up to find the janitor's big, brown, caring eyes staring down at her. He stood in the doorway, strong and humble, sincerely interested to know whether she was losing her mind.

'Yes,' she said in a voice that oozed hopelessness. At her wit's end, she waved the fist that held the note as she established whether Fletcher was still in his office. He'd gone home for the day. 'Somebody's sending me love notes and I have no idea who it is or why they're sending them.'

The janitor stepped into her office and gently but firmly removed the note from her hand. As he smoothed it out, he spoke.

'The why shouldn't be hard to figure out,' he said quietly. She noticed an expensive but understated black onyx ring on his hand. The setting was surprisingly elegant, sprinkled with diamonds just large enough to catch the light.

Once the paper was flattened, he took a pen from her desk and signed his name to the note.

'And now you know the who.'

She stared at him, dumbfounded. She felt foolish and

thrilled, confused and aroused. His dark eyes never left her face, speaking volumes about the appreciation of beauty and the value of consciousness.

'I'm sorry if I upset you. It's just that I find you so beautiful and I didn't know how else to tell you.'

His directness, so foreign at Silverman–Hart, put a lump in her throat. After the week – no, the years – of game playing and subterfuge, his honest proclamation touched her to the point of tears. Something inside her budged, like an iceberg breaking free. Everything she thought she knew about investment banking and love seemed suddenly utterly wrong.

He read her face and smiled. Not the self-satisfied, arrogant smile so cultivated by the likes of Fletcher and Thompson, but the warm, unpretentious expression of happiness that's inspired by the simplest of pleasures.

'Would you like to have coffee?' she asked, glad that Sarah wasn't there to witness how thoroughly she was ignoring her own advice.

'Yes,' he said. 'That would be very nice.'

Sex with Benicio begins as a tentative exploration, a timid introduction to slowly yielding flesh. Everything about his body is firm, hard and powerful – from his smooth, chiselled pectorals to his pronounced abdominals right down to the taut tendons of his calves. There is a burgeoning, uncompromising masculinity in his stance, his expression, his movements, and this is an endearing contrast to the restraint he exercises. He seems to know that, if unleashed, his passion may overwhelm the both of them.

He touches her with discovery in his soul. Though he is interested in pleasing her – even seems to exist to please her – he wants to feel what she has to offer, too.

'Excite me past my boundaries,' his eyes implore.

She is aware of her body when he kisses her breasts and tongues them like they are cherries coated in ice cream. She is at one with it when his big hands burrow into her folds and stroke her to new and feverish heights. She merges with him when he enters her and exclaims in Spanish what she cannot define in English.

There is no one-upmanship, no power exchange, no test of wills. Instead, there is affection and joy and enthusiasm. Though all of it is new, it is also strangely familiar.

She asks about his ring as they lie in each other's arms.

'It is the last remaining possession I have from my investment banking days,' he says, grinning at her.

Her eyes widen. 'You were an investment banker?'

'Years ago, yes. I had your boss's job at Shafer and Howe. What's his name – Thompson. I quit one day after a meeting where I suddenly realised that nobody in the room was saying what they meant. Not a person present felt genuine to me and I knew that I had been one of them. It felt good to let go of the mask. I left the company with enough money to retire comfortably. The ring reminds me of what I left and why.'

For the second time that day, her throat tightens with emotion. That she should learn love from an investment banker is both richly ironic and entirely fitting. She holds him close and kisses him until he is hard again.

She suddenly remembers that Sarah is interested in the man whose cock she now fondles. 'Do you know my friend Sarah Boyd?'

'Oh yes. The blonde woman.'

'That's the one,' Etang says. 'She told me today she is going to ask you out. I feel a bit guilty, being with you like this. It will probably upset her.'

'Investment bankers weather disappointment fairly well, don't you think?' He smiles. 'I pursued you, remember? Don't feel guilty. She will find someone else. I notice she does that easily.'

Etang laughs and makes his beautiful cock disappear down her throat.

Marigold Primula Bond

I'm already mucky, and that's just from twenty minutes sitting on the tube – half-moons of grime in my finger-nails, a blackening rim around the cuffs and collar and puddles all over my pointed boots. I should have learned by now that wearing snowy-white cotton around London is doomed, let alone honey-coloured suede, but I can't let my standards slip, no matter how basic the job.

Because, when I get to work, the shirt, the boots and, this morning, the tight black pencil skirt, will all be coming off. I wonder what the others wear? Scruffy jeans or jogging bottoms, no doubt. Leggings. Who knows? Maybe some of them come dressed as princesses, or ice skaters. I never see them. I arrive first, and I'm done before their shift begins. I relish the peace and quiet of the very early morning, and I love to work on my own, high up in the sky suite, with no one but the dawn chorus for company.

It's still dark. I'm instructed to go up the backstairs, or use the trade lift, but forget that. I'm not walking up thirty flights, nor sharing the lift with laundry baskets stuffed with dirty napkins and stained towels. Who do they think I am?

The posh lift spits me softly into the upper echelons, where the night lights glow and London grumbles faintly down below. The workforce up here is, unusually, pre-dominantly male, and you can tell from the way they leave their workstations – beautifully tidy, actually, apart from the odd basketball ball left lying around to trip me up. Female workers are far messier.

I glide through the scented silence. I think of all those ruthless managers and directors tamed into brief boyhood as they doze in their glitzy apartments. They'll be sprawled across black satin sheets, a trophy blonde or some stranger picked up in a bar curled awkwardly beside them, already awake, or even tiptoeing away. Their big dicks will start rising soon, hardening against their thighs while they sleep, surging with their morning erections.

And all the while I'm here, preparing their little empire for them. It'll be hours before they arrive.

When all the other offices are pristine I key in the code and the door of the presidential suite ushers me inside. This is my favourite part. This is why I come in so early. El Presidente has a dirty great glass desk the size of my kitchen, and a big, white leather chair which you can swivel while you watch the sun sliding up the smooth phallic sides of the landmark Gherkin building opposite. He obviously likes the finer things, too, as there's no sign of anything so aesthetically unpleasing as a computer or a filing cabinet. Only a wire rubbish basket, piled with empty champagne bottles. So there was a party here last night, was there?

I put my bag of utensils down and go across to the mirrored back wall of the big man's office. The panoramic views are reflected everywhere; it's either mirror or window up here, and there's little me, smart as any executive wife, floating in the clouds as they float past. For a minute I rule the world.

But first things first. I study myself in the mirror. Grimier fingernails, dirtier neck. I unbutton my overall. Sooty specks in my cleavage. Never mind. I have just the thing. I bend to unzip my bag, and there is the bag of wipes along with my other equipment and, of course, my fresh pink gloves.

I spot movement outside the window and walk across the silencing carpet to look. There are men jumping, no, literally *spraying* out of the top of the Gherkin building, like James Bond, as if it's a giant showerhead. Or the tip of a penis, shooting its load. Ooh, I always feel so turned on at this time of the day. All kinds of sexy thoughts invade me, enough to make my usual self blush scarlet. It's prowling round this room, smelling him, his wealth and power reverberating after years of tyranny. The action men on the Gherkin seem, with the sunrise behind them, to be dressed all in black. They're abseiling down the curved sides. Other buildings have scaffolding or absurd cages for cleaners. Those guys will do it on the move, sliding down their ropes, polishing and buffing.

I carry on unbuttoning and pull open my overall. I like to keep this tight, too, like all my clothes. It accentuates my considerable curves, and helps me to concentrate. But, ah, the freedom when I'm undone. I press myself against the cool glass for a moment. It's warm in these offices, central heating going all night.

The abseiling men aren't far off. I could almost call to them, but they're too busy to see that there's Miss Moneypenny a few feet away, dark hair pinned up demurely, rubbing her tits against the window. That's what they would call my breasts. Tits. It's a great, naughty word. Short, like a shock. How I love to see men cleaning.

I toss my outfit across the great man's desk. That's part of the fun, letting it lie there haphazardly on that virginal surface. Now my skin's covered in just a kiss of lace. Is that one of the men glancing over, swinging from his harness? I turn slowly, rolling my hips. The day is getting brighter. I'm sure he can see me, because his mouth is open and his wiper has stopped moving over his section. I wonder if his section's getting hard.

Oh, I have work to do. There's always a bit of a rush, but that gets my adrenaline pumping, the risk of discovery, the deadline before I have to vanish like Cinderella. I whisk a wipe out of my bag of tricks, dab it over my neck and sweep it down to those grubby specks I spotted between my breasts, where they catch in the murmur of perspiration on my skin. It's warm in that shadow, and I allow the wipe to nudge each lace cup away so that my nipples perk up from their hiding place. I flick each delicate point, and the cleansing fluid is deliciously stinging.

I do it again so that they tingle. I can see them change from wintry pale to an engorged, berry red. There's an answering twinge just inside my pussy. As if there's a wire connecting the two places. Perhaps I could do with a rub somewhere else. I draw the cold wipe slowly down my stomach, over the wispy knickers I like to wear underneath my severe outfits, and start to slide it over the soft crevice, but I can't. Time's ticking on. I must work my magic on this office and be gone before he knows it.

I throw the dirty wipe onto the clutter of bottles in the rubbish basket. The white leather chair looks so comfortable. Is that a stain just where his shoulders would go? Not lipstick, surely? I'll just give it the once over. And no one will ever know if I just have a twirl. The sun's swinging round. The men on the Gherkin have swung down out of my sightline, and I'm alone up here again.

The leather sinks beneath me, creaking and caressing as I wriggle into its contours. I cross my legs primly then lift my feet up onto the desk, more comfortable that way. What would the boss think if he could see me now? He doesn't even know I exist, hoovering and polishing for him, making this my personal domain while on the other side of town he's standing under his shower, bubbles of soap running down his chest, following the trail of hair over his stomach to his groin.

I've heard he works out. None of your overweight, paunchy businessman image for him. As the water sluices him, he'll be lifting his big cock to clean it in that dazed, tender way men have when they're washing. He'll be

thinking about the deals, the conference calls, the bollock-ings of his staff he'll have to undertake when he gets in to work.

There are no trinkets on his desk, no simpering photos of a trusting wife or girlfriend like the others display; no rugged picture of him on a ski slope or a beach, or kids or dogs. There's just a discreet trophy, a silver letter opener, and a laptop, closed and unplugged.

And a cluster of champagne glasses from last night. That's good. The whole team will be hungover. That'll make them even later for work. I must take the empties to the kitchenette, dump the bottles in the trash, but my hand has been trailing over my body while I've been picturing the boss in the shower, and my fingers are back between my legs, easing under my knickers, rubbing into my crease. The chair has moulded itself around me and, as I swivel from side to side, first towards the window, sky turning blue, now towards the door, which I've left ajar, my sex lips part slightly, and they're already sticky.

The movement invites my fingers to dig a little deeper into the shadows, forage through the velvety folds into my warm, waiting slit. I keep it almost totally waxed apart from what my beautician calls a 'little landing strip'. Not because there's anyone around to admire it; no one is begging to go down on it, or lick it out – there's a little twitching grab down there as I think this – but because it's cleaner. I sigh. And because I'm saving myself.

I can't help it. I'm moist now. I draw one finger out, sniff it and the sweet salt aroma, and then probe back inside. My eyes are closing as ripples of pleasure start their lazy progress, but I glance at the clock on his desk. No one here for ages yet. I slide down so that my pussy is on the edge of the chair, tipped up, my legs splayed outwards while my feet grip the desk to rock me faster from side to side. The juice trickles over my fingers. It'll make the chair damp – white honey on white leather. It

creaks louder as I laugh to myself. If only he knew. If only his uptight secretary, perched at her computer, knew. What would she say, coming in with a pile of phone messages, if she saw the wet spot on her master's chair?

I know what she looks like. She wears Chanel suits and one string of pearls; her face is inscrutable, her hair always so, her make-up discreet, none of that pouting red gloss which makes a woman's mouth look like vulva. When she's at work she wears glasses with pointed frames and an expression of ice. I'll bet she fantasises about his strong, powerful body under his Jermyn Street tailoring when she watches him shaking hands with important clients. I'll bet she peeps through his door when he's in meetings, thinks up excuses to call him when he's abroad on business.

She'd do anything for just one smile. Go down on her knees. Oh, imagine that, on her knees in front of him, sliding down his zip, opening his trousers, taking the brunt as his secret weapon thumps into her face, bold and erect, beads of spunk welling up at its tip, forcing its way through her lips.

She's called Marigold, just like the rubber gloves, and she's worked for him for twenty years, woman and girl. All she's ever had from him is a pat on the shoulder at the Christmas party. She'd go mad to see my lustful ooze all over his precious seat. She'd know straight away what it was, because she sits on her own chair creaming herself most days. I'm almost tempted to leave it there, my bitch smell on the seat of his trousers for the whole day, the sharp tang of sex snaking up into his nostrils every time he leans forwards to bark into his speakerphone or sign a cheque.

Both my hands are working now, one spreading my snatch wide open, the other pinching, tickling, delving. Me and the chair have a wonderful rhythm going, rock, swivel, slide, dig, my thighs opening and closing, the

sunshine slanting through my eyelashes as I start to gasp, my tits bouncing, the nipples poking up rigid where they rest on the lace seam. I'm rubbing myself harder, opening and closing my sex, my buttocks sliding on the sticky chair, heating up the leather as if it's still alive.

Is that movement through the glass panel of the door? I shake my head, no, no no, not possible, far too early, this is my secret time of day. If anyone asks I'm here to clean, and the ripples have gathered into a knot, ready to roll, like a snowball, through me, my lonely journey to the peak, this sister used to doing it for herself . . .

It's not my imagination. There's the flash of a dark figure outside, near Marigold's desk. Not one of the team, trespassing on my patch? If it is, let them come in, let them see me frisking myself, writhing and moaning on the big man's white leather throne; they'll soon scarper; they wouldn't dare try to stop me . . .

The door is opening. Is there time for me to bring myself off, quick? I'm hanging on the edge here, my cunt twitching, my clit throbbing, the snowball of pleasure tight as wire, so close to rolling. Just sitting here does it for me, right here in the hot seat, up in the clouds, before the hum of life starts to rise through the building like flame up a torch. I'm so close that a touch on my little button will push it right over. What a show that would be for Humphrey and Donald and Jake coming in early to take up their workstations; or Jackie or Madge coming up with their dusters from their shift on the floor below to see what's going on.

'What the fuck do you think you're doing? This is my office!'

I've never had a bucket of cold water thrown over me, but now I know that it would be the most ecstatic experience.

'I'm here to clean,' I moan, my words swallowed as my throat stretches; all of me stretches to catch the strands of pleasure starting to fray, but far from turning me off this great booming voice flicks all my switches. 'Really. I've been here since dawn. I come here every day.'

'You're here to clean?' He strides right up to the desk, leans his fists on it gorilla-fashion and stares straight at me. At part of me. Well, any man would.

'Yes, yes, Mr Flint,' I gasp, clamping my knees together and pushing myself away from the desk. He must be able to see my pussy, its slice of red silk yanked to one side, but at least closing my legs quells the insane quivering. 'See my gloves, over there in the bucket, and my fluids?'

There's a long pause. Not a sound. Not a telephone ringing, not an aeroplane overhead, not the ding-dong of the approaching lift. My eyes are on a level with his crotch. He's wearing charcoal grey with a chalk stripe, perfectly pleated.

'So when were you going to make a start?' His voice is a rasp. 'On the cleaning.'

'I thought I had plenty of time. The party, the champagne. I suppose that was your retirement do? I assumed you'd be late.'

'I'm never late. And you're in my chair.'

Now's the time to recoup some dignity, if that's possible. My underwear barely covers the essentials. My overall is on his desk. I could grab it and flee, lose my job for sure, or I could brazen it out. After all, he's a fit, healthy, attractive man of the world, isn't he? Red blood in his veins, a girl in every bank, presented with a practically naked creature pleasuring herself in his chair like a horny Goldilocks.

You don't get to the top without a rampant libido, all that stress needs constant release, doesn't it? Didn't President Kennedy need sex four or five times a day?

Even at this hazy hour, probably. Especially at this hazy hour. Remember those morning erections?

'What are you going to do about that, big bear?' I breathe, my voice still husky.

That's brazen for you. Not only that, but I sit upright, lean my elbow on the arm of his chair, stroke my chin, my mouth still open as I gasp for breath. I lower my legs, cross one over the other, swing my foot. My pussy's still burning, furious, cheated, but it's hidden for now. Let him see what else is on display.

I arch my back a little, thrusting out my tits. One strap slips down my arm. My nipples are raw with longing.

'I should call security,' he warns, and now there's a catch, a definite warp, in his voice. 'This office should be sacrosanct.'

My eyes linger on his trousers. So well cut, but is that a big bulge, extending to the left of the zip? He's standing, as leaders of industry do, or politicians, with his hands on his hips, both edges of his jacket flipped out of the way. Dazzling white shirt – who irons it for him? I wonder – dark-red silk tie, small knot at throat, and now the craggy, handsome face.

'Oh, it's a shrine, all right. And I'd love you to call security. All those men in uniforms.' I can't believe myself, and what I'm saying, but now I'm standing up. The chair tips, knocking behind my knees. I lose my balance, falling on to the desk. My breasts bounce forwards, swollen in size. 'What do you think they would do? Frisk me?'

My hand flies up to cover my mouth as a crazy giggle bubbles up. My fingers smell of sex. And now I look straight into his eyes, grey like his suit, piercing through my display of insolence, not moving from my face.

'Would you like it if they did? Because, believe me, they're not gentle, those guys,' he answers, coming round the desk towards me. 'Especially when I give them the order.'

He's inches away. I can feel heat radiating out of him. I

look away from his eyes towards his mouth. There's a seam of moisture between his tightly closed lips. I sway towards him so that one breast brushes against his shirt. Warm round flesh on cool white cotton, but there's a real man underneath. I'm not going to budge. Not after these years of anticipation, wondering what he would be like up close like this, isolated from his colleagues and clients.

He doesn't flinch as I bump him. In fact, there's definite pressure so that my breasts are squeezed up against him, and I'm pushing harder. His breath blows on my forehead, raising a sweaty strand of hair. I can smell his cologne, patted onto his dark face when he got out of that shower this morning, much earlier than expected. What was he thinking about as he gazed over the London roofscape from his penthouse?

'They can manhandle me all they like,' I say, throwing caution to the wind. The Marigolds and the J-cloths will have to wait. 'But I'm not going to let you slip through my fingers. Not now that you've caught me.'

'Not had a good rogering for a while? Is that it? You have to get your kicks from the boss's seat?' he growls, taking my arms and turning me as if in a slow dance so that my back is to the desk, to the window, to the world. The glass edge digs into my butt, a nice pain, and I focus on a greying lock of his hair falling over one eyebrow. Cruel words, but the gamble has paid off, because he can't keep those steely eyes off the thrust of my tits.

'So sack me, while you're still in charge.'

I start to gyrate very slightly against him, because that makes my nipples grate against the buttons on his shirt, friction burning and kick-starting those shafts of desire that he so rudely interrupted.

Some of the others call him a stuffed shirt, and I daresay he can be a bully in the boardroom, his features stony with stress, but how many of them have penetrated the inner sanctum? I can clearly see lust sparking in his eyes, a new flush infusing his face and, best of all, an unmistakeable response in the way he sighs and shifts his weight towards my body, and not away. That's enough encouragement for me.

He glances over at the door. He must be the only one who doesn't have a hangover this morning. The entire department can peer through, if they want to, but they wouldn't dare barge in. I catch his instant of distraction and shove my damp sex up against the fabric of his trousers. There it is. The blunt instrument, hard and ready, whatever he denies. Exquisite tailoring, to hide it so well. Does anyone else ever notice or wonder how big it is, how good it is, as they dawdle by the water cooler?

No point pretending I'll be cleaning this morning. He looks as if he's about to give me a good caning. Like I'm giving him the horn. Oh, this scenario is making me so wicked. There's only one thing to do about it now he's here.

'I'll decide whether writhing about on the presidential chair is a sacking offence or not. But while I ponder the matter, I'd like it back.'

He lets go of my arms and sinks into the white leather. Has he shaved this morning? There's shadow on his cheeks and chin. He looks dark against the white, his eyes glittering, the mouth parted to show me his teeth.

The lift bell dings. A big square of sun is advancing across the carpet. Over the top of his head I can see myself in the vast mirror – my hair has come down a little from its pins, my eyes without the spectacles are big and crazy, my breasts huge and dominant, pointing into his face.

'And while you're pondering, Mr Flint, why don't you fuck me?'

I can't believe I've said it, perhaps I only thought it, but I won't bottle it now. I've come all this way, waited this long to take what anyone else could only dream of. I straddle him, lower my crotch, slide myself up his long legs until I'm right in his lap, groin to groin, and now the length of his cock is nudging against my slit. I'll let it rest there for a minute, relishing the promise. Let him push me off right now if he doesn't want what I'm offering.

But he doesn't move. He has astonishingly long lashes, I notice, and his eyelids are relaxing very slightly. He'd never show the transatlantic team even the slightest weakness, would he? But here he is, already dissolving into a pure human.

I raise my arms to unpin my hair and watch myself in the mirror. My breasts are inviting white mounds in the daylight, punctuated by those tight red berries, enticing him to touch. There's a taut moment when all I can hear is our mutual, harsh breathing, then with a grunt he starts to caress my breasts, flicking the acorn-hard nipples idly through the slippery silk.

The reaction sizzles instantly through me so that I jerk my hips, opening myself against the rigid shape of his cock tucked inside his trousers, while he, smooth operator that he is – how many women has he undressed in his time? – easily unclips my bra so that my tits bounce freely into his face and he catches one, bites the nipple, no preamble. I rise on my knees, always worshipping, and grip the back of the leather chair so his face is forced against me, his mouth wrapped round the aching bud.

I arch and stretch, desire crawling through me as he bites and sucks, and I'd willingly freeze this moment but I can't wait to see his majestic prick in all its glory. I get at his zip, my legs shaking with the effort of keeping upright, wait for him to stop me, but although he pauses there's little he can do, and now I'm easing the solid length down from its upright position, clamping my fingers around it, taking it prisoner.

My pussy is yearning towards it, twitching to kiss and swallow it, the damp curls tangled with moisture as I hover over him, and still he's licking each stiff nipple and there's an urgency in me, that knot is tight and growing. I start to sink, my legs giving way, raking my hands through his hair. I thought it would be wiry, but it's soft, mostly dark, only grey round the temples. The urge to grind myself onto him is overpowering.

'Who would have thought it,' he groans, muffled by my soft flesh. 'A temptress under that severe tweed.'

That does it. The man is mine. Why didn't I do this years ago? Walk into his office, strip off and sit on his face? See, they're all the same underneath the wrapping, although I have a feeling he's more magnificent than most. To find out, I rest on the rounded tip of his knob, letting it nudge about blindly just inside my crack, setting fire to that most sensitive part of me, but now, although I'm loving the sharp delight of his teeth on my nipples, I want to look at him while this happens.

'Admit it. You don't even notice the uniform, let alone the underling inside it,' I chide, holding his face between my hands as I rock very slightly, letting his knob tease my burning clit, no further inside, just tickle the surface, prepare me, use him like a toy before I lower myself onto him, down that long, thick shaft. The smooth surface is already damp from where I've slicked it with my honey, and that shoots stronger thrills of excitement through me.

'I'm a busy man. Everyone in this company knows that.'

'Not too busy for some morning delight, though, Mr Flint. Not busy at all, now you've officially retired.' I close my eyes for a moment as his life of future ease unfolds. I intend to be part of it. 'Let me show you how it's done.'

My playing with myself has built up such a head of steam that I could come at any second, but I want to be fucked by him, every last bit of him buried and coming inside me.

I grind down hard, no more messing, and his cock makes contact with the burning nub of my clit and my brave words die in a filthy sigh as I savour the length fitting hard inside me, a hot beast filling me, attached to the man everyone admires but whom I really, really want, impaling myself on him so that I could spin on it. I pause, my breasts rubbing his face as he watches me.

'I'm never too busy for the right woman,' he murmurs, tightening his grip on my hips as I reach the base of his cock and we wait for the rhythm to begin.

'Well, you've found the right woman now,' I tell him. I can't wait any longer. I catch my eye in the mirror. I'm licking my lips as I start the stroke up and down his cock as it goes on growing inside me, no choice but to move, engulf him, every inch of him grazing every screaming inch of me so that I can only go so far before slamming back down on him, groin on groin, and, each time I do it, his knob is as hard as rock.

'What's the rush?' He grabs my hips to slow me down. 'Now that we're here . . .'

He settles against the chair but I'm not fooled because he's not slacking, far from it, because next thing he's slamming right up inside me as I descend to meet him and when we collide, over and over, my voice gabbles in a crescendo, trying to articulate what it's like to be impaled on the rod of steel whose sole aim is to stoke up and burn the exquisite pleasure I've already kindled.

He's getting harder, and I'm getting wetter. Rivulets of fire streak through me; my breasts bounce frantically, and then, the most incredible thing of all, as I'm curving and arching, trying to curb the inevitable, it's flooding through me and his eyes are glazing over. Then it peaks and floods – my climax, up here on the top floor, astride the top dog, and the most incredible thing of all is that the top dog is smiling. No one's ever seen him smile; his lips curl back not in their habitual snarl but a real, splitting grin of pleasure and triumph as he pumps his spunk into me, throwing me upwards with the force of it as I fail to bite back my screams.

'What have I told you about keeping perfect silence in my office?' he mutters into my hair, pulling me across him so I can milk his dying erection with my own pulsating muscles.

'Speak when you're spoken to, Mr Flint,' I whisper, rising and falling on his chest.

There are muffled voices, whispering and tittering outside the door. My legs are aching from being spread so wide, working so hard, and with a sly chuckle he heaves me off him, packing away his subsiding cock and zipping up his trousers.

I slide back into the white leather chair, leg hooked over the arm, totally sated, already lusting for more of him as he marches across the room, wags his fingers at the prying faces outside, and lowers the blind.

'Who would have thought it, Marigold?' he says, coming back and spinning the chair until I'm dizzy. 'All those years of sitting out there, taking calls, organising my life, the ice queen, hair perfect, boobs perfect, ankles perfect – what's come over you, slumming it as a cleaner?'

I sit up, stick my chest out and my hair falls out of the last pin. I stretch across his desk and pick up the pink-checked pinafore and dangle it off one finger.

'Moonlighting, if you please. Or rather sunlighting. Human resources are so hectic they didn't twig who I was when there was a vacancy for a cleaner. It got me going in the mornings, Mr Flint. Cleaning your office was the closest I could get to you.'

'Well, we'd better rethink your job description, hadn't we, Marigold? Who would have thought there was a bitch on heat under that face powder? And, as for my job, I'm not sure I'm ready to retire after all.'

He pushes the lock of hair back, and instantly he's the

tough company director again. That's better. I've unleashed the animal in him, all the more exciting when it lurks under that impeccable suit. Oh, I've felt it exploding inside me. So there's no golf and gardening yet awhile for Mr Flint.

And as for the Marigolds? Well, perhaps in time he'll learn to love the feel of rubber on his skin.

FOOTSIE 100 Heather Towne

Vanessa Sanchez tentatively approached my desk, unsure of herself and what I wanted. I was sure, though; very sure.

'You wanted to see me, Ms Williams?' she said in a soft voice – a voice soft enough and warm enough to suck into your mouth and swallow down like a luscious chocolate.

Easy, I told myself, easy. You don't want to scare her off. So I nodded in a businesslike manner, stood up, walked past her, and shut the door to my spacious, well-appointed office. Ours was a gleaming, modern building taking pride of place in the financial district of the City. I was part of a team of investment brokers working for a private bank that had a long and impressive history of securing handsome rewards for wealthy clients. I spent my time keeping ahead of the TSX 300 and the world markets, nosing out the best deals in futures and bonds – number-crunching for profit and investment. But recently, since Vanessa Sanchez had sashayed her fine frame my way, I had been devoting more time than I should to idle daydreams of an erotic nature.

I turned to face her. Her green eyes briefly met mine, then dived down into the thick carpeting. She was dressed in a simple black skirt and white blouse like any one of a million other office workers, except that the skirt was short by anyone's standards and the blouse was tight – too tight not to draw attention to itself. The skirt show-cased her round firm ass and her long, toned, supple dancer's legs sheathed in glistening black sheer stockings, all the way from her spike-heel-encased toes to somewhere just above her shrink-wrapped skirt. Her full blatant breasts pressed against the thin, see-through fabric of her blouse and, in the air-conditioned atmosphere of my office, her dark, erect nipples were clearly visible through the flimsy material – large and hard and begging to burst free. Her hair was chestnut with red highlights, and her delicate face was doused a golden brown, advertising her sultry, sexy Spanish heritage.

'Yes, Vanessa,' I said briskly. 'Have a seat, please. I wanted to discuss your performance evaluation. Your three-month probation period is up today, as I'm sure you're aware.'

She seated herself on the edge of one of the comfortable leather chairs that fronted my vast antique desk, while I stood facing her, leaning against the wall with my arms folded, feeling aroused by her very presence, knowing my thoughts and designs on her were wholly unprofessional. I couldn't help myself. I watched her cross her lithe legs and fight with the ever-rising hem of her skirt as my pussy juiced up and my face flushed. I could plainly see a stripe of bronze flesh on her right leg, between her skirt and her stocking. My eyes journeyed on an arresting course from that hot starting point, past her fleshy thigh, her rounded knee, her muscular, moulded calf, her slim ankle (narrow enough to easily wrap my fingers around), and down to her foot – a foot dramatically displayed in black, imitation-leather stilettos.

'Yes, I am aware,' she mumbled, leaning forwards to nervously grasp her knee, interlace her fingers around it, her manicured nails flashing. Her bountiful breasts almost tumbled out of her overstretched blouse as she leaned over her legs, and I could see and appreciate the warm, deep cleft between those two magnificent, mocha mounds.

I was that unusual thing – a leg-woman from way back, when the days of ballet lessons and summer vacations at the beach and gym classes had triggered my

first longings for my own sex. And that's where my eyes
returned and lingered. Nothing, absolutely nothing, com-
pares to a well-turned set of legs when it comes to driving
me wild, as my guilty collection of specialist leg mags and
tapes hidden away in my bedroom attested. I'd fast-
forwarded and rewound my way through *Flashdance*
maybe a hundred times, till the spindles groaned in protest, and the hosiery sections of the last five years of
Victoria's Secret catalogues were as dog-eared as a basset
hound. Female lower limbs are erotic works of art to me,
things to be studied and admired, fondled and fucked
with.

'You've been doing a good job, Vanessa,' I intoned.
'Everyone thinks so. However, I've had a couple of complaints about your ... business attire – the way you dress.'

She squeezed her legs and her emerald eyes flashed fire
at me, her blood going to boil instantly. 'Who's ... I mean,
what are these complaints about specifically?'

That was a good question, since I'd made them up. I
stared dreamily into the burning jade depths of her eyes,
momentarily lost, then I gave my head a shake and
returned to the reality of deception. 'Well, take your skirt,
for example,' I said, making up policy on the fly. 'Our
company dress code clearly states that skirts cannot be
more than four inches above the knee.' I reached back and
picked up a metal ruler off my desk; it was time to get
tactile with the Latina heart-throb. 'For the record, I need
to substantiate these complaints by measuring what
you're wearing now. Stand up, please, and we'll see just
how far above the knee your skirt is.'

Vanessa rose swiftly from the chair, tugging her skirt
down to make it look as long as possible, which was a
futile effort.

'I think it's awfully petty of people to complain about
their co-workers' clothing behind their backs,' she said.
'They're probably just jealous,' she added saucily.

'They probably are,' I agreed, my eyes locked on the young honey's gorgeous frame. I flushed and swallowed hard as I gazed at her stockinged legs – luscious limbs that seemed to go on forever, straight to my heart. I licked my lips with a wooden tongue and dropped down in front of her; in front of her silky legs.

I could smell the faint, sweet warm scent of her body spray, and perhaps even the musty dampness of her pussy. She was a passionate girl, easily aroused, of that there was no doubt. She jumped when I gently cupped the back of her right leg with my shaking left hand. My fingers lingered on the soft sheen of her stockings, and I surreptitiously caressed the fine black material and the hot brown flesh that it covered.

'OK, here we go,' I croaked, grasping the back of her thigh more firmly. I placed the cold, steel ruler against the bottom of her skirt, on the front of her leg. A quick glance told me that her hemline was a good six inches above the knee, but I'd known that much from a visual inspection; to an experienced leg-watcher like myself, hem length is all important. I pressed the ruler firmly against her leg and then slowly, slowly, slid it underneath her skirt, until the tip of the metal barely touched her burnished flesh.

'Oh!' she gasped, her emotions running quickly from anger to pleasure, hot to hotter, just as I'd anticipated.

I kept sliding the ruler up, until it tickled the edge of her panties, while, with my left hand, I began openly caressing the back of her leg, stroking up and down from her thigh to the vulnerable spot at the back of her knee, and then back up again – higher and higher each time, slowly and sensuously. My hand slipped underneath her skirt and touched the top of her stocking. Then I felt the rounded flesh that led up to her big, beautiful bum.

'Oh, Ms Williams,' Vanessa breathed, her voice breaking.

I reluctantly pulled my eyes away from her lush legs and glanced up at her face. Her eyes were closed, her red, pouty lips open, her body quivering with excitement and her chest heaving with mounting desire. 'Call me Karen,' I cooed, for lack of anything poetic to utter. My mind, like my sex, was now a muddled mess thanks to the brazen leg-heat of the young Spanish hussy. I sensed that we were well beyond words, anyway, and that's exactly where I wanted us to be.

I slid the edge of the ruler underneath her panties, rubbed it against her superheated skin, firing her pussy, while I caressed and squeezed her butt cheek, revelling in its firm over-fullness. 'God, you've got beautiful legs, Vanessa,' I whispered, mesmerised by the feel of her soft, smooth flesh, my reverent hands damp with perspiration.

'I've seen you admiring them, Karen,' Vanessa confessed quietly. 'And wondered when you would take matters into your own hands.' She stared down at me, her emerald eyes misted over with lust, her nostrils flared with passion-heavy breath, and then she slowly began to unbutton her blouse.

I dropped the ruler as quickly as we dropped all pretences, and moved directly between her legs, squatting in front of her, eagerly gripping her with both of my loving hands. I began stroking her, running my hands up and down her thighs, down the backs of her legs, then the fronts. Her knees buckled slightly and she gasped, overwhelmed by the fierceness of my leg lust, but I kept right on feeling up her luxurious limbs. I couldn't ever get enough of them, but I'd die a blissful death trying.

She tore her blouse open, peeled it off her shoulders, and threw it aside along with her remaining inhibitions. The Venetian blinds on my floor-to-ceiling twentieth-storey office window were open, exposing our wanton lesbian leg lust to the big bad world beyond, but neither of us cared. My own world had shrunk down to the busty young lady's long, stocking-clad legs, and the wet, smouldering pussy that I knew lay at their apex.

Vanessa frantically unfastened her chaste, pink bra and tossed it away, and her beautiful bronze tits spilled out. They were huge – round and heavy, peaked by thick, long dark-brown nipples that were already fully engorged, as a compliment to my preliminary leg work.

'Take off your skirt,' I commanded in a choked voice, my busy hands never taking a break from groping her stunning legs.

She fumbled with the fastener on her skirt, her hands shaky and clumsy, until, finally, she succeeded in unhooking it, and let the skirt puddle at her dainty feet.

'Yes,' I murmured, staring at her satiny, pink panties. The contrast between her skin's deep, rich brownness and the sleek black of her stockings was simply and utterly breathtaking. Her panties were damp at the front, and I breathed in the wonderful scent of young female arousal, barely able to keep my hands from rubbing her where it mattered. 'Sit on the edge of the desk,' I ordered, and she obeyed.

I stood up and slipped my quivering fingers under the top of her right stocking, then began to carefully unroll it. She lay back on the desk and stuck out her leg, whimpering softly and breathing hard as I unrolled her seductive leg-covering. I tore off her sexy, slutty shoes and pulled the stocking from her foot. And, as I repeated the same process with her left leg, she began to play with her tremendous tits, squeezing and kneading them, gripping their heavy thickness in her small hands. She rolled her inch-long chocolate nipples between her fingers and groaned.

I had both of her stockings in my hands now. They were still warm from the heat of her hot, hot legs, and I rubbed them together, rubbed them against my face, drank in the silky sensuality of the heavenly garments, smelled the sweet smell of young, dewy womanhood in them. Then I carefully placed them to the side and grabbed up the fleshy reality of her bare legs. They shone brown and smooth in the light, and I held them by the ankles, pressed them together, and began sucking on her toes.

'Yes!' she hissed. 'Make love to my legs.'

That had been my intention all along. I held her feet together and sucked on as many toes as I could cram into my hungry mouth at once. Then I pulled them dripping wet out of my mouth and flicked my tongue up against them, against the underside of her feet. Her legs jumped in my hands, but I held on tight.

I swallowed two of the toes on her left foot – sucking on them, tugging at them with my mouth, playfully biting them. My tongue coated them with saliva, bathed them with my grateful admiration, my mouth worshipping them. I put her feet back together and sucked long and hard on both of her big toes at once, then licked at the soles of her feet again, lapping at the sensitive skin in long, slow –

'Karen! Hello! Karen!'

I gave my dizzy head a shake. 'Huh, what?' I looked around. Ms Sanchez was standing next to my tiny desk, looking down at me with a stern expression on her face. 'Yes, Ms Sanchez?' I asked, hanging my head. I'd been daydreaming again. And, judging by my boss's angry face, she didn't know and didn't care what an important role she had played in that dream.

'Karen, I'd like to see you in my office. Right now!' She abruptly turned around and walked away, my bleary eyes following her bold butt as it bounced joyously underneath her tight black skirt.

The other girls in the open-plan area were looking at me and smiling. I grinned stupidly, got up, straightened out my skirt and stumbled away from my desk and after Ms Sanchez, knowing that I was going to catch hell – again.

'Yes, Ms Sanchez?' I said glumly, when I arrived at the door of her spacious, well-appointed office.

'Come in and shut the door, please, Karen,' she replied briskly. 'Have a seat.'

I meekly did as she said and seated myself on the edge of one of the comfortable leather chairs that fronted her vast antique desk. She stood in front of me, staring at me with her large, green eyes.

'Karen, your three-month probation period is up today. And this is the fourth time in the last three months that I've caught you daydreaming when you should have been working.' She held up my personnel file, and then continued in a businesslike manner, 'What are you thinking about when you're supposed to be working, anyway?'

I blushed scarlet and looked down at my hands, twisted them around in my lap.

'Do you have some personal –' She was cut off by the phone ringing. 'Just a minute,' she said, walking around her desk and picking up the phone.

I sucked some cool air into my overworked lungs, pondered the possibilities and made up my mind. It was now or never. I stood and walked over to Vanessa, took the phone from her hand and replaced it into its cradle. Then I pulled her from her chair, and walked her in front of the desk.

'What are you doing?' she exclaimed, startled by the bad, bold look in my baby blues.

Her words caught in her lovely throat when I bent down in front of her and began caressing her legs. 'This is what I've been dreaming about, Ms Sanchez,' I confided, 'day and night.' I urgently felt up her legs with no intention of taking no for an answer.

And in a matter of a few fleet minutes that seemed

like sexually charged hours, I had my boss flat on her back on the desk, her hands groping her overripe tits, polishing her jutting nipples while I excitedly pulled off her inky stockings and started sucking on her slender, brown toes. I sucked both of her big toes into my mouth at once, and my head bobbed up and down like I was sucking a rock-hard cock. I licked the soles of her feet, my tongue tracing trails of fire on the bottom of her delicately arched peds.

'Yes,' she moaned, like I knew she'd moan, her body jumping each and every time that I licked at her feet – and I licked hard and often.

I bathed her beautiful, bronze feet with my tongue, sucked on her toes again, kissed and nipped at her sculpted ankles, and squeezed her fleshy calves in my hands. Then I placed her sparkling feet between my legs, squeezed them tight, holding them upright with my knees, and quickly pulled off my stylish cashmere sweater and lacy, black bra. I lifted her legs back up and pressed her naked feet against my full, bare, creamy-white breasts. 'That feels so good,' I murmured, rubbing her feet against my tits and chest.

'Let me do it,' she said.

I let go of her legs and watched and felt her use her tender feet to massage my tingling breasts. The sensual delight of her sun-kissed feet on my big, pale breasts and pink nipples made me weak in the knees, and the head. Vanessa rubbed my juicy globes with her feet, played with my rigid nipples with her toes, then took one over-sized tit between both of her feet and squeezed and fondled and caressed it.

I closed my eyes and threw back my head and groaned, my long, blonde hair cascading wildly down my naked back. The air in the office turned hot, my voluptuous body hotter. I felt loose and limp, and my head swam as my senses were rocketed unchecked along an erotic roller coaster by that Latin vixen massaging my flesh. And before I knew it, and way before I wanted it, I found myself teetering on the brink of a catastrophic orgasm.

I grabbed on to Vanessa's loving feet before I exploded in premature ecstasy. I opened my eyes and said, 'I want your toes in my cunt.'

She smiled up at me, then stood up and brushed the unimportant business paraphernalia off her desk. Her butt cheeks quivered with the effort, and I reached out and grabbed her big behind. She straightened up with a sigh, leaned back into me and I wrapped my arms around her massive treasure chest and held her close.

She turned her head and parted her lips, and I pressed my wet mouth against hers. We kissed ferociously, hungrily, our slippery tongues fighting a frenzied battle in which there were no losers, only winners. I gripped her huge, tan breasts and squeezed them, feeling the incredible heated heaviness of them, pulled and primped her fully flowered nipples, all the while mashing my mouth against hers – tasting deeply of her.

Finally, we broke apart. She pulled down her panties and stepped out of them, and I clawed off my skirt and my panties and joined her on top of the desk. Her pussy was slick with dampness, gloriously naked except for an inverted triangle of soft, brown fur at the very top of it.

'I want you to toe-fuck me,' I hissed, as I sat back on the gleaming surface of the oak desk, facing her. I stuck out my left leg until my twitching foot was only inches away from her beautiful face.

She let me dangle there for a while, like the toe-teasing scamp that she was, staring longingly at my foot, her thick, pink tongue flicking out and brushing lightly against my toes. My leg began to quiver with the effort of holding it up and out, and the raw sexual anticipation of what Vanessa's mouth would do to me, until, finally, finally, she gently took hold of my foot and steered my outstretched toes into her mouth.

'Yes!' I cried out, oblivious to the strictly business setting in which we were consummating our lust, and to the staff working just outside the thin confines of Vanessa's office playground.

She fed on my toes; sucked them, licked them, bit them. I closed my eyes and let the scalding waves of sensuality wash up from my trembling leg and engulf my sodden snatch. I shuddered as her mouth attacked my foot and her tongue slapped against my toes. She licked and kissed the bottom of my ivory foot, the top, my ankle, my calf. She was obviously an experienced foot-worshipper herself, as evidenced by her practised, patient technique. I desperately stroked myself, rubbed my swollen clit, then jammed a couple of digits inside my sopping wetness and started finger-fucking myself.

'No!' Vanessa snapped. 'Not like that.' Her green eyes were blazing with desire.

I nodded my head and yanked my fingers out of my red-hot pussy; let her watch me lick the juices off. Then I pulled my foot away from her and spread my legs, extending her an open invitation.

'That's more like it,' she said, smiling wickedly.

She held out her right leg and I caught it in my hands and sucked on her toes until they were good and wet. Then I steered her sexy ped to my burning, blonde pussy and brushed it against the glistening lips. I was jolted with pleasure. She pushed her foot forwards and her big toe pressed against my aching clit. I screamed with joy. My body rippled as if with electric shock, and I knew that I wouldn't last long with Vanessa's toes in my pussy.

'I'm going to fuck you,' she said flirtatiously, thrusting her big toe up against my clit and into my sex. Getting the hang of this somewhat unusual task for the first time, she easily built her confidence, shoving it further inside me. I grabbed on to her tapered ankle and helped her plunge in and out of my volcanic cunt.

As she frantically toe-fucked me, she began rubbing her own steaming puss. She shoved three fingers into herself and frigged fiercely, all the time rubbing her foot around my sex with abandon. We stared fiercely at each other, at our sweat-dappled, heaving bodies, our eyes glazed over with suffocating passion and towering desire. The sight and smell and feel of that sultry, bronze goddess was rapidly becoming too much for me to bear. I hammered her foot into my flaming lovebox, her toes penetrating deeper and deeper and deeper – to my sexual core, where lay mind-shattering ecstasy. I pulled her foot out slightly, to angle her big toe onto my button as I pumped my hips and writhed my lust onto her, using her as an aid to my impending moment of ultimate delight. I was in femme heaven.

'I'm going to come!' I cried at her, my body on fire.

Vanessa's pouty lips were set in a voluptuous pucker, her face contorted with the awesome effort of staving off her own explosive climax until the very last possible moment, as she finger-fucked herself to the searing edge of all-out orgasm. 'I'm coming too!' she yelled, all too soon, her body shaking. Her magnificent brown melons were jolted over and over again as a powerful climax detonated inside of her and thundered through her writhing body.

My mind and sight went fuzzy, and my entire world disintegrated down to her foot and my pussy, my pussy and her foot. And then my clit erupted and scalding waves of super-erotic bliss crashed down upon me, my body convulsing with the most intense orgasm I'd ever experienced; once, then twice, then a devastating third time. I felt like I was going to pass out as I was rocked again and again by earthquake orgasms that had, as their epicentre, Vanessa's toes in my pussy.

Aftershocks of ecstasy tore our bodies apart as we valiantly held on to each other – my hands clenching her foot, her hand squeezing my leg – until the last of the white-hot spasms had coursed through us and dissipated. I weakly raised her darling foot away from my smouldering pussy, to my mouth, and cheekily licked my come off her wiggling toes.

'I want a taste, too,' she whispered exhaustedly, and I let her pull her limp leg away so that she could twist her foot into her mouth. She licked what I had licked, and smiled a satiated smile.

My left foot reached out and my wriggling, mischievous toes began to fondle Vanessa's come-smeared pussy, getting to know it a little.

'Karen! You're doing it right now, aren't you?' Ms Sanchez demanded to know, slamming the phone down angrily.

I grinned sheepishly and looked down at my nervous hands again. 'Doing what?' I asked innocently.

Her Brush Jill Bannelec

I have my own business and I am my own boss. I work when I need to, and I get to pick and choose who I work for. Before you jump to conclusions, what I do is legal. I trained hard for it. I was the only girl in that year's intake at the technical college, and I was ready for the jibes from the others – school leavers like myself, but who were all male. I was the exception, the girl apprentice in a class of 25 blokes, but I wanted to be just what they did – a painter and decorator.

It was a hard slog, which I had anticipated, especially the plastering, but my being there also seemed to make it difficult for my fellow students. Some of the guys seemed distracted by my presence and were unable to concentrate, some even blaming me for their failings with calculations and wallpaper hanging as their eyes wandered to my curvy shape – even clad in regulation blue overalls. And in the warm early autumn days at the start of the course, I must admit that I sometimes popped a button or two open for air as I was grafting hard, stretching and pasting and wielding paper strippers and planes.

The teacher, Ron, announced that no one should treat me differently, equal opps and all that, but it didn't stop them trying it on. I'm an OK looker, so I'm told, and had even once considered modelling as an alternative career. But despite what the tutor had said, nobody took me seriously, even though I'd made a good start, and those I told to sod off when they tried it on told the rest I was a lesbian. Typical. Why else would I want a man's job?

To be honest, Ron probably fancied a go at me from the

day he saw my name on the register. He was twice my age but very fit, and because I showed enthusiasm he took me under his wing, although, inevitably, the conversations between us got a little fruity as time went on. I remember his politically correct behaviour slowly morphing into oh so predictable male patter, and also how we eventually had sex on his desk after the final evening class.

'Don't forget what I've taught you,' he said, climbing on top of me as a pile of paint charts dug into my back. 'Dip your brush in about two-thirds of its length; wipe the surplus off as it leaves the tin, and commence long generous strokes until it's empty.'

Some of the lads dropped out of the course but I stayed, mastering the theory as well as the practical, blistering my fingers, breaking my nails, and getting the odd gloop of paint in my shoulder-length dark hair. I studied hard, ignored the quips and the gropes, and was rewarded by finally getting my articles and venturing forth as a time-served craftsperson, being eventually accepted onto the council decorating team as 'one of the lads'.

After that, I thought I had it all under control until the day we lost a contract and I found myself redundant at 25 with a mortgage around my neck. I'd invested in a small terraced cottage and, of course, redecorated it myself. It seemed a good idea at the time. Unfortunately, one of the first things people do to save a bit of money when things get tough is to put things off, and those things, I found to my cost, always included decorating. But then I had my brainwave.

I advertised as a fully qualified 'lady decorator', a concept I thought might appeal to single women who didn't want cowboys – although there could, of course, be such a thing as a cowgirl – but, more importantly, who felt safer with a member of the same sex working in their home. It was an instant success, and I was soon overwhelmed with work from elderly ladies and career girls to single mums. I was even able to be generous when I thought they couldn't afford my normal rates, and found myself the subject of an article in the local press, complete with photographs of myself in and out of dungarees. It praised my enterprise and entrepreneurial skills, and brought in even more business. I bought myself a van, with my business name, 'Her Brush', boldly emblazoned on the side, and settled down to a lifestyle that I had dreamed of, managing my hours to include plenty of time off for riding during the summer, and keeping the interior work for the cold, wet days of winter.

And then, after the article appeared, so did the other possibilities of my apparently unique service, ones that had never previously occurred to me. Men also started to ring for quotations and estimates. Some were obnoxious, some obviously on the pull, and some sounded genuine, but the truth was I didn't need their work. I put the first few off, saying I had too much on but, eventually, I thought, Why not? I might even meet someone fanciable; be a bit of a cheeky chappess on the job. It had been a while since I had met a kindred spirit, but it never entered my head that they might be married, or a bit odd. If I didn't like the look of a caller, I thought, I could always give an inflated estimate but, if I did fancy him, he might even get it at trade cost. I decided to give it a try, conscious that the customer's motive for choosing an attractive woman to decorate their bedroom might involve more than the usual required tasks of a painter and decorator. So what, I decided. So what?

In the late summer, just when I was on the lookout for a nice lucrative interior job during the cooler days, it happened. Out of the blue, a guy called Josh Ettersby rang from Roland Towers, a select office block that had been built in the late 80s as part of the revitalisation of the former docks area of the city. It was nearly ten miles from my house, but I knew the area was renowned for successful small businesses and Josh sounded quite nice for a budding millionaire. Besides, I might be his neighbour one day, so I needed to check the place out.

I finished early for the day, got changed and took the lift up to the fifteenth floor, taking in the view of the shimmering, sunlit waters surrounding the building, and opened the door bearing the gold lettering: 'J. Ettersby – Actuary'. I looked across the room to see the smiling face of a rather conservatively dressed woman, probably in her early thirties, whom I took to be his secretary.

'Ms Carpenter?' she asked, standing up and offering her hand. I nodded, recognising the standard City uniform of white blouse and regulation-length dark skirt. She beckoned me in. 'I'm Sally Jones, Mr Ettersby's PA. He's expecting you. He thinks you're quite a celebrity, breaking the mould, so to speak. It must have taken a lot of bottle.'

I was thrown by the unexpected praise. 'I suppose it did,' I replied, 'but I just didn't see myself working in an office like all . . .' I heard my voice trail away as I realised I was being less than diplomatic, but luckily she didn't seem to mind.

'I know what you mean,' she said, generously putting me at ease, 'but it has its rewards.' She sat down, swivelling her chair back under her desk and smoothing her skirt under her thighs. She seemed to take an age, and I was sure she deliberately gave me a glimpse of her cleavage as she leaned forwards to speak to me about the job. I did a double take; our eyes met, and there was an uneasy silence for a moment or two as hers challenged mine. I was saved as Josh Ettersby came out of his office.

'Hello,' he said, offering his hand. 'You must be Ms Carpenter.' I'll never forget his firm, yet gentle, grip on my hand. He was gorgeous, and I immediately wanted this job more than any other I'd taken on. He was about my age, well built, with a mass of blond hair flopping across his forehead, and wearing an immaculate dark-grey suit. He even smelled good. I felt his gaze and also Ms Jones's stare settling on me, and my breathing quickened as my emotions struggled with the unexpected situation. 'Come and see what you think,' he said, beckoning me in to his office.

The room was large, filled with a deep rich crimson carpet. One side was taken up with a picture window that afforded a spectacular view over the water below. His large mahogany desk seemed somewhat old-fashioned, with its inlaid bottle-green leather top, massive intricately carved legs and heavy brass handles on the numerous drawers but, if an actuary couldn't have a desk like that, then who could? On top of it sat a laptop and an intercom that doubled as a phone. A row of wooden filing cabinets and an oak bookcase filled the opposite wall, and a table and six chairs matching the desk occupied the space under the window. Behind the desk was another door, slightly ajar, to reveal what appeared to be a shower cubicle.

Josh waited until I had assuaged my curiosity before speaking.

'I wanted a look that combined modernity with quality and tradition, if that isn't a contradiction in terms,' he said. 'My clients like the idea of security and lasting values, but recognise the need for me to invest their hard-gotten gains with some element of risk if they are to be successful. The interior designer came up with these.' He handed me some colour samples – emulsion, gloss and stains – and some very expensive-looking wallpaper.

'What do you think?'

I studied them, and in my mind's eye applied them to the room, nodding in appreciation.

'What's your opinion?' he asked, smiling.

The opinion I was forming at that very moment was unlikely to be the one he had in mind. It was of him sitting on the corner of his desk, pants drawn tightly across his muscular thighs, arms casually folded across his chest. And it was very obvious that he dressed on the left.

'I think it will be very attractive,' I said, actually liking the designer's work, and trying to avoid staring at his crotch. 'But what about the room opposite?'

'No. That's OK. It's just the loo and shower. I go jogging straight after work, so it's useful to have somewhere to get changed and freshen up. Anyway, do your measuring up while I get changed, 'cos it's jogging time right now.' He strode out with an energetic bounce, closing the door behind him, and I set to work trying not to think about him stripping off a few feet away. I tried to concentrate on the real reason I was there, but the close proximity of the vivacious young actuary had succeeded in making me seriously aroused as I entertained notions of inappropriate behaviour that I was obliged to quickly suppress for the sake of my income.

He emerged while I was crouching behind the table, measuring the window, and I had a perfect vantage point to give his lower body a surreptitious once-over as he re-entered the room. He was wearing a snazzy pair of light-weight trainers, a vest top and some expensive designer shorts, every inch the young executive at play, and this look had an even more marked effect on my desire to see what was underneath. I straightened up, fighting the urge once more to look at his crotch, his cock coiled and bulging in his groin, probably aching to be caressed. His face betrayed not a hint of self-consciousness as he casually walked out. 'See you later,' he said. 'Give Sally a shout when you're finished.'

I left, reluctantly, before he returned, my fertile imagination working overtime as I drove home. I worked hard over the next few days, pitching the price as low as I dared, and hoping that any profit would be physical rather than fiscal. The following week we met again, and he and

Sally pronounced themselves more than happy with my references and estimate. The only complication was that the job had to be finished within a fortnight, and I had to work between five and eight each night, when Josh had finished in his office. I made a start the next day, being left to my own devices after Sally had gone home and Josh was out for his daily jog.

When he returned that first evening, still perspiring as he let himself in, I couldn't resist the urge to study him as I sanded the paintwork, dressed in my blue overalls but cheekily wearing only the finest lingerie underneath, just in case he was overpowered by passion for his painter and decorator. Like, yeah, dream on, girl, I thought. His muscular legs were covered in a sheen of sweat, and an intoxicating muskiness filled the room. He peeled his T-shirt over his broad shoulders just enough to give me a tempting flash of his body as he disappeared into the shower room without even a backward glance.

I listened to him singing in the shower and cursing as the soap periodically clanged to the floor of the cubicle. In my imagination, he was thinking of me as he washed himself, using more than enough soap as he handled his cock and lathered it up, which hardened as he fantasised of how one day he would tell Ms Jones to cancel all calls and appointments so that he could concentrate on me. We would do it on the desk and then shower together, making love a second time in the steamy, slippery heat. My fingers were already delving under the side buttons of my overalls and into my coffee-coloured, lace-trimmed satin panties. There was something so decadent about wearing such girlie fabrics underneath the industrial cloth of the overalls. I was being so unprofessional, but it was so hard not to think of the floppy-haired Josh. How I wished I was holding the soap and not my dusty sandpapering block, as I laboriously prepared the woodwork and filled the cracks in the plaster. I heard the water stop, then he emerged, drying his hair with one towel, another around his waist. I looked away, a mixture of lust and embarrassment in my mind. How could he torture me so?

Over the coming week, we exchanged the usual platitudes about the weather and about my unusual choice of career. He was very pleasant and had lovely manners, but I could see that his mind began to wander after a few moments of hearing my 'tales of a painter and decorator'; no girlfriend of his would have such a lowly occupation, I'm sure. It just wouldn't be right, and certainly not feminine. But things were to take a curious turn by the end of that week. One evening, when he had left after his shower, I deftly applied the posh paper that had been delivered that afternoon to one of the walls and took a sneaky few minutes of relaxation and reward, reclining in his luxury leather desk chair, breathing in its delicious scent as I spun around like a kid. I even played with the buttons on the intercom, mimicking his voice.

'Bring me a coffee, Ms Jones, and then lean over the desk while I shag you from behind. No. On second thoughts, bring that decorator woman with you. I fancy a change.' I allowed my imagination free rein now that I was alone. If he could see and hear what I got up to – that as my arousal built to such a peak I brought myself off in his shower while I rubbed his still-warm shorts between my legs – he would have had a heart attack, but that was exactly what I was doing when the phone rang.

I ignored it at first, then realised he just might be checking up on me. I dashed for the desk and flicked the switch.

'I'm glad you know how to work the thing. It took me weeks,' said Josh. 'You sound out of breath. I must be working you too hard. Anyway, I wondered if you fancied something to eat.' I tried to control my breathing as I squatted out of sight from the other buildings and dripped all over the dust sheets. I did my best to mask the excitement in my voice, trying to sound as nonchalant as possible.

'OK, thanks, but I'm up to my neck in it right now. Give me twenty minutes. Where shall I meet you?' I stuttered.

'Actually I was thinking of a takeaway. Chinese? Good. I'll get their special deal. I'll see you there in ten minutes.'

I sat there for a second or two in a nervous puddle, but as I shakily stood up I jogged the keyboard of his computer and activated the screen. And that was how I found his pictures.

He had a folder of JPEGS of a woman in various states of arousal. The first depicted her in a dishevelled but smart office skirt and blouse on all fours looking up at the bulging crotch of an otherwise unseen man. Her skirt was rucked up to her waist, and her long tanned legs were finished off by a pair of ankle boots. She had no underwear on and her naked backside was facing the camera, giving an embarrassingly pin-sharp, glorious view of her exposed and swollen, glistening cunt.

I was speechless staring at it, finding it shocking that such a well-mannered young man had such filthy tastes. I clicked on another JPEG, my heart beating wildly as I wondered what it would reveal. This was taken from the same shoot; an obviously excited male was on all fours, his hard cock pointing at a crimson carpet. The woman was on offer and he was ready to mount her, like an animal. I felt my own excitement building. I'm not innocent or inexperienced, and certainly not prudish, but this was something else. I realised who the people in the photographs must be – Josh Ettersby and the prim, efficient, conservative Ms Jones! My horror turned to excitement and then jealousy as I studied the rest. They were in some sort of chronological order, oral sex on him, several featuring penetration, and ending with Josh coming all over Sally's face and breasts. I had suddenly become hot, sweating in the air-conditioned room. I caught sight of myself in a mirror, noticing that my nipples were hard and peaked, my chest flushed with excitement. I squeezed one nipple gently, and one thing led to another. My right hand slid back between my legs, slipping into my warm, pungent wetness.

As I gazed at the last photograph, my envy for Ms Jones and the power she was able to exert over Josh became a flame of jealousy, and my fingers were frantic over my clit. Ms Jones's sex lips were parted, her splayed legs high in the air, her knees bent like a cat waiting to be tickled. She had a pleading but knowing expression on her face, as if confident of getting just what she was begging for, which she did, as it sprayed over her. It pushed me over the edge and, as I fixed the image in my mind's eye, I came, chest heaving, hips bucking, reeling on the floor with the aftershocks of an intense orgasm. I dropped down onto my haunches, panting uncontrollably, taken by surprise by the strength of my arousal and the intensity of my response. And then I remembered Josh was just a few moments away.

I clicked the photographs to close into the folder, then went into the shower room, my thighs damp with the honeyed juices of my ecstasy. I soaped myself clean, feeling invigorated and almost opiated by the endorphins that rushed through my body, and I dressed in a guilty silence, wondering how I would look Josh in the eye, then I heard his key in the lock, and he wandered in.

'Very nice,' he said glancing at the one wall that I had managed to finish. 'The paper looks really good.' I smiled at the praise, but he saw there was something else in my expression. 'Anything wrong?' he asked with seemingly genuine concern.

My thoughts returned to the images. I stuttered an unconvincing, 'No.'

'Why don't you call it a night?' he suggested. 'You look like you've been overdoing it. It's nearly seven. I'll unpack the Chinese.' The food smelled delicious, and I was hungry after my earlier expelling of energy.

'Thanks,' I said, regaining some composure at last, and thinking I'd got away with it. 'I think I will.'

I tidied up as he unpacked the meal and laid it out on the desk, complete with a bottle of red wine. He brought a chair over for himself and insisted I use his. He adjusted the height for me, hopefully not realising I had moved it only a few minutes before, and slid it under my bottom as I sat down, ever the perfect gentleman, but one with a secret, whom I now saw in a far different light. We ate steadily, the wine excellent and the food delicious. There was a continuing heat between my legs that confirmed my desire to be part of the fantasy. I gradually relaxed as the wine hit me and there seemed to be less chance of me being found out. Then he spoke.

'Just click on that photo file on the desktop, will you,' he said, so matter of factly, but so devastatingly, nodding at the laptop. What could I do? Refuse? How, without letting the cat out of the bag? I tentatively opened it up, turning the laptop to face him.

'What did you think of them?' he asked quietly, standing up and walking behind my chair, ''cos I know you've been peeking.' He spun it round then so that I faced him, but I stared at the floor as if I were guilty of something appallingly rude and, for an instant, I thought of denying it, but the shame and arousal in my eyes told a different story.

'Your silence tells me all that I need to know,' he said, crestfallen. 'I'm so sorry if I've upset you, Jane, but I had to know.' It was the first time he had called me by my Christian name, and I suppressed a shiver, but I detected a genuine concern and self-doubt in his voice as he spoke.

I still couldn't look him in the eye, but heard myself say, quietly but clearly, 'I found them ... exciting. I can't believe that you would have pictures like that; they're so explicit.'

Then there was a long, torturous pause before I spilled out what I really felt, that I wished the woman was me and not Ms Jones. Afterwards, I was genuinely relieved that I had managed to say what I really wanted to, but I felt a different tension blossom in the room. I knew a business relationship had just moved into uncharted waters, and I feared for what would happen. Would I lose the contract? Dare I show such unprofessional complicity in his pervy hobby? Would he want me to get involved or not? Slowly, I looked up at his face, to see the expression of a child who has just unwrapped the one Christmas present he really wanted. He refilled the wineglasses and gave mine to me.

'A toast,' he said, 'to naughty fun in private rooms! You are sure you liked them?'

I nodded, my expression slowly mirroring his.

He then opened his briefcase, took out some printed photographs, and handed them to me. They were stills from a CCTV, of relatively poor quality but quite clearly photographs of me. In the first one I was hard at work, in the second I was sat on the floor of his shower room with his shorts held up to my face; and in the third I was bringing myself off with them pressed between my legs. I felt myself blushing with a mixture of anger, indignation and renewed arousal.

'I take it I'm off the job?' I said, my voice wavering with emotion.

'No. No. Not at all,' he said. 'In fact, it's you "on the job" that I like to see. You see, most of the porn I like features smartly dressed women, or them wearing kinky stuff – the predictable whips and corsets. I like women to look a bit tougher, I suppose. Women in uniform and –' he hesitated '– work wear. Overalls and kind of butch stuff. I like girls who don't mind getting messy.'

I was surprised and puzzled, but there was no anger in his voice, only anticipation. I opened my mouth to speak, only to be silenced by his finger firmly against my lips. I knew better than to refuse.

'I like what you wear,' he continued. 'All the time you were telling me about your painting and decorating antics I had a raging hard-on. I was thinking about you naked under those overalls. It would be so easy to pop the metal buttons and grab you!'

The pasting table was still out and, with shaking hands, I measured a new piece of paper, cut it to size, and laid it out ready for pasting. Josh motioned to the table.

'Go on, let me see you hard at it,' he said, his voice thick with anticipation.

I picked up the broad brush and dipped it deeply into the plastic bowl full of paste, for once not automatically remembering Ron's advice as I began to spread it evenly over the paper. As I leaned across it, making sure the far edge was generously covered, I heard him close the window blinds, then I sensed him directly behind me.

'Don't stop, Ms Carpenter,' he said, slipping his hands around my waist and then up to where the overalls were buttoned down the front. 'I want to capture you on film as you work, but these are not for the local paper, they are just for me. Is that all right with you?' The implications of this were huge, but I felt myself nodding as the words left his mouth. 'Right. Just carry on, ignore the camera.' I tried to concentrate, recharging the brush, as he slowly popped each button until the overalls were baggy on me and my sexy lingerie was exposed, to which he gave a knowing cry of delight. Down they went, over my hips and onto the floor, exposing my thong and fleshy bottom. I stepped out of them but kept my boots on, now looking vulnerable and tough at the same time. He unfastened my bra, removing it to let my full breasts fall free, then started to take the pictures. I felt a strangely arousing sensation as my erect nipples traced patterns in the pasted surface as they were dragged across the sticky paper when I reached for the far edge, and, when I looked down at my glistening, smeared breasts, I felt them swell even more. I shakily folded the paper and climbed the stepladder before hanging it and cutting it to size. All the time he wandered around me, taking what seemed like dozens of photographs. I began to feel incredibly good, and I had a clear idea now what it was that turned him on, and I wasn't going to disappoint.

He watched me intently as I laid out another piece of paper ready for pasting, feeling unusually free and sexy as I leaned across the table. I got paste on me, of course, as he knew I would. He was focused on the view of my rear end, and I shimmied my arse for him as I worked, then, in a moment of unscripted imagination, I removed my pants, stood legs akimbo, still with my back to him, charged the brush, and brought it back between my legs, pasting myself from bum hole to cunt, the touch of the thousands of bristles teasing open my sex lips, paste splattering noisily on the floor as it fell from me in huge drips. I stifled a gasp of pleasure, but he could not deny his.

'Oh yes,' I heard him say excitedly. 'Oh yes, oh yes, oh yes!' I heard the camera one last time, and then suddenly he was right behind me, his cock out, and his hands on my nipples, cupping my breasts, kneading them in time to my sweeping brush strokes. His erection nuzzled between my sticky buttocks as he moved in close enough to press me against the table, then, without warning, he lifted me by the hips and spun me around to face him before sitting me squarely onto the pasting table, completely ignoring the fact that I was dropped onto the glistening upturned, expensive paper.

'Here, watch it,' I warned. 'That's about forty quid a roll, isn't it?'

He looked at me grinning with happiness and arousal.

'Who cares? It's me that's paying,' he said, his outstretched palms fighting for purchase on the slippery surface. Suddenly, and not to my surprise, there was an ominous crack and the flimsy table collapsed, folding in two so that we were both deposited in the 'v' as it landed on the floor, to be hit a split second later by the bowlful of paste as it slid towards us.

Needless to say I came off worst, as the entire pale-grey stickiness enveloped my midriff. There was suddenly complete silence until I began to giggle uncontrollably, and his concerned expression was replaced by one of unbridled amusement. He apologetically surveyed the state I was in.

'Sorry,' he said, faking a serious expression. 'I don't normally come so quickly, but it's been so very, very long.'

'Yeah right,' I said, smearing the paste around his stiff cock. I grasped it gently and clambered to my feet, before placing his eager hand between my legs. 'Fuck me or I'll report you to the Master Decorators' Guild.'

'No, not that!' he said, in mock horror. 'Anything but that! I'll do anything you say!' I knew he meant it.

'What are you waiting for?' I asked, as he hesitated momentarily. He knelt down and drew his fingernails tantalisingly along the inside of my thighs, then pushed me gently towards and into the shower room, where he cleaned me off before kneeling down and lifting one of my legs onto his shoulder. He began to lick me like a cat, long deliberate strokes up along my inner thighs, teasing my clitoris, darting back towards my anus as he lifted me higher, and I held onto him and shivered with delight as he tongued me.

'Are we on camera?' I asked, parting my legs as far as I could. He nodded guiltily. 'So this is my audition,' I purred, smiling.

'Ours,' he replied. The significance was not lost on me. I raised my eyes momentarily, motioned to him to let me go and knelt before him, taking his cock into my mouth. It was the first time that I spotted the little eye in the corner of the shower, filming everything.

He felt and tasted so good, so satisfying, and I licked and sucked, feeling his hips bucking in ecstasy as I worked on him. I caressed his balls and traced my index finger to the entrance to his anus, just pressing inside far enough to take him over the limit, and, at the last moment, as his glans jerked, I pulled his cock from my mouth and directed his spunk across my face and breasts, using my hands to spread it over me, its salty muskiness seeming to envelope us. He returned the compliment, his tongue renewing its interest on my clit until I orgasmed with an intensity that triggered my own shower onto him, his face and hair being marked with the scent of my release. I felt spent, satisfied, animal, and he was still beneath me, panting, when some thing occurred to me.

'Who took the photographs?' I asked.

'I did,' he said, simply.

I was perplexed. I had jumped to the wrong conclusion. 'Then who was . . .?'

'It was Simon, the new interior designer, Sally's boyfriend. Anyway, enough of them. I'm a bit of a voyeur, as you can probably tell. And those two are exhibitionists, of course! When I saw you in the paper, I thought to myself, 'She looks a game girl, a bit tough, just how I like 'em.'

I'd always gone for guys that were earthy and traditional; I'd never been out with a posh suit type before, but I would never judge by appearances again.

'So many girls don't want to get messy,' he said, 'but you don't mind and I love that. I think I may have found my kindred spirit.'

'So do I,' I said, as Josh helped me to my feet, his cock stiffening as he embraced me. 'And the customer is always right.'

I was about to become an apprentice again.

Doing a Number on Him
Lisa Sedara

He rapped on my open office door before I could pick up
the phone and pretend I was busy. 'Yes? What can I do for
you?' I asked, glancing at my Concord La Scala gold and
diamond watch like I had only a hectic few minutes to live.

'I've got some questions, Ms Demmings,' the kid
responded, unfazed.

'Well . . .' I stalled, staring angrily at the phone, willing
it to ring. No dice. I'd been ducking the auditors the entire
three weeks that they'd been examining the company
books for their year-end audit, but it looked like I was
finally trapped. Hefty bank loans and limited stock capi-
talisation made their presence an unwelcome necessity; it
had always ruffled my tail feathers that they could delve
into any aspect of *my* company that they wanted to.

'Come in and have a seat,' I eventually responded,
pouring syrup on to a full-bodied smile.

There were two ways of handling nosy number-
crunchers: the hard way – brushing them off, making
their job and the accounting records as difficult as possible, until they, hopefully, became too intimidated to
question you or your actions; or the soft way – soaking
them in so much sugary kindness and useless documentation that they, hopefully, jettisoned their objectivity as
they rushed to get the job done on time. I knew; I'd
worked for a public accounting firm 25 years before, before
the long hours and short pay sent me in search of private-
industry riches.

'My name's Malcolm,' the short, stocky, brown-haired bean-counter informed me, as he parked himself in one of the big, black leather chairs that stood guard before my big, black desk.

'I guess you guys are just about finished the audit now?' I asked, flashing a picket fence of white teeth dazzling enough to snow blind a Canadian.

Malcolm adjusted his out-of-style tie with one of his thick hands, gripped a pad of green seven-column and a mechanical pencil with the other. 'Yeah, we're just about done.'

'I used to work for one of the Big Five accounting firms, you know,' I said, attempting to lasso the square-jawed auditing foot soldier with our common bond, waste the only face-time he'd ever get with me on idle chit-chat as opposed to tough Q & A. 'An audit is never really quite done, though, is it, what with –'

'Anyway,' he interrupted, 'I know you're busy, so I'll get to my questions.'

'Yes, well, only too happy to help,' I said, glaring at the open door; there was never a busybody secretary when you needed one.

'I've got some questions about some of the income-statement accounts,' Malcolm intoned. 'First, the "Other Expenses" account. I noticed a lot of payments to consulting companies going through that account. One company in particular – T & S International. I looked at some of the invoices and all they said was "Management Consulting Services". What work did T & S International actually do for your company, Ms Demmings?'

I fingered my Waterman Leman 18K fountain pen, leaned back in my executive chair and crossed my long, black-stockinged legs. 'Catherine,' I said, smiling. 'Those amounts are fairly small, aren't they – for your materiality level, I mean?'

He nodded his blocklike head, his clear, brown eyes

unblinking as he glanced from my silk-sheathed legs to my pretty face. 'Yeah. None of the individual invoices is for more than ten grand – way below our single transaction audit materiality for a client with five-hundred million in sales – but they looked unusual, so I thought I'd ask. What'd T & S International do for you?'

I ran the slender, silver-ringed fingers of my right hand through my lustrous, black hair, twirled a shimmering strand around my forefinger as the soft, pink tip of my tongue peeked out from between my crimson lips and moistened them. The kid had a hell of a lot of nerve for someone half my age, and an accountant to boot. I'd run across his kind before, however, in my past life – lily-white untouchables with puritanical streaks wide enough to build a highway to heaven on; plain-looking guys and gals on self-righteous crusades to protect the fidelity of every number they audited; charmless innocents with no real-world business experience, in other words.

'I can't recall off the top of my head,' I replied. 'I'll have my secretary look it up and see that she faxes the appropriate documentation to your office.'

Like hell I would! Ten individual payments of less than ten thousand dollars to what no one but me knew was my own wholly owned shell company, which provided me with jet-set vacations, weren't enough to hold up a large-scale audit. Now, if those personal payments were put together with the other payments to the other subsidiaries of myself and long-dead relatives, then the whole crooked jigsaw puzzle might come together. And that could lead to a qualified audit opinion, possible de-listing, my probable termination. Not to mention nasty criminal charges and shareholder class-action lawsuits.

'I need to see some evidence of the work that these consultants performed, and I need a name, a phone number and an address – so I can get third-party confirmation,'

Malcolm remarked, ignoring my response, making it all sound so damned easy.

I slammed my chair upright, my baby blues turning cold enough to pour Scotch over. 'Your firm collects a significant audit fee from my company each year,' I scolded. 'And I don't pay the partner you report to – Lyle – to waste my time with insignificant, immaterial questions.' I stared hard at the earnest, green-as-money auditor, like any more sass might cause me to bend him over my knee, give him some good, old-fashioned motherly advice.

He didn't flinch. 'I'll need the information I asked for – immediately – otherwise I'll be forced to document your lack of co-operation, and my concerns, in a management point, forward it to the partner-in-charge of the audit, Mr Warkentin, with a cc. to the board of directors. As duly appointed external auditors, we're entitled to full access to any and all records that we request.'

It was quite the sermon, and it made my delicate, manicured hands ball into rugged fists. It was time to implement the last-chance plan. I slowly stood up, swung around my desk and sauntered over to the door, my hips swaying like a fish-tailing Caddie. I closed the door, and then sashayed back over to an antique filing cabinet and pulled it open. 'Well, let me see what I can find for you,' I said huskily, with a smile warm enough to penetrate the darkest heart of any accounting zealot.

I plucked a folder marked 'Miscellaneous' out of the cabinet, and accidentally on purpose dropped it. Papers scattered all over the plush carpeting, forcing Malcolm off his chair and onto the floor, to gather up some of the meaningless pulp. I stood there and looked at his hard, round buttocks, as he squatted at my feet, and then I unlatched my short, black, leather skirt and let it fall to the floor. He heard the seductive plop and halted his paper chase, turned around on his heels and tentatively fingered my abandoned hip-wrap. His eyes wandered up my slim, stocking-clad legs, all the way up to my lacy, black panties and sheer, black garter.

'See anything you can use?' I murmured, unbuttoning my metallic-grey blouse, sliding it off my buff shoulders to reveal a black lacy bra that had its cups full trying to restrain my overlarge breasts. I'd attained the ripe age of 45 only two months earlier, but in my business – in any business where ethics are written in sand – it pays to take good care of yourself, and I had.

Malcolm watched as I unhooked my bra and shrugged my shoulders, forced the stretched-out tit-holder to join my skirt and my auditor on the floor. I cupped my heavy, creamy-white breasts, rolled my jutting, pink nipples between long, silver-tipped fingers and formed a scarlet 'O' with my pouty lips, my eyelashes fluttering. I wouldn't be doing a girl–girl with Jenna Jameson any time soon, but judging by Malcolm's red face and partially unhinged jaw, my performance had definitely gotten some sort of rise out of him.

'What say we forget about the paperwork for a while?' I suggested, before reaching down and grabbing Malcolm's tie, pulling him to his feet, pressing my hot, soft-hard body against his and kissing him.

And after applying a heaping dose of snog to the stunned auditor's mouth, intoxicating him with the sweet scent of my body spray and the sensual warmth of my big tits and velvety lips, I broke contact with his gaping mouth. He tried to splutter a protest, but I placed a calming, controlling finger on his smeared lips. I pushed him back against the desk and dropped to my knees, unbuckled his belt and unfurled his fly in the time it took to cross a t, dot an i. Then I yanked his pants and shorts down in one fluid motion and proudly greeted the hard penis that sprang into my face, brushed my nose and swelled even further with anticipation as I breathed on it.

His aroused cock topped out at the five-inch mark – short and stocky like the rest of him. 'God, it's so big!' I enthused, looking up at him with admiring eyes. Come to mama, little man, I thought, you're playing by the house rules now. I wrapped my fingers around it and his body jerked, and then I began swirling my soft hand up and down his velvety pink length.

'Jesus!' he blurted, his body trembling.

I had the overwhelmed number disciple in the palm of my hand now, and I torqued up the sexual pressure, tugging on him faster and faster, testing his resolve, my scarlet lips mere millimetres away from the mushroomed head, my sure hand a blur.

'Ms Demmings – Catherine!' he wailed, warning me that he was about to bubble over with excitement, so enthused had he become with my sales pitch.

I released his cock, let it twitch in the hot wind of my breath for a moment, looking at it eye to pre-come-glazed eye. And after the spunk in his balls had settled down a bit, I opened my mouth and vacuumed him into my warm, wet mouth, consuming him.

'Yeah,' he groaned, giving tacit approval to my executive actions. His knuckles whitened on the edge of the desk as he looked down at me, and I expertly sucked him, my tongue running a slippery descent down his rock-hard shaft.

I mouthed more and more of him, scrubbing the sensitive underside with my tongue tip as I did so, revelling in my position of power and feeling myself moisten with every enhanced, enthusiastic gesture I made.

'Mmmm,' I moaned, sending oral vibrations coursing through Malcolm's overwrought body, hot, humid breath steaming out of my flared nostrils and against his crotch. I pulled back a bit, released half of his glistening length and then gobbled him up again.

I got a tried and true sucking rhythm going, bobbing

my head up and down with my free hand tickling his balls. He gripped my shiny raven hair in his sweaty hands and grunted, and I gazed up at him from between his legs, my mouth full of his cock, my head full of triumph at the easy seduction I had perfected.

'Fuck almighty!' he called out, blaspheming into the air-conditioned room, yanking my head into his body and desperately churning his hips, frantically pumping himself to oblivion. I wondered what was going through his mind; did he really think that he was the one in the powerful position? He'd probably imagined that he'd been the one to seduce me – the archetypal 'ice queen' older woman. If only he knew. Poor dumb sap. Then he threw his head back, bellowed like a beast and shot superheated spunk directly down my throat.

I grasped his quivering ass with my talons and milked that dick, my cheeks billowing in and out with the effort, my throat constricting around his spurting hood, drinking in his lusty load. And when he eventually squirted his last white dollop of surrender, I disgorged his cock and licked the remnants of his integrity off its softening tip. Then I smacked my slimy lips with the satisfaction at a deal gone down well, and asked, 'Any more questions, Mr Independent Auditor?'

A month or so after my oral exploration of Malcolm's character, he unexpectedly reappeared in my office doorway. The audit fieldwork was long since over, and the financial statements, with a clean, unqualified audit opinion, issued.

'Hello, Catherine,' he said, striding in, before taking a seat without being asked.

I studied his plain, placid face, his bright, brown eyes and his authoritative body language. 'I'm rather –'

'Busy?' he interrupted. 'Sure. But not too busy to hear a

business proposition.' He crossed his stubby legs, folded his oversized hands in his lap. 'I know that you're defrauding this company of hundreds of thousands of dollars, Catherine – cutting cheques to companies you own for services never performed – in order to boost your take-home pay well beyond board-authorised limits.'

'Get the hell –'

'But I'm not going to report what I know to the various authorities ... provided you hire me as your new vice-president of finance.'

I threw my pen down in disgust and angrily folded my arms beneath my breasts. 'You little punk!' I sneered. 'I've spent twenty years building this company – my company – and I didn't get this far by being blackmailed by premature ejaculates like you! There's a camera in this office, child's play, and it's recording your extortion attempt, just like it recorded our off-the-books suck session last month, when you compromised your firm and your accounting designation by consorting with a client. Not to mention set yourself up for a conspiracy charge when you didn't report what you knew. Sorry, buddy boy, no deal.'

He didn't flinch. 'My work has seemed pretty boring since I got a taste of the real world of high finance right here in your office. I used to think that good business was squeaky-clean business, but you showed me the way, Catherine.'

My eyes narrowed to gun slits, fired darts at him, willing him to back down. We were both in a bind – the one I'd fashioned for myself and he'd discovered, and the one I'd entrapped him in – and that was fine, as long as no one tried to tighten the tourniquet.

'You've got plenty more to lose than I do,' he went on, putting the screws to me. 'I'm young and inexperienced; it's easy to suck a guy like me in. But you're old, I mean

old-er and more experienced, with a company and personal reputation to protect.' He smiled a bland smile. 'So
when do I start?'

My brass cupcake routine crumbled like the Enron
empire as I realised he was right. 'Next Monday,' I said
quietly, knowing when I was temporarily licked.

He shook his head, rubbed some salt in my gash. 'Not
soon enough,' he said. 'My father's got a bit of money,
Catherine, and, while he won't give any of it to me, he's
always looking for a good investment. I told him about
your company – not everything about the way you do
business, of course – and he wants to invest. Provided that
I'm in a position of authority to make sure things are
done right.' He stood up and walked around my desk,
pulled me out of my chair and planted a sloppy wet one
bang on my startled pucker. 'And he and I both think I
should start work here right away.'

As Malcolm brusquely pushed his tongue into my
mouth, trapping my tongue, I consoled myself with the
thought that the first rule of business is adaptation:
embrace change or die. So, I wrapped my hands around
the head of the newest member of my executive team
and fought an erotic duel with his sticker. The kid wasn't
the best-looking stud I'd ever fucked for business reasons,
but he was still plenty good enough to bring a tear to a
mature girl's pussy.

He told me to strip, and I unzipped my sapphire-blue
Versace and let it puddle at my spike heels, as he calmly
kicked off his shoes, pulled down his pants and shorts and
let his hardened dick catch a breath of fresh air. The guy
was as cocky as any young gun loaded with come could
get, and his prick pointed directly at my puss, thick and
throbbing. I awaited further instructions, willing to let
him run the show – for now, anyway. 'Let me see those
big jugs of yours,' he said tersely.

'Of course.' I unhooked my satiny blue bra and let my

boobs tumble forth, hang huge and heavy, riding up and down on my chest as I breathed.

He grabbed my tits and roughly fondled the hot, firm tingling flesh. My mouth broke open and I moaned; his hands were feeling so very good on my ultra-sensitive globes and there was a certain new confidence to his manner. I moaned again when the jacked-up exec bent his head down and started licking at my nipples. I gripped his square shoulders and watched as he swirled his thick, wet tongue all over my flushed buds, before inhaling one into his mouth and pulling on it.

'Yes!' I hissed, my head swimming, my body electrified, making the best of a bad, bad situation.

Malcolm spat my glistening left nipple out of his mouth and swallowed up my other, sucking urgently on it. Then my blackmailer shoved my boobs together and bounced his head back and forth between my nips – tonguing, sucking, slobbering all over them until he topped off his tremendous tit-play by jamming my mounds so close together that he could tongue-slap both engorged nipples at once, which he did repeatedly.

'I've always liked older women,' my younger-by-half business associate confided, pushing my right breast up so that I could lick my own slick nipple. 'They can teach me so much.' He rammed his tongue onto my tongue, excitedly helping me to lap at my rigid nipple.

'Fuck me,' I ordered, when I could bear no more of his frustrating tit-play. The upstart never had the decency to try and find my sweet spot down below, or ask what I might want out of the situation, so the least he could do was give me his cock. I was aching for it between my legs, and my panties were soaking with excitement at his rough handling.

He unhanded my overstimulated boobs, led me to the front of my desk, and then spun me around and bent me over the top of its gleaming, ebony surface. He fumbled with the straps on my garter, then tugged my dainty, cornflower-blue panties down my *noir*-stockinged legs. I lifted my heels out of my damp underwear and spread my legs, anxious now to culminate our merger. I'd deal with the ramifications of our unholy alliance later – when I'd orgasmed a time or two.

Malcolm stroked the luxurious silk that covered my lithe legs, then abruptly grabbed my bare ass with one hand and ramrodded his cock into my sopping pussy with the other.

'Yes!' I shrieked, not giving a damn if my entire staff piled into the office to find out just what sort of transaction was going on.

Malcolm's dick dived deep into my greasy sex till he was balls-to-the-walls. Then he started pumping his hips, fucking my sodden snatch faster and faster, spanking my big, pliable butt cheeks with his hard-thrusting body as my damp hands squeaked back and forth on the high-polish desktop.

He sawed in and out for a good, long time. He was certainly getting his fill of high-class executive bitch and he seemed determined to have the upper hand this time around. He was loving the way our roles had reversed, with him the commander and me the subordinate. He grabbed me by the back of the neck and pumped himself to a frenzy, till he finally leaned over on top of me, grabbed my tits and hissed in my ear, 'I'm gonna fuck you up the ass.'

I didn't utter a word of protest – if we were going to work dirty, we might as well play dirty.

He eased out of me, polished himself with spit and pussy juice, and then pressed the bloated head of his cock against my butt hole. I quickly reached back and parted my cheeks. There was no point whimpering and playing the virgin. I went full throttle into slut mode, welcoming his unholy intrusion into my anus. I groaned, overcome with a heavy, languid heat as Malcolm's prick sank into my bum.

'Fuck my ass,' I whispered, 'fuck it.' I was dizzy with the wicked sensation of his cock buried to the hairline in my violated bottom.

He moved his hips, slowly at first, then more rapidly, sliding his meat back and forth in my chute, bum-fucking me with an assurance that belied his tender years. Then he draped his body over the top of mine again, scooped up and squeezed my breasts, tongued up and down my neck, banging away at my back door.

I reached between my trembling legs and desperately buffed my puffed-up clit, frantically polishing it as Malcolm pulled on my nipples, swirled his tongue around my ear, and littered the air with obscenities. The dirty bastard was having a party. It was no surprise to me that this seemingly decent professional employee was an animal underneath. Scratch the surface of any office-bound accountant in his smart suit, with his spreadsheets and forecasts, and a beast will spring out at the right trigger – the sight of a moist slit and a little slutting around. Underneath the pretence to civilisation they all want to get a smart woman bent over and fucked.

The violent slapping of his thighs against my rippling butt cheeks grew more and more frenzied, until he jerked up and bellowed, 'I'm coming!' and blasted sizzling semen deep into my stretched-out anus.

I rubbed myself like a woman possessed, and a mammoth orgasm exploded at the thought of his raw lust finding its fruition. My climax thundered through my quivering body, and the contracting heat of my cunt spasmed and throbbed until I collapsed on top of the desk, exhausted and exhilarated. Malcolm collapsed on top of me; my pact with the devil had been signed in white-hot come.

* * *

Malcolm continued to fuck me up the ass, both literally and figuratively, and it wasn't long before he and his father had virtually taken over my company. He installed himself and his dad on the board of directors, and put an end to my double-dipping in the company till. He used his father's money to pay back the money I'd taken, giving me 'a clean and honest start forwards', as he kindly put it.

I put up with the reduced authority and salary and perquisites, playing the part of the reformed, repentant capitalist cheat, while I secretly worked on some strategic plans of my own. And, when I walked into Malcolm's office late one night and caught him pecker-deep in the accounts receivable manager, I decided it was high time to take care of some unfinished business – old management school-style.

'I've got a surprise for you, Malcolm,' I informed him soon after his bad debts diddling, strutting into his office in one of my sluttiest ball-breaking outfits – a red, latex skirt and black, see-through top. My legs were clothed in their usual night-shaded colour, and I had a pair of silver-tipped stilettos strapped to my feet. My push-up bra had me spilling personality, but I wanted to make sure that young Malcolm realised just what he was going to be missing – and just how low-down dirty the pussy-eat-dog business world can really get.

'Not interested,' he stated dismissively from behind his desk. 'I've got real work to do.'

'Not interested in meeting my new husband?' I pouted.

Malcolm's father ambled into the office. 'Hello, son!' he hollered, snaking a stubby, covetous arm around my narrow waist. 'What do ya think of your new stepmom? We got married last night in Vegas. Surprised?'

I kissed the morbidly obese, sixty-year-old type-one diabetic on the cheek. 'We're all one big, happy family now – at home and the office,' I cooed, savouring the stunned, defeated look on Malcolm's mug. To tell his father about my transgressions would force me to lift the rug on his own sleazy dealings, and that would make sugar Daddy very, very angry.

A smile of triumph graced my full-bodied lips. Malcolm gave me a cold, sour stare, as his father proudly eyed my voluptuous body like it was a trophy he'd just won at the crap tables. It was going to be just peachy living a life of pampered leisure for a change, while my stymied stepson and unhealthy hubby laboured to keep the family business humming. And, if anything should happen to my mate, well, I was more than willing to pick up his controlling interest and take over; I'd had a bit of experience running the company, after all.

Strip Search Angel Blake

I suppose you could have called me naïve back then. Or at least idealistic, although there's nothing wrong with that, is there? I can remember when we were told about drugs at school. A police officer came round and showed us some awful slides and a bit from a video; it made a strong impression, and I was really shocked, though most of my classmates thought it was hilarious. Some of them probably even ended up that way – druggies, I mean. Anyway, I was about to leave school then, and I hadn't known what to do. I'd stayed on for my A levels – the teachers thought I was quite bright – but I didn't think I was really cut out for college, and didn't want to start off my adult life getting knee-deep in debt either.

But the police demonstration had got me thinking of what I could do to make a difference in the world. The idea of catching drug smugglers, using speedboats and trying to outwit carriers – 'mules', they called them – at airports was exciting; more, at any rate, than the dead-end jobs in retail or sales most of my friends were going in for. When someone from where I came from said they were in banking, it meant they were behind the counter at Lloyds. Anyway, I looked into it and found that as I'd done A levels I'd qualify for a fast track, and could have a uniform and actually be on active duty within a month! I'd always fancied the idea of a uniform. People would give me respect, give me credit. So I applied, passed the tests with flying colours, I might add – and got the job.

Needless to say, it didn't quite live up to expectations. The airport was a hellhole of a place pretty much year-round, with the budget carriers making sure we worked hard for our pay every day of the year. They tended to bring out the senior officers for the problem flights – Kingston, Miami, Amsterdam and pretty much anywhere in South America – and leave us to do spot checks, which mainly involved checking people's shoes; if they were really tatty, or if they were wearing those slippy snakeskin numbers, we often called them over and checked out their luggage. It had struck me as a weird way to go about it, but that was the received wisdom – look at the shoes – and all I'd found so far was a matchbox full of cannabis resin some long-haired posh kid said he'd forgotten was in his backpack, but I still had to ask him to part his cheeks and bend over, lift himself up, all that kind of stuff – and he stank, no question, probably hadn't had a bath since he'd left England, the bloody soap-dodger.

I didn't like that part of the job much – though rummaging through people's luggage was OK as it was amazing the stuff you found sometimes – but my colleague did. Lisa had been on the job a couple of months longer than me, and frankly I fancied the hell out of her. She had dark hair in a fairly short crop, pouty lips, and a really ballsy attitude. The admiration didn't seem to be mutual, though. I wanted to be friends with her – we'd be working most of the same shifts, after all – but when I tried to talk to her about the kind of stuff I was interested in she wasn't impressed. I still don't think there's anything wrong with Billy Joel, but when I asked her about her taste in music she just muttered something about 'darkwave' or something. I'd never heard of them. I couldn't help blushing when she actually laughed at the crucifix I wear round my neck. It's not like I'm that religious, but why not hedge your bets, that's what I always think.

Anyway, she seemed to have the hots for this tall, skinny goth guy, Vincent, who worked as a baggage handler but was always hanging around the customs area talking to Lisa. It was funny, him being so skinny and working in baggage – me, I like to work out, keep a nice build, and I could never understand why a girl would want to be seen with a man like Vincent, who didn't look after himself. He was all lanky hair, vacant expression and scuffed shoes. He didn't even wear his baggage-handler's uniform properly. I tried to talk to Lisa about him once; he was slowing down her work, which reflected badly on us as a team, and so made me look bad. This was unfair, and I told her so, but she just swore at me, and we got on even worse after that.

Still, I wasn't about to run to Miss Sims and tell her. I may be many things, but I'm not a grass. In any case, she was scarier than Lisa, very smart and strict, always properly turned out, prim and neat, with her little half-moon glasses. She was young, too, only just thirty probably, and she knew where she was going. I admired that in her, but she was way out of my league, and always kept things on a strictly professional level that I was in no mind to mess with. After all, it was up to her when I moved up a level, so it didn't do to rock the boat. What eventually happened was far worse than me just being overfamiliar with the boss, but you never know what's just around the corner, do you? So I spent most of my time at work alone, reading a thriller on my breaks or taking the sandwiches my mum made me outside to eat at lunch, rather than deal with the unfriendly faces in the staff canteen. It was just as well that I spent my time alone, though, because I soon found out that Lisa was a pervert.

Don't get me wrong – she wasn't into anything really rough, and I'm open-minded when it comes to sex, but Lisa just got into the whole body-check thing a bit too much. We'd been shown how to do it properly – you didn't want to give the passenger any cause for complaint, as they could sue, so it was strictly men searching men, women searching women, and no funny stuff. Not that

I'd want to get close to a man's tackle anyway, no thanks, but Lisa didn't seem to mind when it came to the women she dealt with; quite the reverse, in fact.

First time I noticed was when we were both patting down passengers, and I heard a cough from the woman Lisa was doing. I turned round and saw that her passenger had gone bright red. Her arms – they had to stretch their hands out, you see – were shaking, and she looked like she was about to start crying. I could see why, too. Lisa's hand was right up at the top of her thigh, her forefinger pressing between the woman's legs. I couldn't believe it.

I started watching her more closely, and saw that she only gave this special treatment to a few of them. Not just the cute ones, but girls who looked like it probably wouldn't give them a heart attack. I suppose Lisa didn't want to get any complaints if she could help it, and I wasn't going to tell Miss Sims, but when I got told off it was a bit unfair. Lisa had a routine. She'd be all brusque and officious, not looking the girls in the eye at all, but running her hands up under their armpits, down the sides of their chests, her thumbs just skimming their nipples, which usually got the first gasp, then down to their bums, which she'd actually pull apart to run her fingers along the crack. They'd all go deep red, but none of them ever seemed to file a complaint against Lisa; and once, when I was watching her, and I admit I wasn't giving my own passenger much attention, Miss Sims caught me and gave me a bollocking.

It was fair enough insofar as my mind hadn't been on the job, but I was upset that I'd been singled out – hadn't she seen what Lisa had been doing? But mainly I was glad that the uniform trousers I was wearing were heavy-duty, thick cotton; the kind that won't bulge too easily. Because I'll admit it – watching Lisa with these women gave me a hard-on. The first time it happened I had really mixed feelings, like I'd done something dirty, getting off on seeing Lisa taking advantage of these women, like I was responsible for it as well or something, but after a while I started to look forward to these little displays.

Because it wasn't like she'd stop at just feeling them up, either. When she searched through their luggage, she'd have a field day going through everything they had, holding it all up just to humiliate them, as far as I could see. It wasn't on, really, in my opinion – we were meant to be catching the bad guys, fighting crime and all that – but to be frank it all turned me on, and I didn't really want it to stop. Sometimes I even had to rush to the toilet afterwards to bring myself off, though if Lisa noticed she never let on.

That was another thing. She'd keep a poker face through the whole thing, whatever she was pulling out of their bags and dangling in front of them. Most of the women she did had probably just come back from package holidays, a bit of fun in the sun, and they had the clothes to match: skimpy thongs, tiny boob tubes, that kind of thing. She'd just hold them up and gaze sternly at the passenger, and most of them would start trying to make some excuse, stammering their way through their 'you see's and 'it's just's. A few boldly stared back, and then occasionally she'd make comments, put-downs, really, but subtle enough that she could get away with it. I remember one woman going scarlet when Lisa pointed out how many condoms she'd brought back, implying she was some kind of slut, or, worse, an unsuccessful one.

Another time she'd gone through someone's bag – a tweedy woman this time, not quite the type she normally went for – without finding anything, just plain bras and knickers, nothing racier than a pair of hold-ups, until she got to the bottom of the bag and pulled out an electric toothbrush. This she held up in front of the woman, who looked stunned and confused that such a thing could be thought in any way suspicious, then, in full view of all the people walking by, Lisa switched it on. Almost every head turned, the buzzing noise pitched just so you could hear it over the clatter of trolleys and the hushed voices. It was nothing, really, that toothbrush, nothing to be ashamed of, but Lisa holding it up like that made all kinds of insinuations. She didn't even have to say anything and the woman blushed. She always got to them in the end.

Once she'd picked a smart businesswoman, again not the type she normally went for, and I wondered how she'd known who to choose, because, after she'd unpacked the laptop, office odds and ends and a few identical sets of business suits, she found a crop – the kind of thing a jockey might use on a horse, only she didn't have any other horsey stuff with her. That was one of the only times I saw Lisa's mask slip. For a split second she looked triumphant, then, as she held it with one hand and slapped it lightly against the palm of the other, she just raised an eyebrow and looked at the woman quizzically.

God only knows how long it all would have gone on if it hadn't ended the way it did. It's probably just as well it did finish, because things were getting a little out of hand. I could have sworn I saw Lisa notice my hard-on a few times, and she didn't need to be a genius to work out what was going on when I went off to the toilet after one of her shows. Still, it could have ended a bit less disastrously.

She came in on a flight from Brussels. I was going to sit this one out – what would anyone want to smuggle from Belgium? Extra-strong lager? But Lisa had seemed excited all morning, and zeroed in on her when she came through. She was dressed simply enough, in a pair of jeans with a rollneck top, a leather jacket and a smart pair of trainers; early thirties, I'd have said, with brown hair pulled back into a ponytail and everything in the right place, but nothing extra-special. Still, Lisa had a talent for nosing the right people out, and she hadn't lost the knack with this one. The woman flushed as soon as Lisa called her over, and gulped visibly as she was told to stand with her legs apart and her arms stretched out.

Lisa took even more time with her than usual, and I couldn't help enjoying watching her go to work, surreptitiously just flicking the nipples as she went down, then running her hands slowly up each thigh in turn, to end by pressing hard against the crease of her jeans and skimming a hand over the cheeks of her bum, almost stroking it. I was amazed that she could still get away with it, and was starting to feel a little uncomfortable at how upfront she was being, but it must have been nothing compared to what the woman felt when Lisa unzipped her bag and half-a-dozen hardcore porn mags and DVDs spilled out onto the counter.

They must have been packed in a hurry, an impulse buy perhaps, as she'd made no effort to hide them at all, but now they were all out, one of the magazines even opening out on a centrespread of some tart with her arse stuffed with a huge cock, her eyes closed as another one spurted all over her face. For a moment neither of them said anything, and the lurid display lay there for everyone to see, then the woman, crimson now, hurriedly picked them up and started to put them back in the bag, muttering, 'I don't think this –'

But Lisa stopped her, saying, 'I'll take those, miss' and spreading them out along the counter, each one face up, all of the magazines full-colour with names like *Hustler XXX*, *Anal Sluts* and *Teen Debutantes*, and the DVDs were even worse. I was shocked. Regulations clearly stated that any pornographic material seized should be taken away immediately so as not to offend other passengers passing through. I could already see a couple of elderly ladies looking over with appalled expressions, and the poor woman whose passport Lisa was now slowly leafing through looked like she was about to burst into tears. I glared at Lisa, but she just ignored me, then gathered all the stuff up, to the woman's clear relief, and put it in a separate bag. But her relief must have been short-lived, as Lisa then said, 'I'm afraid that these DVDs are contraband material, madam. They aren't allowed into the country without being classified by the British Board of Film Classification. Do you understand?'

The woman nodded mutely.

'I'll have to confiscate them. As we've found you with this illegal material, I'll also have to give you a more thorough search. If you'd like to follow me into my office, please.' Lisa beckoned to the door behind the counters, which led to a handful of inspection rooms, and the woman, flushing an even deeper red, walked towards it with her head bowed.

It didn't take me long to make my decision. There was only a thin straggle of people coming through now, and there wouldn't be any problem flights for a while. I had to know what Lisa was doing to that poor woman. I'd never known her to use one of the interrogation rooms for her games, and couldn't help but be excited by the idea that maybe she'd push it even further this time. I knew I couldn't get into the room, but there was a keyhole which I'd be able to see something through, and I'd be able to hear them too. I left it a couple of minutes, then left the desk and walked through to the corridor.

The first room was empty, so they must have gone into number two. My heart pounding, I put my ear to the door. There weren't any voices at first, but when I heard a snapping sound I realised what was going on. Lisa must have just pulled on a rubber glove to give the woman an internal inspection. I crouched down, and could make out the shape of the woman's thighs as she lay on the trolley.

'Spread your legs.' Lisa's voice was quiet but clear, and more of an order than a request. I could see the woman's thighs twitching, closing.

'I don't think this is really necessary. I don't have anything hidden up there. Do we have to do this?' The woman's voice was quavering now; it sounded like she was about to cry.

But I didn't expect this would slow Lisa down, and sure enough I saw her come towards the woman, take hold of her thighs and pull them apart. The woman groaned.

'Normally we'd use some Vaseline for this part of the procedure, but you don't seem to need any extra lubrication.' Lisa said this so matter-of-factly that it took a second to sink in, then the woman sobbed and my cock twitched in anticipation. There was a squeaking noise as Lisa spread the woman's thighs further still, and I caught a glimpse of pink, a tantalising wetness, before Lisa moved to block my view.

This was unbelievable. I stared at Lisa's moving arm, and imagined her gloved hand teasing the woman's slit and probing deep inside, pushing her way into the most private place and leaving nothing untouched. I was sure I could hear wet, sucking sounds as she made her inspection, and the woman's sobs were soon replaced by sighs.

Abruptly, Lisa moved back, and I saw a flash of the woman's open wetness before her thighs moved together again. Lisa walked away, then came back and snapped on a new glove.

'Bring your knees up towards your chest. No – keep them open. That's right.'

I heard the woman gasp.

'Bit dirty down there, aren't you? Didn't have time to have a shower this morning?'

I couldn't hear the woman's reply, and nor could Lisa, it seemed, because she asked her again. 'Speak up, then. I didn't catch what you said.'

The woman's voice trembled as she explained, 'I ... I had to go at the airport this morning.' She almost didn't make it to the end of the sentence, sucking in air as Lisa probed deeper inside her. All I could see was a hand held tightly against a thigh, and Lisa's arm working back and forth.

'Not very tight down here, are you?' The woman whimpered. 'Been sticking things up your arse, have you? Or maybe your boyfriend likes to take you in the shitter, does he? Do you like it like that? I bet you like rubbing yourself while his fat cock plugs up your hole. Look, you're soaking wet!'

I couldn't believe Lisa was talking like this. Surely this woman would complain. This was sexual harassment, no bones. Banter with suspected drug smugglers was frowned on, in any case, and we were surely facing a lawsuit after something like this. But I didn't hear her make a squeak, and nor could I help my stiff cock; I moved a hand down to my trousers to make it more comfortable.

'Here, wipe yourself off. You've made the trolley damp.' Lisa handed the woman something, a tissue perhaps, and moved away again, and I saw the woman's hand rubbing between her legs with something white. Then she spoke, sounding half out of breath.

'I wonder – I need to go to the toilet. I didn't go on the plane, and I'm bursting to go now.'

I heard Lisa snort. 'We don't allow passengers to visit the toilet in the middle of inspections, madam. You could take any contraband you had on your person and flush it down the toilet! You'll just have to wait.'

The woman sobbed again, and her voice broke as she said, 'But you've just given me my inspection. You have to let me go now.' There was a pause, and then, in a faltering voice, 'I might wet myself if you don't let me go.'

Lisa sighed in exasperation, and I could hear her moving around in the corner of the room. Finally, she moved something to the floor. 'You can use this, then.'

The woman sounded astonished. 'But I can't do it in front of you! Please, let me go to the toilet.'

'If you can't go in front of me, you can't need to go that badly. I'll put this away, then.'

'No! No, all right then. But please don't watch.'

I heard Lisa snort again. 'Hurry up, we've got to go through the rest of your luggage yet.'

The thighs shifted, and the woman got off the trolley and walked across the room. I moved, and could just make out a yellow shape on the floor, with the woman starting to squat over it. It was a bucket. Lisa was making the woman piss in a bucket. I heard zips being undone – Lisa must have started looking through the rest of her luggage – then a couple of drips and a clatter and a sigh as she finally started to let it go.

Suddenly, I saw something out of the corner of my eye, a shadow just about to turn the corner, and heard footsteps. I stood up and walked away as quickly as I could without running, down to the other end of the corridor. I could hear someone behind me, but I didn't dare turn round to see who it was. But, when I heard them knock on the door, I thought that was it for Lisa's game – whoever it was wouldn't be impressed to find some poor woman squatting over a bucket, with the whole room probably thick with the smell of arousal. But I heard the door open, and looked back just in time to see a trouser leg and a shoe go in and the door close again. A man's trouser leg!

Even considering everything else Lisa was doing, this was highly irregular. Men weren't allowed in inspection rooms when women were being inspected and, whatever else the woman knew about customs, she surely knew that. But there were no shrieks from the room, no sounds of screaming and protestation, and I warily made my way back to the keyhole.

The woman seemed to have got back on the trolley, and I could hear a man's voice, no mistake, but it was too quiet to work out what it was saying. There were footsteps, a rustling sound, then I heard Lisa again. 'We found this in your luggage as well. Would you like to show us what you use it for?'

There was a low chuckle – a man's chuckle – then the woman replied, 'I think it's obvious, isn't it? Haven't you ever seen one before?' She sounded different now, bolshier, but if she thought Lisa would be easily intimidated she was wrong. Lisa crossed the room and blocked the view once more. I heard a buzzing noise, then a squeal.

'Is that what you use it for? You like wanking yourself off with that? I wonder if you like it more rubbing on your clit or –' she paused and I heard a distinct moan '– to fuck yourself with it. Go on, show us what you like doing.'

She moved back, and I was rewarded for a split second with a view of the woman's legs splayed, her hand teasing some kind of vibrator slowly along her slit, before a leg swung round and blocked it from my view. But I could still hear it, louder then quieter as she pushed it inside herself and, on top of it, the sound of the woman whimpering.

I heard footsteps, then a zip being pulled down. At one side of my view I could see a man's legs, standing, with something dark in front of the crotch. It took me a second to realise that it was Lisa's head, and that she was sucking a man off in front of the passenger, forcing her to wank herself off. My cock was ready to burst, and I reached down in my pants and started tugging on it, feeling my balls tighten as I imagined what was going on inside.

'Adam? What the hell do you think you're doing?' Suddenly Miss Sims was there, staring at me from one end of the corridor. I hadn't heard her at all. She walked towards me, her heels clacking on the lino as she fixed a steely gaze on me from above her glasses.

I don't know what made me do it. I panicked, really, unable to come up with a story in time, and stood up, watching Miss Sims's gaze flicker down to the telltale bulge at the front of my trousers. That was it – I had to deflect attention from myself.

'I think there's something going on –' I started to explain, now blushing as deeply as any of Lisa's victims as I fumbled with my set of keys in the lock, then swung the door open.

It must have happened too quickly for them to react. The room smelled strongly of sex, and the woman was naked from the waist down, with her top pushed up and her bra pulled down, her face and chest flushed, her eyes shut and her tight long nipples sticking straight up as she caressed them with one hand. With the other she still had the vibrator, rubbing it against herself, but she soon snapped out of it, opened her eyes and stared at us.

'Lisa? Who's this? I thought you said there'd only be one man?'

Lisa was still on her knees in front of Vincent. She looked appalled, but Vincent was grinning, as though he didn't mind being caught in one of the interrogation rooms with his cock out in a colleague's face. Lisa's trousers were undone, and her fingers were wet, like she'd been rubbing herself.

For a few seconds the only sound was the vibrator, still buzzing in the woman's hand. Then Miss Sims, looking slightly flushed herself, spoke to the woman, 'I don't know who you are, and I don't care. Please get dressed, and I'll show you out.'

As the woman swung herself off the trolley, her eyes down and her face scarlet, Miss Sims turned to the rest of us. 'Vincent, put that ridiculous thing away. All of you, I want to see you in my office in five minutes.'

My hard-on still hadn't gone down by then. Lisa and Vincent were sacked, for misusing company property. I don't think Miss Sims wanted to know about what Lisa had been doing to other passengers, but Lisa actually knew this one, and they'd arranged it between themselves. I was suspended, but decided to leave anyway – I couldn't face Miss Sims after what she'd seen, and the stories would have been around the staff room in no time. I didn't want to have a job where everyone thought I was a pervert, so I handed in my notice, and now I'm in training to be a bouncer. It's not so different, really – we get a uniform, and I'm fighting the bad guys, but this time it's a bit more hands on. Not in Lisa's style, though.

Short Circuit
Maddie Mackeown

Sally could not believe that she had reached this particular point in time. It was only two years and two months that she had been working for this company and tomorrow she would be leaving.

It had been good at the beginning when she was the new darling, a bright young executive with great promise, not yet thirty, a graduate with some years' experience. It was generally considered that she was to have a highly successful future. The way she saw it she was going up in the lift while others climbed the stairs breathlessly. She was good. Everyone thought so. She thought so. No false modesty. What was the point in that?

She had expected envy, even malice, for sparkling talent often rankled, but she had not been prepared for the latent obduracy and stasis of those whom she had to deal with on a daily basis. She had got up the noses of too many in the upper echelons of the company. They had closed ranks against her in a subdued panic of self-preservation and she had been firmly placed outside the magic inner circle.

It had also been politely suggested to Ms Sally Howell that 'she move on in order to gain further experience elsewhere: to fulfil her potential'. Yeah, right. On the understanding that she is never to lighten the portals of this company again. For if she so does then proof of certain known facts would be handed over to those whom it may concern. They were voiding the company of sneaks.

Meanwhile, she was being closely watched until the day she left when a glowing reference would be handed to her directly.

It was not revenge that she desired. Not exactly. It was more like a continuation of the game. At the moment it stood at deuce. Well, maybe advantage company. It was her task to choreograph a more satisfactory ending. To her advantage, needless to say. To redress the balance.

Why no one else had noticed the discrepancies hidden deep within the spreadsheets of the networked system she did not comprehend. Unless they had and decided to leave well alone. She had a highly intimate relationship with her computer that had proved to be rewarding. There had been a small trickle of money on a steady continuum of some years duration to clients with indeterminate and exchangeable aliases. Mind you, it did require a certain amount of logic, lateral thinking and financial acumen besides the knowledge of various passwords that were held separately rather than corporately. A soupçon of Morse mixed with Poirot and Tennison was necessary.

Maybe she had not been entirely honest. Well, OK. Maybe even some procedures had been a tad illegal. But such is life. She knew that she and her computer were now being closely monitored. Scrutinised. Cornered. But she was not one to give up easily. It was simply that she had so little time in which to achieve satisfaction. But they had not reckoned on the persistence of Ms Cool. Her motto? Don't mess with me.

Stalemate? Ha! Watch this space!

The office was currently in a state of hectic refurbishment with plumbers, electricians, carpenters and glaziers crawling all over the place. Nowhere, it seemed, was sacrosanct. Why the building hadn't been closed even a section at a time during this upheaval she did not understand. Not cost-effective, she supposed.

She passed through the gamut of the open-plan section

amidst varying remarks: some genuine, supportive, caring; others knowing, two faced, amused. There was the eternal background hubbub of computer hum and quiet voice, the professionally efficient sound of a well-oiled corporate body dulled by the thickness of relatively new carpet.

And there was Hugo right on cue, looking as suave and impeccably dressed as always, just happening to be where she was to pass. Predictable. She could read him like a book. She suspected that it was he who had dobbed her in; whether to protect his own back or because she presented the only serious contender for the promotion he wanted, she did not know. Whichever, the metaphorical toad held certain incriminating evidence against her which he would hold no qualms about using if required. It was a shame really because they could have made a strong team if either of them had been good team players.

He stepped in her way as if by accident and she was forced to stop. Predatory stalking was his style, the enjoyment of smooth seduction technique leading to the kill and he always got his way. Well, almost always.

'Sally.' Slimy smile that she wanted to flick into his out tray. 'I was wondering if we could consult on the Foster file. Have you a moment to spare?' Ingenuously innocent.

'Hello, Hugo. No. I don't.'

'Busy to the end. We are all going to miss you. Some more than others.' Suggestively compassionate. 'How could you decide to leave us so soon?' Snide.

She made to move on but he held his ground and continued, voice now lowered to a confidential whisper, 'Only a day to go and you've not had me yet. We could adjourn later to conference room two where we won't be disturbed. I know for a fact that it will be free at two thirty.' He pressed himself lightly against her. 'What do you think?'

'That your cock is as big as your nose,' she said. 'Or so I

hear from half the females in this office.' Although this was quietly spoken there were sniggers from those nearby.

'Only when in repose, sweetness,' he carried on smoothly. 'Aren't you longing wetly to experience the awakened version?' She had to admit that his slick recovery was attractive.

'Excuse me, Hugo, I have work to do.'

'A little tidying up and sorting out perhaps?' Sweet smile, raised eyebrows.

She made an elegant sidestep and escaped to her office.

Leaning against the closed door for a moment to free herself of Hugo contamination, she realised that she was not alone. An electrician was elongated on a stepladder reaching up to do something interesting with the smoke alarm. Her eyes travelled up the length of long legs with taut thighs encased in worn denim to a cute bum. His T-shirt was trying unsuccessfully to make a bid for freedom from his belt. She watched him stretching and imagined the muscles moving beneath the fabric.

'Sorry,' he said speaking to the high ceiling. 'Won't be long. I'll be leaving shortly.'

'So will I.'

He twisted to look at her. 'Bit early to be finishing.'

'That's what I told them.'

She went over to her computer, slipped off her jacket to place it on the back of the chair on which she then sat straight-backed. She took a deep breath and settled into stillness. She perfected her poise and began to click the mouse repetitively, her eyes intently scanning the information brought up on to the screen.

He was drawn to her focus and worked quietly so as not to disturb her but surreptitiously kept watching her. She was in a lone place of concentration, wandering, lost in a world of files and data. She created an ambience of 'do not disturb'. Calm, self-contained but with an underlying energy closely reined in. He watched as she picked up a water bottle, unscrewed the lid gently but firmly and touched it to her lips, her eyes never stopping their search. She fascinated him. The information continued to scroll. Her eyes continued to explore. As she tilted her head and swallowed, he watched her exposed neck, imagining the water trickling coolly down her throat.

Then she stopped, swivelled the chair and crossed her legs. Her skirt slid slightly up over her stockinged thighs, revealing glossily covered litheness. She idly picked up a pencil and began tapping it against her teeth in nervous rhythm while she considered an implosion of loose con-nections. Total concentration permeated the atmosphere. Suddenly, she threw down the pencil, turned back to the screen and frantically keyed in a series of commands.

The flickering words halted.

She read attentively. Her face gradually relaxed from its scrutiny and she smiled. 'Yes!' she said, pushing the chair eagerly backwards straight into a pile of equipment that was on the floor behind. There was the jarring sound of metal collapsing. She swivelled in the seat.

'Shit!' Her eyes went from the tangled pile to the man. His eyes went from her to the wreckage and back again.

He was standing on the ladder looking down at her. Another type of woman might have giggled or shrieked. She didn't and he liked that. Ms Cool. Her breath came through slightly parted lips. She was doubly excited by the recent discovery on the computer and now the metal-lic attack. She did not apologise nor attempt to explain but returned his look directly. Something fizzed in the air between them. A coiled control ready to spring.

'That was unfortunate,' he said stepping down. He stood tall and self-possessed, an aura of alertness veiled in nonchalance. 'Do you want to discuss this?' he asked knowing that she would say no.

'No,' she said.

He appeared to consider options. Mr Detached. 'Shall I

put in a claim for compensation to management for chair negligence?' He paused. 'Or would you prefer immediate punishment?'

Her gaze did not falter as she continued to look at him but a slight blush belied her composure. He was intrigued. 'I'm in enough trouble with management already.' He had his answer.

He went calmly over to the door and locked it. A thrill shot through her. He came over to the tangled mess at her feet and crouched to inspect the damage. His thighs stretched leanly muscular inside his jeans and his hands hung relaxed and powerful as he rested his arms on them. He tapped the screwdriver gently on the carpet. A tension continued to build in the silence. Sparks began to gather. He lifted his head to look at her, tutting and shaking his head theatrically. Inscrutable.

Their eyes locked. She looked down from the height of her chair into the glowing embers of brown velvet, soft but invasive. However, she did not feel that she was in complete control of this situation as management courses would have you believe. At least, she was allowing him some degree of control.

He sat back on his haunches. 'Stand up,' he said quietly. She stood.

'Take off your skirt,' he said.

Shit. The giveaway blush of Ms Cool. A fluttering filled her belly but she would not give him the satisfaction of seeing this, although she suspected that he knew. She carefully undid the button and slid the skirt down in a single fluid movement, stepping out of it and dropping it casually on to the floor. She watched his eyes move slowly from her high-heeled shoes upwards over the hold-up stockings to the smoothness of skin above where hairs were escaping from her knickers. She held herself proudly still. A challenge presented. There was an exchange of calculation. She decided to grasp the initiative. 'So how do you want to fuck me?' she said. 'Over the desk or on the ladders or –'

'I am not going to fuck you,' he interrupted. 'I am going to spank you.'

A shock wave spiralled through from her belly to fingers, toes and nipples, making her skin tingle. Shit, she thought, as she felt a wetness seep between her legs that he must have noticed.

'Kneel down,' he said.

She did.

'Bend over,' he said and she did.

She felt strong hands at her waist to pull her across his thighs. She waited, expectant, tensing her buttocks, holding her breath. Fingers began an inexorably slow climb as he stroked from her ankles upwards along the length of her legs, teasing across naked flesh at stocking-top, exploring the dampness of silky fabric. She could not believe that she heard a whimper as she opened her legs wider and lifted her bum to press herself onto his touch but then she yelped as she felt a stinging slap on her buttock.

'Naughty girl! Lie still.' The arm that held her at her waist clasped her more firmly. He reached to pull her knickers down, sliding them slowly to midway on her thighs. She was excited by the thought that he was seeing his finger marks on her naked flesh. She bent her head, twisting towards his leg and biting her lip to stop herself from crying out as his hand began to spank her. She bit onto his thigh but it was not hard through the denim. Then she realised that the slaps were more of a tease than anything. Playful. It was excitement not pain that flowed through her. She began to squirm in pleasure and he began to laugh. The giggles bubbled inside her.

The smacking stopped and a hand slid beneath her camisole to stroke, while a finger slid slickly into her. She raised her hips and opened her legs for him as far as the knickers would allow. His finger was deliciously questing and intrusive. He turned her over so her back was lying against his belly while he pulled her knickers down completely and carefully lifted them over her shoes. She turned onto her back, lying across him once more, a glance of appreciation flashing between them. There was a moan as he lifted her legs, bending them at the knee and spreading them. She closed her eyes to merge with the pleasure as he rubbed her clitoris. She pulled up her camisole, running her hands across her skin and knew he would be looking at her body. A veritable eye feast.

But on opening her eyes to check this, she was surprised to find herself looking straight into his and felt a surging connection. There was a fusion so strong that both were surprised. They were momentarily arrested. Her questioning eyebrows received a slow smile in response. He held her gaze as he continued to fondle then blinked lazily to look where he was touching.

He withdrew his finger. Already she was swollen and building to climax. He was pacing her. Breathing quickly, she raised her head to see what he was doing. He picked up the discarded screwdriver and turned it deliberately in his hand so that the handle was uppermost. Her eyes widened. He placed it against her clitoris. She held her breath and, as he rotated it, waves of sensation rippled through her belly. She stifled a gasp and lifted herself to lean on her elbows to watch what he did to her. The handle was disappearing gradually into her pussy where it twisted to touch interesting places. She closed her eyes to enjoy the feeling of the smooth blue coolness inside her and began to rock her hips in counter undulation as he thrust gently. He recognised that she was on the climb to orgasm.

'Look at me,' he said quietly and she immediately opened her eyes again. He pulled the handle from her. She opened her lips in a silent protest. Was this her punishment? To be masturbated nearly to climax but not allowed to come? But he had not finished yet. He lifted her leg, resting it on his shoulder, then looked away and she felt bereft. She reached to grab his wrist. He placed the handle on her anus where he pressed and, after a slight resistance, it slid into her easily, because it was so wet. He looked back at her and she felt complete once more. She lay back, sprawling across his thighs, letting go of his wrist but clasping his shoulder.

'Keep looking at me,' he demanded. 'Good girl.' He continued to rub her clitoris while the handle pushed deeply inside her. Her orgasm was rebuilding quickly. She put a wrist to her mouth to stifle a moan. Her eyes widened and she writhed to his control. He held her gaze. 'Come for me.' She instantly bucked and he felt the rippling waves as they broke into spasm, gripping on his fingers as he slid them into her, feeling the gradually subsiding pulse and her fingernails as they bit into his flesh.

There were a few moments of almost stillness, sparking with residual electrical charge.

The phone suddenly rang into the almost silence.

They both blinked to break contact. They shifted reluctantly and she stood to answer. 'Sally Howell,' she said somewhat huskily. She sat on the chair as her legs were tremulous. She felt a need to look back to him but didn't. 'I can be with you in ten minutes.' She listened and nodded vaguely a couple of times. 'I'll give you twenty minutes max. I'm in the middle of something.' She glanced at him, replacing the receiver, and bent to retrieve her skirt. After stepping into it, she pulled it up, efficiently smooth, slipped on her jacket, then went over to unlock the door. He liked the way that there was no fluster or fussing with hair.

'I'm sorry,' she said.

'About the equipment?'

'About going when I've just come.'

'That's OK.' He smiled but was not as calm as he would have her believe judging by the extra tightness of his trousers. He threw her knickers to her. She noticed nail marks on his arm. 'By the way, you didn't break the equipment. It just came apart.'

'I know,' she said. 'And I knew it was behind the chair.'

So who was manipulating whom?

He gestured vaguely with the screwdriver which he still held, its blueness taking on a new quality as it glistened with her fluid. 'I'll be here for a while if there's anything you need.'

She hesitated. 'Actually there is. You have many skills. Don't go away.' And she was gone.

Sally could not believe that she had reached this particular point in time. It was her final day and she was pleased. She manipulated her way through the open-plan section with minimal fuss. Tonight there was to be a leaving party without its guest of dishonour.

And Hugo? Where was he? Come on, Hugo, don't let me down. Mm. Yes! There he is; right on cue. He stepped in her way as usual to block her passage, bending close in subtle intimidation. 'Sally. Wonderful perfume. You smell delicious.' A small light of awareness flashed an imprint onto her memory. 'And so it's come. Your last day with us.' Smug. 'We're all going to miss you. How can you leave us so soon?' Confidentially friendly. 'It's a sad day.' Sad expression. Slight shake of the head.

'Yes, Hugo. It is. Do you know, I think I'm actually going to miss you.' She smiled up at him from beneath lowered lids and set the trap with just the right amount of flirtatiousness. No flicker of eyelashes. That would be too much, too suspiciously un-Howell like, although she was tempted to play the game to the utmost. But no. Nothing too OTT. She allowed a hint of fluster.

He was momentarily disarmed but held his composure well. His smile never faltered.

'Peace?' she offered.

Only momentarily thrown off balance. What was this? Sally Howell, compliant? 'Peace,' he agreed. He pressed his advantage. 'Maybe we could meet later for a private goodbye.'

She hesitated, as if considering this suggestion. 'I think I would like that,' she said, managing a small blush. 'One for the scrapbook, so to say. Shall we say three o'clock in conference room five? I know for a fact that it will be free.' She failed to add that she had booked it before this chance encounter.

He looked at her with what she presumed was meant to be a smouldering 'come to bed' expression. Yawn! 'Until later then. I must control myself for a little while longer.' Then he walked away with the barest hint of a swagger.

There was organised chaos going on all around. Carpenters were in the main entrance by the reception desk erecting a classy new screen that was to be camouflaged by environmentally enhancing plants. Glaziers were hanging precariously out of windows and climbing agilely across scaffolding. A plumber was making a miniature water feature in Sally's office while moving a radiator. That was fine. She was on the brink, ready to dive.

And an electrician had been busy in Hugo's room all morning doing interesting things to the smoke alarm.

At three minutes to three, Sally made her way down to the lower ground floor in the bowels of the building. Her flowing skirt swished seductively about her knees as she walked. The heels of her shoes sank silently into thick pile.

At three o'clock precisely she opened the door to conference room five to find Hugo already there, jacket free. He slipped his arms around her from behind in a lazily greedy hug. She wriggled just the right amount and pushed her

bum back against his lower belly. Already she could feel a slight development. She turned in his arms to face him and his hands slid to fondle her bum.

'There are those who think that Ms Howell is untouched goods but I think not,' he muttered into her neck and began to pull up her skirt to feel beneath.

'Patience, Hugo.' She pushed his chest firmly to make him step backwards until he reached a chair in front of a supporting pillar. The backs of his knees pressed up against it and he sat. 'We have a whole half-hour and I'm worth waiting for,' she whispered, resting a knee on the chair, bending to kiss him and sneakily checking her watch behind his head.

She rubbed his nose gently with hers and he looked delightedly puzzled. 'Just checking for size,' she said. Then straddling him she felt the hardness of his erection. Mm. Definitely bigger. His hands dropped to the hem of her skirt. She stopped him and raised his hands to her scarf. He slowly undid the loose knot and slid it delicately from her neck, leaning forwards to lick in the hollow where neck meets collarbone. He pulled her blouse from her skirt, to uncover the breasts that swelled above a lacy see-through bra.

She's dressed specially for me, he thought.

Knew he'd like it, she thought.

His touch on her skin was surprisingly gentle, an experienced touch from much practice, knowing how to stimulate. Oh, Hugo, I'm almost sorry. But not quite. She leaned forwards to bite his ear before slipping from his lap to pose before him.

'Take off your knickers,' he said.

'No.'

'Why not?'

'Because I'm not wearing any.'

Sexy woman, thought he.

Quick getaway, thought she.

'Show me,' he said. He wanted to look at her, to see all that was hidden.

She turned her back on him, looking provocatively over her shoulder. He smiled at her, narrowing his eyes. She proceeded to slide the skirt up to her waist. Placing her hands on her hips she began to caress herself, then ran her fingers in meandering paths across suspender, buttocks and down to lacy stocking tops, even showing him a glimpse of what he was not going to get. His prick twitched. She swayed her hips seductively in a teasing movement and he wanted more than to look. He reached to pull her to him, holding the fabric clear so he could kiss and nibble her ass.

She took a discreet glance at her watch again.

When he became more insistent, beginning to bite and part her buttocks, she twirled and slowly lifted the skirt until there was a glimpse of pubic hair. Taking the scarf and holding it behind her, she reached to pull it between her parted legs. He watched it sliding through the moisture at the apex of her thighs. She crumpled it in her hands, gave it to him and he held it to his face. He breathed in the musky smell of her and felt his hardness increase. She took hold of his hand, licking the palm and sucking the fingertips while tying the scarf round his wrist. He laughed as she lifted it and looped it over a hook screwed into the post above his head.

Strange, he thought fleetingly, never noticed that hook before.

With his other hand he pulled her onto his lap again, skirt round her waist. She felt the rigidity of his penis through his trousers. Impressive. She writhed onto him, effectively stopping him from trying to stand. He began to mouth her breasts, pulling at the bra to free them and licking across her skin to suck the nipples. She closed her eyes to appreciate this feeling until he fingered down her

body, sliding the tips round to touch between her buttocks and unwittingly encouraging her to her purpose.

She grasped his hand and lifted it with the weak resistance born of surprise, her breasts pressing enticingly against his face as she leaned towards the post. He breathed in the perfume that wafted from her warm skin.

Having now secured both hands, she stood calmly in front of him. Oh yes! He liked these games.

'You've been a naughty boy, Hugo. You told them about me.'

Maybe she would make use of his belt: designer leather, the best. He smiled at her. 'All's fair in love, war and business.' Then added in an exaggerated whisper, 'And sex.' An image of leather on skin flashed through his mind. He tugged on the scarf to no avail. What would she do next? he wondered. Was she going to hurt him? He wanted her to undo his trousers and suck his prick. Suck until he was tender. Maybe use her teeth on him: make him come in her mouth. The thought made him thicken and throb.

She remained calm. Very calm. Ms Aloof. Too calm. Ms Ice. She straightened her clothes discreetly while watching realisation dawn.

Suddenly he wanted to tear his hands free and rip her clothes askew, bend her over and spread her legs wide, face to the floor and bum in the air offering herself to his rough thrusts while . . .

She looked at her watch. 'Goodbye, Hugo.'

The lights suddenly went out. 'What the f –' came from the darkness.

Sally left the room closing the door behind her. She had twenty minutes. One nearly gone already. She ran up the stairs as the lifts would not be working. Eighteen minutes. She was fleet of foot and sure of her way as she took a circuitous outside route to Hugo's room, gazelle-like in her nimble swiftness. The scaffolding was secure as was to be expected. She easily located her goal. Fifteen minutes.

She could see the cable from the Uninterrupted Power Supply which snaked suspiciously into Hugo's office. Climbing in through the window, shadowed by an over-hanging platform, she could hear groans and incredulous exclamation from outside the room where the power cut had caused blackout and immediate system shutdown. And to cap it all, failure of the backup to cut in. Crash! It would cost them buckets in people time. Ha! Advantage Ms Howell.

She went over to Hugo's PC, logged on and punched in some commands. Yes! Information started to scroll rapidly across the screen.

'Come on, come on!'

Strong arms slid round her and she smiled. 'It's OK. Fourteen minutes to go,' he said. In the absence of natural light, she could not see the burning depths in the velvety brown eyes but she knew they were there. He held her close, completing a circuit that promised the energy of continually renewed excitement. She did not like to think of the dependence creeping up on her. She refused to go there yet.

The moving symbols stopped. She read. 'Shit! Wrong file.' The arms squeezed her. She typed in another command.

'How is Hugo?' His breath tickled her ear and she liked it.

'Probably deflated by now. And working at those knots. Hope he was never a Boy Scout.'

'What if he talks?'

'And ruin his pride and reputation? His infallibility? I don't think so. And he's not totally innocent.' She kept watch of the screen. 'Anyway, all's fair in business and sex. I have it on good authority.' Though some actions are maybe fairer than others, she thought.

'Twelve minutes left.'

The hieroglyphs on screen halted. 'Yes, that's it,' she said and ordered to copy information which could incriminate certain key people at the top. 'We've nearly done it.'

'Eleven minutes.'

'Finished!' She ejected the disc which he took.

'Be careful,' he warned. 'Don't outrun your time.' And he was gone.

Nine minutes. She turned back to the monitor, pressed a key and began to click through windows. Seven. The Hugo not-persecution was definitely proving to be fun. Six. 'Damn. Where are you? Where have you hidden it?' she whispered to herself. She perched on the edge of his chair as tension mounted. A minute later and she had found Hugo's death knell, lurking in a strange place. The Mclaren and Arkwright file represented Hugo – promotion and a highly substantial profit.

Five. Her soft laugh manifested into the dimness beyond the brightly lit screen. 'Got you! Sorry, Hugo, but you did not quite fulfil the electrical charge.' She calmly pressed Shift/Delete. Mclaren and Arkwright were sent into the great blue yonder along with ten months of Hugo's successful wheeling and dealing.

Game, Ms Howell.

She logged off, disconnected the UPS, attended to one final task and left, quietly closing the window behind her.

And so it was that when power returned Ms Sally Howell was never seen again and the electrical team was one man down.

It was considered that she was too upset at leaving. It was suggested that she could not face a party that would be more like a wake with a live corpse and so had made an early escape under cover of the power failure.

It was thought that the electrician had gone AWOL

because he had made a terrible mistake that had caused the failure. Embarrassing.

As the power returned, Hugo walked nonchalantly back from where only he and one other knew. His path took him directly to his office amidst the surging hum of the rebooted system, muffled cheers and a collective moan for the loss of unsaved data. It all seemed rather distant to him. Like a disintegrating dream on waking. He was seen to dab with an immaculately white handkerchief at a light sheen of sweat that glistened softly on his brow.

He calmly closed his door before rushing in panic to his computer.

There on his desk was a neatly placed screwdriver with its blue handle pointing to the screen where was attached a friendly bright yellow note with the beautifully written words: 'Well and truly screwed.'

Hugo could not believe that he had reached this particular point in time.

Shift Change Sasha White

Everyone has fantasies. But not everyone does something about them.

However, after a night of drinking with my best girl-friend, Julie, who is absolutely fearless when it comes to ... well ... everything, I decided to tear a page from her book and go after what I want. Or perhaps I should say *whom*.

His name is Joe Carson. He's a security guard at the small casino on the edge of town, where I work in the cash office. I see him every afternoon at three thirty when we make a run to the vault with the cash from the previous night's take. He's been the star of my fantasies ever since I first laid eyes on him two months back. His quiet strength, black wavy hair and intense blue eyes give him a dangerous air that makes me want to be bad right alongside him ... or underneath him ... or on top of him.

I decided that last Monday was the day I was gonna make my move. Only I hadn't figured out quite what before I went into action.

Three fifteen.

It was almost time to start loading the cash bags up, which meant it was almost time to see Joe again, and I still didn't know how to get his attention. I glanced around the casino and knew it was going to be a quiet afternoon.

A half-dozen people sat at the slot machines, but the rest of the place was quieter than a nun in a sex shop.

Mondays were like that. Not many people had money to gamble with after the weekend.

With no one waiting to cash in or change money, Suzy and Marianne were preoccupied with reliving their clubbing exploits of the night before, and I was free to make a quick bathroom run. I washed my hands and checked out the image in the mirror.

My short plaid skirt and plain white blouse would've looked quite schoolgirlish if the shirt had been a bit longer. But, as it was, the short skirt showed off my firmly muscled thighs, and the shirt lifted up to show off my pierced belly button every time I raised my arms above my shoulders. Would it be enough to peak Joe's interest?

My reflection showed long straight blonde hair framing a soft, classically pretty face dominated by big brown eyes. Despite the clothes, I look like an innocent young thing. And, to be honest, I *was* fairly innocent. Well, my body was anyway. My mind, on the other hand, could lay no such claim, thanks to Julie's escapades and the shelfful of erotic novels in my apartment.

I swiped some clear gloss across my lips, fluffed my hair and exited the washroom. I got back to the office just in time to meet Joe at the door to the cash cage.

After a quiet hello he followed me inside and held the cart while I piled almost a dozen canvas bags onto it. He didn't talk, and I couldn't get my lips to form the words, 'Will you go out with me?' So we were both quiet as we left the office and headed for the elevator.

Joe checked the inside of the elevator before waving me forwards and pushing the cart in behind me. I stood with my back pressed against the rear wall and gave myself a quick pep talk while he put his security key into its slot and punched the button for the basement.

God, he was fabulous!

At six-plus feet every inch was solid muscle. His uniform was a major turn-on, too. There's just something about a big man with handcuffs and a nightstick that makes my pussy drool and my knees weaken and I had a few minutes to do nothing but ogle his tight behind and broad shoulders. It was enough to send my imagination zooming into the fantasy realm.

I wondered if he could feel the heat of my gaze on him; maybe even read my lustful thoughts.

I wished he could. And I wished he would act on them – turn and pin me to the wall, holding my wrists captive above my head in one of his large hands. His thigh, between mine, would force my legs apart. His hard cock would be pressed against my trembling belly. He wouldn't kiss me, because he'd know that was what I wanted. He'd tease me instead, licking and biting my neck as his free hand ran down my side and then back up to cup a large breast and play his fingertips over the puckered nipple.

He'd groan in pleasure when he realised my full breasts were real and pliable, not silicone, and without padding. His head would dip down further, his hot mouth sucking me through my blouse. Impatience would make him a little rough as he ran his hand down my body and under my skirt to –

PING!

Fantasy interruptus. The elevator shuddered to a stop. We'd arrived in the basement, and I was brought back to reality with a jolt.

Straightening up from the wall, I realised I'd been completely lost in my daydream. Joe was standing just outside the doors, looking at me with bemused expectancy. His eyes dropped to my nipples, visibly hard beneath my flimsy shirt. Heat flared in his eyes before he glanced away.

If only I could read his mind.

I pushed the cart out of the elevator and followed him down the near empty hallway, glad that the people passing me could only see the blush on my cheeks and not the dampness between my thighs. Joe nodded to the security guard at the door to the camera room as we passed by, and a reckless plan formed in my mind.

'It's that time again, Tom,' Joe greeted the guard at the door to the vault room.

'Great, that means it's almost shift change. My wife cooked lasagne last night and I can hear it callin' my name all the way from the lunch room.' Tom rubbed his stomach appreciatively as he stepped aside to let us enter the room.

'Lucky man.'

'Yeah, she's great. She even sent along a plate for you,' he said with a chuckle. 'Feels sorry for you, being such a "sweet" guy and all, with no woman to cook for you. Don't know how she got the idea you were sweet.' With a shake of his head, Tom pulled the door closed behind us.

We went to wait by the vault for the timer lock to switch off. At exactly three forty-five the red light would change to green and signal we could then enter the combination to the vault itself. The small smile that had played across Joe's face during his exchange with Tom was gone now. He didn't look so 'sweet' to me either, but, then, I wasn't looking for a cutesy lover.

'Do you guys take turns monitoring the surveillance cameras, Joe?' I asked casually.

'Yeah, it can get boring, so we rotate every half-hour to keep sharp – sometimes standing guard, sometimes watching the monitors.'

'Ever see anything interesting?'

He eyed me curiously. 'Define interesting.'

'You know, maybe a couple getting friendly in the corner, or sneaking into the bathroom together.' I let a smile play over my lips suggestively, hoping he would flirt back. My earlier slip into fantasy land had made me horny, and given me just the boost I needed to chase my shyness away.

He was the right guy to fulfil my fantasies, and it was time to stop waiting for him to make the first move. I was going to have to peak his interest myself.

With a quiet click the vault light changed. I stepped forwards and entered the combination. After turning the big metal spoke, I grabbed the handle and put all my weight into pulling the heavy door open. When it had creaked open a few inches, I let my fingers slip off and stumbled back against Joe with a phoney gasp of surprise.

His arms wrapped around me quickly, clasping me to his chest. They felt like bands of steel clenched high around my ribcage, with his hands nestling just under my loose, full breasts.

'OK?' His husky voice tickled my ear.

'Mmm, hmm.' I was a little breathless as his thumb played against the curve of my tingling breast.

With a little lift he set me on my feet again and reached around me to open the vault door completely. His chest brushed against my back as he did and, when the door was open, he gave me a playful swat on the ass.

'Shoo, I'll pass them in to you.'

As he handed me the bags off the cart and I placed them in the vault, he resumed our conversation. 'Personally, I've never seen anything that exciting. It's always been boring. I guess that's good for the casino, though, nobody trying anything funny.'

'What would you do if you did see something interesting? Would you call the other guys to watch also, or send someone to break them up? Or maybe you'd just enjoy a bit of voyeurism yourself?'

'Depends on who and what I saw.'

'Done.' Turning, I dusted my hands off, and left the vault. I looked into Joe's eyes as I stepped out to where he waited for me to lock the vault back up.

I gave him a small smile while my pulse kicked into high gear. He'd noticed my subtle flash of skin as I worked in the vault. The mixture of lust and curiosity in his dark gaze told me so. But he wasn't going to do anything about it.

Joe opened the outer door for me and we exited, him telling Tom that someone would be there to relieve him in a minute.

When we got to the door of the camera room, I thanked him for the escort, and continued on to the elevator, twitching my tail as I went.

As I waited for the elevator to return to the basement, I watched Joe disappear into the camera room. Then Steve came out and stood at the door while the guard from that door headed down to the vault room to relieve Tom. Perfect for the plan I had in mind.

The elevator arrived and I stepped in, my mind quickly sinking back into fantasy land on the ride back up. The all-over body flush I felt ensured that this was it. The time had come to act on my impulses and, hopefully, get what I deserved.

I swiped my pass card and entered the cash cage where the girls were busy exchanging coins from the slot machines into bills for customers. They'd get back to their gossip when the line finished so I headed straight for my office.

'I'm going to try and catch up on some paperwork so don't disturb me unless it's important, OK, girls?' I said.

I waited for their calls of 'sure' and 'no problem' then closed and locked the door behind me.

Highly aware of the security camera mounted in the corner of the room, I walked towards my desk. When my back was to the camera I pretended to see something on the floor, and bent over at the waist to pick it up. I hoped my round ass, barely covered by my plaid kilt in that position, would draw Joe's attention.

I glanced at the clock as I slipped behind my desk. It was four minutes to four. Suddenly appreciating that my desk faced the security camera, I shuffled some papers around a little then leaned back in my chair with a mock frown creasing my brow. As I sat in apparent contemplation, my hand trailed from the side of my neck around to caress my throat, much as I liked a lover's lips to do.

Closing my eyes, I let my fingers play up and down the collar of my blouse to the buttons. I undid the top button, and let my fingers trail across the upper swell of my breast. My nipples poked out firmly, aching for attention. To tease myself a little more, I ran my hands lightly across them, circling the rigid tips, enjoying the feel of rough cotton abrading them.

Arousal and anticipation mounting, I leaned forwards and picked up the phone. After punching in a three-digit extension, I sat back in my chair and waited. I had my eyes closed and was playing with my nipples again when he answered on the third ring.

'See anything interesting now?' I opened my eyes and stared straight at the security camera.

'Definitely,' he said, his answer firm, his voice tinged with arousal. I was finally getting the response I wanted.

'And what are you going to do about it?' I asked, promising him a real treat in not so many words.

'Enjoy a bit of solo voyeurism.'

A shiver ran down my spin, and I gave a naughty chuckle as my fingers traced from my nipple to my blouse buttons. Closing my eyes, I imagined he was right in front of me instead of in the basement watching me on a monitor.

'Do you want to see my tits?' I asked. 'They're aching for attention right now.' I slipped another button from its hole and moved on to the next one. When they were all undone, I left my blouse hanging open but left my breasts still covered.

'If you don't answer, I won't show them to you,' I teased. The firmness in my tone surprised even me. It was almost as if some other daring and dominant woman had taken over.

'Show me,' he ordered.

'Say please.' I teasingly ran my fingers under the flap of my loose shirt and cupped a heavy breast firmly in my hand.

'Please,' he politely growled.

I pulled back the flaps of my blouse and could almost feel the heat of his gaze as I let my generous breasts come into view.

I knew without looking that my nipples would be a deep red that contrasted sharply with my pale skin, and that the lace of my bra did little to hide them. With a flick of my hand the front clasp was undone. I shoved the cups away, leaving my breasts naked and exposed. I licked my fingertip and placed it directly on a puckered nub before rolling it around. A small sigh escaped my lips into the phone, and then I let rip with the teasing like a phone-sex professional.

'This feels so good. My nipples have been aching ever since we were in that elevator. You saw them when we got to the basement, didn't you? It was the sight of your tight ass that got me revved up. Did you know that?'

I transferred my hand to my other breast. Pinching the nipple firmly between my thumb and finger, I rolled it around, starting to pant as sensations flooded my body.

'Seeing your handcuffs on your hip, and imagining what you would do to me if I let you cuff me to my bedposts. I fantasise about it being a little rough sometimes. I think you'd enjoy that. I know I would.'

The breathing in my ear was growing harsher, but not harsh enough. I wanted him panting, and me coming. I thought about how hard he must be straining against his uniform pants as I let my hand fall from my chest then pushed my chair further back from the desk so he could see my lap.

'These are your fingers I feel lifting my skirt,' I said. I walked my fingers on my thigh, gathering up my skirt, slowly baring more and more. He groaned softly when he saw that I had no panties on. 'You like that? It gives me a thrill to know that while I look so innocent, and everyone thinks I'm so innocent, underneath I'm just a horny little girl looking for a man who can satisfy her. A man that will look at me and see what I'm truly like.'

I brushed my fingers over the coarse curls between my thighs. Sliding my legs apart, I ran a finger up and down my slit, dipping in a little. 'I'm wet here. Aching too, but I think I'll stop now. Wait until I get home and have my vibrator handy.' I started to pull my skirt back down.

'No,' he stated firmly in my ear, 'don't stop.'

I stayed exactly as I was. Waiting.

'Please.'

I smiled as I imagined him pushing the plea out from behind gritted teeth.

'Does the camera have a zoom on it, Joe?'

'Yes.'

'Will you zoom in? Or have you already? I'd like you to see my pussy up close.'

I lifted my feet and braced them on the edge of my desk. My legs spread crudely open, not unlike the vulnerable openness of a doctor's stirrups. I dipped my finger between my thighs and spread myself open for him. 'Can you see how wet I am? How hungry my cunt is?'

A groan echoed through the phone, and my sex clenched in response.

Joe's breathing was much more noticeable now, but he never answered my question. 'Can you see, Joe?' I asked. 'Because, if you can't, I'm going to stop.'

'I can see every luscious inch of you. Don't stop now, play with your clit.'

I ran my fingertip over the nub in question, causing a shock of pleasure to jolt through me. I moaned, forgetting about teasing him with words. Lust swamped me, and I began to work myself over.

I frigged myself for a few seconds before dipping a finger right in. The slickness of my juices spread quickly as I worked my finger in and out. I thrust in a second finger and increased my pace. I began to pant when I added a third finger, stretching myself, pumping my hips in a steady rhythm.

The phone rested on my shoulder and I moved my other hand to pinch a nipple roughly. More sparks of pleasure pulsed through my body, and a small whimper escaped my lips. I slid the hand from my nipple down to play against my clit as my hips pumped away in time with the fingers filling me up. My tension mounted and my thoughts became increasingly dirty, imagining Joe's cock; imagining Joe not taking no for an answer after all this teasing.

My orgasm hovered, close, yet still unreachable. My hand pumped faster as my other fingers rubbed rapidly over my swollen clit. Then I gripped my slick button and pinched firmly, thrusting my other hand deep and holding it there as my hips jerked and an explosion happened between my legs.

I stayed in that position, catching my breath for a moment, before pulling my fingers out. I forced my feet back on the floor, and straightened up a bit before putting the phone to my ear again.

Gazing into the security camera, I licked my sticky fingers clean. 'Well?'

'Who knew little Katie Long from the cash office was such a bad girl?'

Click.

That was it? That was all he had to say to me after I'd put on such a show for him? Well, shit! Now what?

Still aware that he could see me, I made a point of shrugging my shoulders. Picking up my pencil, I started on the balance sheets. I wanted Joe with a hunger he'd never felt before, but I wasn't about to put myself out there any more than I already had – if that were even possible.

I was just filing the last of the balance sheets in the metal cabinet when I heard the buzzer signalling someone had entered the cash cage. Unconcerned because it was close to shift change, I kept working until I heard his husky voice.

'I need you to come with me, Katie.'

I looked up with a flirtatious smile ready, only to have it fade fast when I saw how serious he looked. I asked what was wrong, but he just shook his head and repeated that he needed me to go with him.

'And bring your stuff.' He gestured to my coat and purse.

We stopped in the cage and I filled my replacement in on what I'd done and what still needed to be done, and then was on my way, following Joe once again, worried about what was going to happen. Could I be dismissed for such a thing? Of course! And he'd have the shocking proof on CCTV recording. Oh my God, how could I have gotten so carried away?

This time when we stepped into the elevator, Joe moved to the back, I stood in front of him. The doors slid closed and the lift shifted as it began its descent. Holding my purse and coat in front of me, I turned and looked straight at him, waiting for some hint as to what was going on.

He stood silently, his intense eyes full of blue fire as they locked with mine. Recently sated arousal unfurled in my belly and started my juices flowing again.

Determined to have him make the next move, I bit my lip to keep quiet. The lift stopped with a loud chime and the doors slid open. I turned from him and strolled into the hallway.

'This way,' he said firmly and took off down the hall.

I watched his tight butt and swinging nightstick, and hoped to hell he wasn't really angry, and hadn't told anyone else. Perhaps there was still a chance we could work something out...

At the door to the surveillance room, he stepped in and motioned me to follow. Tom got up from the corner monitor and left the room, closing the door behind him.

When we were alone, Joe took my belongings and set them on the table in the corner. Then he stepped closer, invading my personal space. The air between us vibrated with sexual tension. My nipples puckered to the point of pain and I fought against jumping on him.

'That was quite a show you put on for me,' he commented softly. He rested his hands on his hips, his eyes roaming over my face, my neck, my cleavage.

'Is that what this is about?' I pushed the words past the tightness in my throat. 'Am I in trouble?'

'You are definitely in trouble.' He reached out and rested his hands on my shoulders. With a sharp spin he had me facing the wall. 'Assume the position.'

My heart pounded in my chest and an excited gasp escaped. I leaned forwards to place my hands on the wall. Joe's front pressed to my back as he reached around me and adjusted my hands higher, stretching me out for a good frisk.

His hands skimmed down my arms, across my shoulders and back before settling on my hips. He held me firm, and kicked my feet apart.

My breath hitched in my throat and my insides trembled. I'd dreamed of this so often I didn't know if I could stand the reality. Strong masculine hands smoothed over my ribcage and moved up to cup my breasts, dragging a small moan from my lips.

'Oh, you're enjoying this, aren't you?' Joe's words whispered across the sensitive skin of my neck, his hard-on brushing teasingly against my bum. 'You've been hiding your true nature for too long, Katie. With a thorough search, who knows what else I might uncover?'

He pulled back and I felt bereft. Then a hand encircled each ankle and began a slow leisurely trip up my legs. A trail of fire followed as he skimmed over my calves, lingering at the back of my knees before continuing up my outer thighs, and under my skirt.

Rough fingertips brushed over the bare flesh of my inner thigh before he cupped my plump butt cheeks, firmly kneading them. When his thumbs delved into the crease of my ass, my back arched automatically, thrusting myself deeper into his hands. Another ecstatic moan escaped my lips.

Abruptly, his hands left my flesh and he stood once again. Pressing his body against mine from behind, his lips brushed against my neck when he spoke.

'You're such a tease, you drive me crazy,' he growled, nipping my earlobe. 'The things I want to do to you . . .'

I felt the struggle in him, in his unfinished sentence. As big and bad as he was, he still had doubts about me.

'Anything,' I whispered, just loud enough for him to hear.

Gentle fingers cupped my chin and lifted my face until our eyes met. I could see lust, tinged with wariness in his fiery gaze.

'Anything,' I repeated, not backing down. 'I'm all yours, to use any way you want.'

It was as if my words freed us both. Joe's full lips tilted into a wicked grin seconds before his lips covered mine in a fast hard kiss. Then he reached for one of my wrists, and pulled my hand behind my back.

A shiver racked my body at the feel of cold metal wrapped around my wrist.

'Give me your other hand,' he commanded.

When both of my hands were secured in the handcuffs,

he pulled me away from the wall and brought me to stand in front of the bank of security monitors. He kicked the chair aside and pressed my hips against the countertop.

Reaching around me, he flipped a switch and images of me bending over in the cash office filled all the screens.

'Look at that ass. I want that ass.' He bent me forwards and lifted my skirt, baring my bum, and everything else. He stood slightly to the side of me, his hard cock pressed against my hip as we watched the images on the screen together, the rough palm of his hand rubbing over my cheeks briefly before dipping between my thighs.

Pleasure bolts shot through my body at the invasion of his fingers and another, louder, moan filled the room. 'You are a little slut, aren't you?' Joe chuckled and thrust his fingers deeper into my hole.

I bit my lip to try and keep more telling sounds from escaping. I'd never been so vocal before, but I couldn't help it. I'd never been so aroused before either.

'Admit it, Katie.' His thrusting fingers withdrew and lay still against my juicy quim. 'You're a horny little slut, aren't you?'

To tease us both some more, I refused to answer him. Instead, I spread my legs wider, arched my back rudely, and let out a quiet moan.

Joe shifted his weight and his hands left me. I heard him undo a buckle and then the thud of his utility belt hitting the floor.

'I've been wanting to do this for months, but I always thought you were too much of a good girl to appreciate it.'

I felt the hot hardness of his exposed cock slide between my thighs and along my wet slit. One of his hands wrapped itself in my hair and tilted my head so there was no way I could escape seeing myself displayed so rudely on the monitor six inches in front of my face.

The head of his cock probed my entrance. 'But with an invitation like that I'd have to be a saint to turn you down.'

With one forceful thrust, he filled me up and I squealed in pleasure. 'And I'm no saint,' he grunted as he thrust into me fast and hard.

'And I'm no angel,' I gasped out as the walls of my cunt clenched around his cock. 'But I am *your* horny little slut.'

A guttural groan filled the air and I knew my words pleased him. 'Mine, eh? To use any way I want?' One hand gripped my hip tightly, holding me still for his rapid fucking. The other hand shook free of my hair and travelled down my back, and over my rump. Then I felt a fingertip probe surely at my exposed anus.

My sharp cry of pleasure bounced off the walls as he pushed that finger into my virgin hole. He didn't pump it in and out. He didn't need to. The sensitive nerves of my anus lit on fire and the flames spread rapidly, an intense orgasm shuddering through my whole body.

It was too much, the sight of myself masturbating all around us, the feel of his cock hitting deep inside me, my cunt spasming around Joe's cock as he continued his fierce fucking. Another orgasm washed over me when I felt his cock swell, and throb violently, hot jets of come flooding my insides. His grip on my hip tightened so much I knew there would be bruising as he let loose a long low groan before falling forwards to rest his forehead against my shoulder blades, his cock still twitching inside me.

I let my own forehead rest against the cool countertop, flexing my cuffed wrists so that my fingertip could brush against his belly. That small touch cemented my connection with him, while we both took a minute to recover.

Soon, he braced his hands on the counter beside me and pulled away so I could straighten up again. My knees were so weak, I stumbled back against him. His arms surrounded me and held me gently against his chest for a minute, his stubbled cheek resting against my smooth one.

'My slut, huh?'

I turned in his arms, uncaring of the fact that I was still handcuffed and come was dripping down my thighs. 'Yours. To do with as you please, whenever you please.'

He leaned down and kissed me gently, his tongue sliding into my mouth possessively. When he pulled back my knees were weak again and it took me a minute to remember where we were.

He stepped behind me, his hands reaching for mine. I heard a metallic click and felt the pressure of the cuffs on my wrists eased. Once the cuffs were off, he returned my purse and coat, and looked me in the eye.

I smiled when I saw no doubt clouding his expression. A smile that grew impossibly wide at his next words.

'Then go home, clean up and wait for me. I expect to find you naked, and ready for a complete body search. Because I intend to discover all your secrets.'

A Dirty Job Melissa Harrison

When her boss finally pushes into her, it's so deep that she gasps, an involuntary flinch making her pull away for an instant before his grip on her right hip tightens through her indecently short skirt and she arches back into the rhythm of his stroke. Her face is pressed hard into the glassy shine of his deep mahogany desk, her unseeing eyes fixed on the vast river-view his huge corner office affords over the sparkling bend of the river. The desk is cold on her breasts, her nipples hard where her unbuttoned blouse has exposed them; her full weight rests on her chest, as with his left hand he holds both her wrists pinned high behind her back.

He pulls out (the loss of him inside her sudden, shocking) and moves his right hand up slightly to the small of her back, finding the dimple above her buttock and he places his thumb into it, gently, possessively, almost meditatively. Kate can still feel the head of his cock, wet with her, nudging gently at her pussy, which aches for him again. She feels his foot kick her legs even further apart; not gently, but dispassionately. She does what he wants, teetering slightly in her heels, making herself even more available to him, and he drives back into her again, hard, his resumption a reward for her acquiescence. Each stroke ends in a bruising thud as he fills her up; it's almost painful, but deeply satisfying nevertheless. She longs not so much to come, but to feel him come inside her.

The seat covering is hot and scratchy against Kate's face as she rouses herself from her fantasy, the lilting rhythm of the train having conspired to lull her into a dreamy half-sleep. Squinting against the dying rays of a glorious winter sunset, she sees the evening light catch the windows of the tall office block where she works, winking at her from across the water as the train carries her away. She finds herself shockingly aroused, here amongst dozens of closely packed strangers, and feels a guilty flush rise from her neck to her face as if the images she has involuntarily summoned are somehow visible to her fellow-passengers. Looking down at her lap, she lets the fantasy go, knowing how impossible it is; Mr Stevens may technically be one of her bosses, and only a couple of years older than her at that, but as a part-time cleaner at the huge insurance firm she is under no illusions that he would even know her name.

The next day Kate's eyes are fixed on the office block again as it swings back into view around the bend in the river. She times her arrival to coincide with the main flurry of departures at the end of the day; unlike the rest of the six-strong cleaning team, who come from jobs at other buildings, the company is her only employer. During the day she works in a clothes shop, part of a big chain selling overpriced fashion to dead-eyed teenagers with too much money and no sense.

Though she's still slim, Kate's body is made imperfect, in her eyes, by stretch marks. She can still fit into the strappy vests and hipster shorts she spends the day sorting and folding and, at 26, she's certainly not too old; but Kate feels a world away from wanting to show off her body in that way. She's tired a lot of the time, and has got into the habit of avoiding mirrors, though, when she does catch sight of herself, what she sees isn't what the men who pass her slowly on the street see, looking back over their shoulders, or, like here on the train, surreptitiously glancing over at her. There is a raw sensuality to her every movement that marks her out as a woman, not a girl, and which shines out – to everyone but her.

At the office Kate pushes her way through the smart, be-suited crowd surging out through the revolving door, working her way slowly against the flow. They are putting on their coats as they leave, making calls on their mobiles; in black, dun and grey they barely register her, flowing around her like a pebble in a stream. She swipes her card at the turnstile, smiling at the guards who are just changing shift. They smile back, two pairs of eyes following her as she hurries to the lift. They like her; she knows their names – on top of which, she moves with an easy grace that is somehow different from the tailored office girls that stream past them, none of whom ever look over. Even the secretaries with their short skirts and blusher, their hair uniformly straightened, their acrylic nails defiantly impractical; even they have nothing on Kate.

A couple of hours later and she's nearly finished the floor she's been allocated this week; disappointingly, it's not the one that houses Mr Stevens's office (secretly she thinks of him as Adam, the name on his desk), but the next one up. This floor contains meeting rooms and conference facilities; it doesn't need much in the way of cleaning, as a rule; just the bins emptied, the hoover run around and the desks and tables wiped down.

Dragging the squat, red vacuum cleaner with its incongruously smiling face by its electrical flex (in contravention of all the safety instructions), Kate begins to make her way into the boardroom, backwards, the heavy door silent in the deep pile of the carpet, a J-cloth and trigger spray in her other hand. There's a few bars of a song going around in her head; she's not sure what; it's been stuck there all day. But turning into the room, the door still only ajar, she sees something that drives it out of her mind for good.

To one side of the polished expanse of the huge mahogany table, Mr Stevens is moving gently, his eyes closed, his chest bare. There is a moment when Kate's brain struggles to keep up; wonders not why his shirt is off, but only what he's doing in the boardroom so late at night. But a second later and, with a rush of blood to her face, she understands. And in another second, she understands yet more: though the face is turned away from her, the feet she can see under the table, in front of his, are still shackled by the unmistakeable folds of a pair of men's overalls. Mr Stevens is fucking a man.

Kate doesn't move; despite her shock, she's transfixed by the concentration on his face, as well as by the breadth of his shoulders and the pleasing shape of his torso, which she can see tapers to a nicely trim waist. She had imagined his chest to be smooth, for some reason; in reality he's neatly hairy, with the hair converging into a dark line which points down his flat stomach to where it is obscured by the round buttocks he now grips with such concentration. As she watches, he pulls slowly out; she can see the length of his cock, rigid and swollen, for a second only before he plunges it back into the other man's body.

Instantly she feels that she's wet, her pussy aching, an irresistible pulse starting up deep inside her; her heart pounds as she watches his slow movements of a moment before become fast and urgent. A few thrusts later, each one deeper and more merciless than the last, and he pulls out again; but this time he takes his straining cock in his hand and, in a second's work, shoots spurt after spurt of come onto the flushed buttocks before him. Still looking down, he smears it, full-palm, over the other man's skin, his thumb disappearing briefly and exploratively into the crevice of his ass; only then does Mr Stevens break his trance and look up, his eyes instantly meeting Kate's and locking on to hers where she stands only partially concealed by the door, the three of them making a bizarre, yet highly charged tableaux. And in that moment, despite her surprising arousal and overwhelming embarrassment, something passes between Kate and her boss; something she doesn't yet understand.

The bath is hot and deep and Kate sinks back into it gratefully. She's exhausted. She imagines what a luxury it would be to have someone run her bath, cook for her, look after her and put her to bed. But that person doesn't exist, so the next best thing is to do it herself. So now, here she is, her hair pinned up, her body hidden beneath mounds of bubbles, a cold beer balanced on the edge of the bath.

As if waiting for just this opportunity, the image of Adam fucking the unidentified man sidles inexorably into her head. Can he really be gay? She can see so clearly his look of total and utter concentration, the sheer sensuousness of his movements. Although still attended by a flush of something – maybe guilt – at having caught him in so intimate an act, Kate finds no revulsion or distaste at what he was doing; in fact, as she examines her response now, with the benefit of a few hours' grace, she finds her attraction to him remains undiminished. How strange; watching men fuck is not something she's ever fantasised about before. Could it be that she'd never really considered Mr Stevens available in the first place? Or is it just that it's fucking she loves and misses so much – fucking of any kind?

Now Kate's hand trails down through the water to gently explore herself; just thinking about sex has made her pussy swell and she can feel that telltale warmth curling through her. She takes a swig of beer, then dangles the bottle onto the floor and hooks one leg up over the side of the bath, the better to touch the soft folds of her sex where it blossoms under the warm water. In no hurry, she circles her clit where it is starting to harden, her eyes closing, her mind clearing of everything but the sensation she is producing. Slipping a finger inside, she feels the smoothness of her cunt, here at the centre, and suddenly remembers how she used to love to keep it all this smooth; how sensuous it was, how naked. Why did she stop shaving, and when? She can hardly remember. But now, as turned on as she is, she wants to be clean-shaven again.

She stands up, letting the soapy water ooze down her body, and reaches for a small mirror and the razor and gel she keeps for her legs. She sits on the side of the bath, spreads her legs and positions the mirror on the opposite edge so she can clearly see the pinkly engorged lips and the downy hair. Gently massaging the shaving gel around her cunt to form a lather, she feels an actual ache start up inside, she's that aroused; but she takes the razor and, with firm and definite strokes, shaves her entire pussy smooth and pink and clean.

Splashing water on to it from the bath makes her realise how much more sensitive it is like this; her clit in particular feels sensitised, as well as oddly vulnerable. She pauses before removing the mirror, choosing instead to leave it there and stay sitting on the side of the bath, where she can watch her fingers as they play with her newly denuded pussy. Pushing one finger, then two, inside, they emerge slick with her juices; she can see them glisten as she brings the moisture up to coat her swollen clit. She keeps her legs spread wide, liking what she sees, as the sudden vision of Adam's cock, rigid in his hand, shooting spurt after spurt of come tips her over the edge into a bucking, dizzying orgasm.

'So he's not gay?' Kate fails to keep the surprise out of her voice. 'I mean, I suppose I'd just assumed . . .'

'Adam?' Crystal, her supervisor, laughs richly. 'No, he's

not gay. He's fucked every secretary who's worked here, love, and a few more. I'm surprised he's not had a go at you'.

Confused, Kate turns around, busies herself in the store cupboard. It's the next night and she's arrived for her shift a little early, hoping, uncharacteristically, to have time to talk to the others first, see what she can turn up. It's proved to be much easier than she'd expected.

'Why are you asking, anyway?' Crystal narrows her black eyes at her 'What have you heard, girl? Or are you carrying a torch?'

Before the blush rises and gives Kate away, Crystal is distracted by a crash, followed by curses, in the corridor. Going to investigate, with Kate at her heels, they find one of the building's many maintenance man sprawled on the carpet, his ankles tangled in a metal bucket, floored by a mop handle. Though his blue overalls give Kate a jolt of recognition, she wouldn't have been sure if, looking up, he hadn't blushed to the roots of his blond hair.

Scrambling up, apologising, his eyes never leave hers. 'Well, I've got to get on, love,' says Crystal, glancing, amused, at the two of them. She winks broadly at Kate before picking up the mop and bucket and making her way slowly down the corridor. Kate suddenly finds herself looking at her shoes. Must get changed, she thinks. Can't clean in heels.

There is a long silence.

'The other night,' he begins, 'I saw you leave. I know you probably think – I mean, it must seem to you like – and I'm not – I mean, Adam's not. He's not – you know. I've never done that before. He just –'

Here he stops, discomfited, his shoes suddenly holding great allure for him too. Kate wonders why he's telling her at all.

'It's none of my business,' she begins. 'I don't even

know him. I've never spoken to him. I just come in and clean. I'm not going to say anything to anyone, you know.' She looks down again, smoothes her skirt.

'No, I know, I just – it's not that; it's just that I know he has a reputation. You know, for the girls. The secretaries. And I thought you and him might have, too. I mean, you're so –'

'No. No. We haven't,' interrupts Kate, missing whatever he was about to say. 'Like I said, I don't even know him. And I didn't even know about the reputation. I don't really hear much gossip. I'm not really in the loop, I suppose.'

'Oh, right,' he says, grinning suddenly. 'I see. Bit of a shock, then. Sorry.'

She grins back. 'It's OK. Most interesting thing that's happened here in ages. But, I mean, I know it's none of my business, but I can't help wondering ... if he's not gay, and you're not, how come ...?'

'I know. Weird, isn't it. He's just...' Here he looks slightly wistful. 'Adam's just one of those people, I suppose. He likes sex, and he's not fussy. Broadminded, I suppose. I know he's done it before. I hadn't, though. We'd chatted a few times, but then it just seemed to happen, really.'

Kate finds this hard to believe; how can something like that 'just happen'? But it's clear he's not going to go into any more detail without her asking some quite pointed questions, so she leaves it at that. 'I'm Kate, by the way,' she says, feeling an introduction is long overdue.

'I know,' he replies. 'Adam told me. The other night: it's not the first time he's noticed you, you know. And it's not the first time he's talked about you, either. I'm Chris.' He offers his hand, a little awkwardly. 'I've got a feeling you may be next on his list.'

* * *

It was ridiculous, but Kate had to see him. In that second, everything else was driven from her mind – including the shift she was supposed to be starting. Chris had watched her as she turned, just like that, and walked away, down the long, featureless corridor, to the lift bank.

And now here she is in the mirrored lift, twisting her hair into a hasty ponytail in the dark mirror, heart hammering, wondering what the fuck she is about to do. Operating, it feels like, under someone else's volition.

She knows he'll still be in his office; there is a pattern, a logic, to what is happening that renders her helpless, and which she knows will not end in an empty room. She knows where it will end, and her whole body is alive with that knowledge.

'Come in,' she hears from the other side of the heavy door. Why did she knock at all? Usually she just walks into the various offices and meeting rooms, assumes their incumbents have left for the night, works around them if they haven't. Now she takes a second to gather herself: she fills her lungs, exhales, straightens her spine, raises her chin. Then pushes down the stiff door handle and walks in.

Adam is regarding her calmly from behind the expensive monolith of his desk, leaning back in his chair, a pen in his hand. Behind him stretches the panorama afforded by the 90° windows of his corner office; it's dusk, and lights are coming on all over the city, reflected in the broad sweep of the river. Kate's eye picks out the winding shape of a commuter train making its way across the bridge, nosing its silent way east, leaving the two of them suspended, far above the city streets.

She looks back at Adam, and there it is: that spark again, jumping between them. She leans back on the door, making sure it's pushed to behind her. And waits to see how he will begin this.

It feels like an age until he gets up. Unhurriedly, never taking his eyes from hers, he shucks off his jacket and hangs it carefully on the back of his chair. Loosening his tie, unbuttoning the top button of his shirt, he approaches Kate across the silent expanse of carpet. When he's still a couple of feet away, he stops and regards Kate in absolute and minute detail: searching her face, examining her breasts where they push against the fabric of her top, scrutinising her hips, the shape of her, staring intently at her legs. It's both anonymous and deeply personal, and Kate submits to his scrutiny, though she aches for him to touch her.

When he does, it's a glancing touch, but one that makes her whole body shudder. He reaches out a hand as if to signal her to stop, but gently brushes her nipple with his open palm. It hardens instantly and appreciably, and she closes her eyes, feeling that irresistible confluence between her breasts and her clit, causing her pussy to come immediately to life. She keeps her eyes closed as he pinches her other nipple through the thin cloth between his thumb and forefinger, rolling it gently. She longs to step forwards and kiss him, press herself against him, but something keeps her standing there, her arms by her sides and her back against the door.

When she opens her eyes he has his cock in his hand, emerging through the opening in his trousers. He's so hard that the skin of the head is shiny and taut; she can see a few drops of pre-come emerging as he moves his hand gently but firmly up and down. The effect of such a private act performed at such close quarters, and by someone to whom she's not even been introduced, is electric. Instinctively she steps forwards, reaching for what he seems to be offering her. But it's not what he wants, not yet, and taking a step forwards Adam pins her back against the door with his forearm across her neck, his mouth hovering only millimetres from hers, but, though she strains forwards against his arm, he moves back fractionally, just before she can kiss him.

He is still masturbating, but right up against her now, his hand disappearing up her skirt with each stroke, the rhythm unmistakeable against her thigh. Before he can stop her, Kate raises one leg and hooks it behind him; suddenly, the head of his penis is pushing against the damp fabric of her knickers where they tautly cover her aching sex. She is begging him, in every way but verbally, to fuck her.

Now her pants are sopping and sticky with a mixture of her own juices and his pre-come where he is rubbing himself directly across her swollen clit. Still looking at him, Kate reaches down and pulls the fabric aside. Surely he won't be able to resist pushing himself inside her, especially when he sees how smooth and pink she is. And, indeed, she feels Adam take a great, juddering breath as he breaks their gaze for the first time and looks down at the picture his cock makes at the lips of Kate's pussy, open and wet, displayed for him by her hand pulling the lace of her knickers aside.

But it seems he has much more self-control than she had bargained for. Moving his forearm from where it traps her against the door, he reaches around to the back of Kate's head and gently, but so firmly, pushes her down to her knees, guiding his cock into her mouth with one hand on the back of her head. Kate licks gently around the swollen head, tasting the salt of him, and runs her tongue around the shaft. He's incredibly hard, and she is desperate now to feel him inside her. But his hand still rests on the back of her head and she knows it isn't time yet. Instead, she slips one hand down to play with herself while she sucks his cock, taking him deep into her throat. Her knickers are still pulled aside and, as she kneels, it's easy for her to push her fingers inside herself, then pull them out, slick enough to tease the hot little nub of her clit where it pulses and glows.

Suddenly Adam's had enough. Roughly he pulls himself away from her, out of her mouth and, grasping her arm, pulls Kate to a standing position. Unceremoniously he turns her around, twisting one arm behind her back, and frog-marches her forwards to the picture window where he lifts her arms, placing her hands against the glass above her head. From here it feels to Kate like she's about to fall, forwards and downwards into the darkening city; but he's behind her, wrapping a hand in her ponytail, pulling her head back and pushing her skirt up. With Adam there, she can't fall.

She's already opened her legs in readiness. But what comes first isn't his cock, but his fingers, trailing a surprisingly slow progress up her thigh, over her exposed buttocks, and finally sliding into the wetness between. She feels his thumb slip into her ass, giving her an involuntary start, before his fingers begin to tickle at her clit. She is helpless now, her hands pressed on the glass, her head pulled back, her back arched, her whole body alive to what this man is doing to her.

Then, just when she thinks she can take no more, Adam's fingers are at her mouth, where she tastes herself. He lets go of her ponytail and grips her hips instead; Kate moves back a little from the glass, spreads her legs slightly wider, moves her hands down the panes so that she is steady, and cocks her ass back towards him, inviting him in.

And finally, finally, he pushes his cock deep into her swollen cunt, making her almost weep with the joy of it, the sheer shape and size of him filling her and making her close her eyes. After a few long, slow, hard strokes his hand reaches around to her clit; it seems as if all he does is pass his fingers across it and she is overtaken by her orgasm, perfectly in time with him and at his command, his hot come blossoming deep inside her, her pussy tightening around him, the two of them leaning against the cool glass.

But it isn't over yet. As she opens her eyes the first thing Kate sees is the reflection in the darkened window, of Chris, his overalls undone to the waist, his erection standing proud, his back against the door. As Adam withdraws from her, she turns and looks at the two men, a pulse starting up again somewhere deep inside, and she wonders what will become of her, working a little late tonight.

The Silk Seller Maria Lloyd

Newly arrived in London, I discover that I am something of a voyeur.

I live in a Georgian house on a neat little square behind Oxford Street. The area is a quiet cul-de-sac, a no man's land between the rag trade, Soho, college buildings, and the exclusive medical clinics of Harley Street. Opposite my house, across the tiny square, is a discreet shop front – a Georgian Bay window filled with a peacock fan of beautifully coloured diaphanous fabric. There is a discreet brass plaque next to the shop's heavy, black-fronted door. It is inscribed simply, *R Sebastian, Purveyor of Silks*.

At night, the shop-front window is softly illuminated and the coloured fabrics – rich ambers, delicate mauves, crimsons and golds – all glow hyper real, a beacon that draws the eye away from the dark-railed gardens at the centre of the square.

In the morning, on my way to work, I often pause to admire the silks more closely. Sometimes the morning sun catches their hues through the shop window and makes them shine like liquid gemstones.

I watch with interest as the silk-shop customers arrive or depart. It seems business is mostly wholesale, but occasionally a rich private client deals with Mr R Sebastian direct.

A mother and daughter arrive by limousine, dressed in beautiful saris, and seem destined to discuss a bridal outfit of vermillion and gold. A woman in dark glasses, perhaps an actress incognito, departs carrying a sample of swatches. She is still flicking through them when she steps into her cab. The most intriguing customer so far is a man in a sober business suit who arrives carrying a hold-all near the end of the working day – yet the only person to depart an hour later is a suspiciously tall woman, clad in a red silk dress, knee-high boots and ... clutching a hold-all.

People have a right to their private indulgences, their harmless vices, and I feel a little guilty becoming so familiar with the secrets of the silk trade across the way. But still I sit on the window seat of my little lounge, nursing a cup of coffee or forking up take-away noodles, watching the haven of exotica provided by R Sebastian, purveyor of silks.

I grow fond of Mr Sebastian, who regularly, with old-world chivalry, accompanies clients to their waiting cabs on the corner of the square. He is tall and elegant in the masculine sense. He is almost Mongolian in his looks, having dark wavy hair, high cheekbones, heavy eyelids, and skin like polished walnut. He has large dark eyes that dance with brandy and green-gold lights as he smiles and shakes hands with his customers. He wears tailored linen suits, always with immaculate silk shirts and ties.

He is a dedicated man. I watch him working late into the evening in a small office above the shop, dealing with outstanding paperwork and queries on the internet. He even lives above his business, in a neat bachelor flat on the top floor.

I like watching him, in the evenings, in his tasteful office. It is decorated a warm terracotta with silk prints hung in frames around the room. He works at a large desk, with an old-fashioned, green shaded lamp to supplement the glow from his laptop screen as the light dims. He looks stern yet serene in concentration.

Sometimes clients are invited into his office to conclude special orders, and they sit positioned to one side of his desk upon a stylish Mackintosh chair, with its distinctive high-backed lattice design. While he is talking to such clients he sometimes moves forwards to adjust the window blinds, which intrigues me, as I then cannot see what is going on and it drives me mad.

Sometimes, in the very early morning, Mr Sebastian goes jogging in shorts and vest, displaying tightly honed muscles. Occasionally, late at night, before he draws his bedroom curtains, I notice a light on in his flat above the office. I often make myself a mug of hot chocolate before going to bed and, if I angle my window seat correctly, I can see his handsome torso, the wide shoulders and the strong chest with its fuzz of dark hair. I am pretty certain he sleeps in silk pyjamas, or naked against silk sheets.

Wouldn't you, if you were a purveyor of silks?

One lazy Saturday afternoon, fresh from a late shower and wrapped in my kimono, I sit at my window seat with a glass of orange juice and watch Mr Sebastian as he welcomes another client. The sun briefly dazzles my eyes, and I swear that Mr Sebastian looks directly up at me. Has the light illuminated me? My pulse races as I guiltily return his half-smile, just in case, even while I retreat into shadow.

I have been so entranced with my clear view of his office and bedroom that it never occurred to me he may have watched me also, these summer mornings and evenings as I travel naked or in my kimono about my front room.

I know I should move away entirely. But my little game of voyeurism has become far too addictive. Still I sit and sip my juice and watch in the hopes of another glimpse of my neighbour.

I do not expect what happens next.

His office door opens, and he walks inside with his client. I shift in my seat until I can see them both, and the whole room, clearly illuminated by the slanting afternoon light.

She is a willowy blonde wearing an expensive tailored suit and spiky boots. He is very solicitous of her, seating her in the Mackintosh chair, while they continue deep in conversation. She is holding a glass of cordial, which she drains and places on the desk as Mr Sebastian leaves the room for a few moments.

I place my own drained glass on my coffee table, conscious of the parallel.

When he returns he is carrying several bolts of silken fabric, different pastel colours, a few vivid ones, all expertly chosen to match his client's complexion. She fingers each one reverently, deep in thought. Then she points to one of palest mauve, which she evidently finds soft and attractive.

Mr Sebastian rolls the other bolts up and places them in the corner of the room, ready to be taken back down to the shop.

Then he takes a pair of scissors and cuts a swatch of the fabric his client has selected. He strokes the square against her cheek, and then holds it against her lips. She sits very still, letting him play with her in this way.

Eventually he leans to kiss his client, with unhurried grace, through the chiffon fabric. Her face turns upwards like a flower, expectant, hungry for more as his lips travel down the silk to explore her pale neck.

I am shocked. Maybe this is no client, but a lover, or fiancé, even, picking out her trousseau, enjoying a stolen afternoon with the one she loves. I fight the stab of jealousy this brings as she shrugs off her jacket and begins to unbutton her blouse.

Surely she is just a client, I reason to myself, or I would have seen her before, being intimate with him? But this must be a special client, one he has known for many years, one he has had a relationship with. She has the look of one who wishes to rekindle something they have shared before.

I watch as she teases Mr Sebastian. She takes an age to unhook each button on her blouse, watching his expression with a look of defiance that barely masks her hunger for him. Something tells me they have indeed done this before; I wonder if she then betrayed her need for him too easily, and this time she wants to keep the upper hand. Well, that's what we voyeurs do; embroider the scenarios we are lucky enough to stumble upon.

She slowly shrugs out of her blouse. Her bra cups small round breasts. Even from here I can see the fabric is fine lace, the very best designer lingerie, in a pale conch colour, ruched to flattering effect. No doubt she knew he would appreciate such things, because his long fingers reach out to reverently brush the fabric moulding to the breast beneath.

After a short while, impatient for his touch on her skin, she unhooks her bra, and lets it fall to one side. She arches her back to display those pale, perfect breasts, and her rosy nipples are firm with desire.

I kneel closer to my window, rapt with attention. I can feel my nipples swell in response to the way Mr Sebastian strokes her breasts, rolls her nipples between his fingers, bends to kiss and lick and nibble them.

His client remains perfectly still, but her lips part with pleasure and her delicate shoulders rise and fall in little sighs at Mr Sebastian's ministrations.

Again I get the sense they've played this game before.

Next Mr Sebastian kneels before the woman as she shrugs out of her knickers and trousers to display long legs, delicate blonde fuzz between them hiding her coral sex. A woman aware of her body, she is still wearing her high-heeled boots. She rests them in Mr Sebastian's lap, and scrapes the spiked heels gently along his inner thigh, against his groin, as he stoops to kiss her ankle, her knee, her thigh, her swelling cunt.

At this she throws her head back and moans, wrapping

her legs around Mr Sebastian's torso, digging her heels into his back. He still wears his linen jacket, but he must feel the rake of those spikes and he seems to like it as he feasts between her legs.

I can almost feel the heat of his breath on my own sex, and I grow wet watching them. I let the silken folds of my kimono creep between my legs and I gently ease back and forth against its slippery silkiness, feeling nectar ooze from my sex as my own clit swells.

Mr Sebastian stands up, takes up the scissors once more, and cuts a few long strips of the delicate mauve silk.

She sits up straight and offers her wrists, neatly placed together, with charming eagerness. He takes them and he binds them expertly with a strip of silk. Then he ties her wrists loosely to a cross bar that hangs from the low ceiling. She writhes a little in protest but I can tell she loves it, the way he is testing her out, taking her to new places. After some discussion he gives her a silken blindfold.

Now that she is blinded, Mr Sebastian and I are both voyeurs to her naked body, the blush across her breasts, the quivering of her belly. She parts her lips, runs a tongue along them in nervous expectation, but she does not say anything. She is content to be admired, to feel his eyes upon her, to wait for whatever he is moved to accomplish with her.

I wonder if she can sense that more than one person is feasting on the sight of her. I want to kiss those vulnerable lips, twist those stiff nipples and lick her teasingly around her sex. I'm impatient to see what Mr Sebastian will choose to do.

He has more self-control than me. Slowly he wraps a swathe of silk around her breasts, and again he licks and nips at the flesh, the aching nipples, through the soft fabric.

I rub and stroke my own breasts, tweak my own nipples, through the fabric of my kimono, moaning with delight as the silk adds to the open abandonment of my skin and body to these caresses. I envy Mr Sebastian's client, feeling his lips and tongue and teeth as well as his fingertips. I want to bend and lick my own nipples, which I can just about do, but that would mean tearing my eyes away from the lovers across the little square.

And this I simply cannot bear to do, voyeur that I am.

Mr Sebastian takes another swatch of silk and binds it cunningly around the waist, thighs and hips of his captive, so that a length of soft fabric crosses her sex. It looks like a Japanese rite of bondage, designed to constrain gently yet give ultimate pleasure. Again he strokes her here, and kisses her there, and uses his fingers to gently torment her through the silk, so that she is at his tender mercy. He even strokes her clitoris with his index finger, and unexpectedly ploughs the silk inside of her while she spreads her knees wide and seems to beg for more.

I writhe gently in my longing, fingers finding my own sex, stroking through the kimono's silk.

Mr Sebastian abruptly stops what he is doing. The woman is panting, she seems to entreat him to continue, but he backs away, circling her, watching the quiver of her skin beneath the silk. Eventually he kneels before her and takes off her high-heeled boots, and wraps a separate strip of silk around each bare foot. Slowly he strokes and nibbles each toe, each ankle arch, while his client sways and moans softly, brought to the brink and left waiting for more.

I cannot see his face but I imagine his enjoyment, his sense of bringing his lover to the point of total abandonment by exquisite torture with his precious silk. The client bends her head to one side and seems to beg, in earnest supplication. The game must have proceeded to the next round. Mr Sebastian then undresses, leaving his clothes upon the leather chair beside his desk.

His body is lithe and well honed, dense with healthy muscle and bone and sinew. I can see even from here that his penis is fully erect. There is dark hair around his balls, across his chest and forearms that accentuates the smooth warm tones of his skin. I can see the muscles in his back and buttocks flex as he turns to stand above the woman, as he trains his cock against her lips. Gracious in his bounty at last.

She opens her mouth to eagerly embrace the swollen glans; the morsel she had obviously begged to receive is now delivered gently, tantalisingly. She is powerless against the rhythm and thrust he chooses, and he seems to choose exceedingly well. She licks his shaft and balls and lets her lips slide down, all the way down, with absolute abandon. I crane to get a better view, and my tongue travels across my lips when I wonder how that must feel, how Mr Sebastian's cock must taste. I long to accept the full weight of it in my mouth.

I moan with frustration.

Then Mr Sebastian pulls away and takes yet another strip of the exquisite silk, draping it around his genitals. He spits on his fingers and then dampens the diaphanous material so it clings to his contours. He returns to his client so that she can give fellatio through the silken fabric, which she proceeds to do in earnest.

I moisten and then bruise my lips upon the sleeve of my kimono, taste the flesh of the inside of my wrist through the slick silk, in an attempt to feel something of what she must feel, what he must feel.

It feels good. It heightens every sense of touch, addictive and languorous as opium, until I feel hot with desire yet tranquil with sensuous pleasure at the same time – an exquisite knife-edge of longing and procrastination.

Eventually Mr Sebastian pulls away from his lover's lips, and I wonder if he has come. But he has evidently bypassed the point of orgasm and, with some tantric stamina, still holds himself erect, his balls tight, poised to ejaculate.

He unfolds the silk, to reveal his arched, glistening erection, and he pulls his lover up so that she can turn around. Then she bends over, still tethered, as Mr Sebastian strokes her buttocks before he takes her from behind, through the soft film of silk, now wet with her juices, that still shrouds her sex.

She is crying out with the ecstasy, and that he has to hold her hips steady against the sudden onslaught of orgasm as he fucks gently, expertly, for maximum effect.

I plough my fingers through the damp silk of my kimono into my sweet swollen cunt and massage my clit, sliding the silk against me and inside me until I am in a frenzy, until finally I allow myself to cry out with sweet orgasmic release as the couple in the office opposite fuck themselves into coming.

After our mutual climax I watch, slowly stroking myself to cessation, as Mr Sebastian unbinds his client, and they both dress.

Then she becomes quite businesslike. She confirms her order for the silk, takes out her pocket book from her purse and writes him a cheque. I wonder if it includes hidden extras for services rendered. He watches her, detached and considerate, although I detect a trace of amusement on his face.

Moments later she is at the shop door, shaking hands and bidding polite farewell to Mr Sebastian. They both look well groomed and calm, as though nothing untoward has taken place. Then she hails a cab and is gone.

I wonder how many private appointments of this sort go on behind the lowered blinds and the locked door of Mr Sebastian's office. Quite a few, judging from the activity I have seen. But why did he conduct this particular 'interview' without lowering the blinds, so I could see everything clearly, when he was usually so discreet?

Before he goes inside the shop, Mr Sebastian looks up at my window once more and this time smiles directly at me. Even if he cannot see me now, because I lurk in the shade, he is confident that I am still there, watching him.

I have to reach the conclusion he has conducted this particular session of business with me in mind.

A few days later I am walking past the shop when Mr Sebastian suddenly emerges, shaking hands with a well-dressed American woman who saunters towards Oxford Street as though eager to indulge in more shopping. I falter, swerve to avoid them and the ankle strap of my left sandal gives way.

I curse softly and hover unsteadily on one high-heeled sandal while I examine the broken strap. I take both sandals off, decide it would be best to walk the final stretch home barefoot rather than try to rig a repair, when someone brushes my elbow.

'May I help you?' Mr Sebastian asks in a slow sonorous voice.

I feel a jolt of pleasure, and also a frission of fear. This man may be mad, bad and dangerous to know, as well as an incredible and sensuous lover. I must be cautious.

'It's nothing. My sandal strap is broken.'

'It's not good to walk the city pavements barefoot. Let me help you.'

'Please don't trouble yourself. I only live across the way,' I mumble, feeling a strange guilt as I look at his well-manicured hands, which I have seen do such outrageous and seductive things.

'I know. You have been my neighbour for a while now, yes? I am glad of the opportunity to finally make your proper acquaintance.' My nervous smile falters as his grows. He knows, he must know, how I have watched him. I feel that he can tell what I am thinking, how my body is feeling, tense and expectant with longing at his closeness.

'Please come into the shop, and I'll see if I can make a temporary repair to your sandal. If you like, I can show you around a little. You seem like the kind of woman who may appreciate fine silks.'

I blush and nod. I have no strength to resist such a gentle, teasing invitation. From the way I smile, that must be obvious.

'Very well. Thank you,' I manage to say at last.

Inside, the shop is simple and elegant, with comfortable leather chairs, a heavy coffee table of dark wood and brass. There are a few samples of coloured silks on a low counter, thick books of sample swatches, and a vast tree of silk scarves tied to a central pole which glistens and dances in the sunlight.

There is also a reception desk in one corner where a pretty young brunette sits leafing through a catalogue. She glances up, smiles.

'It is all right, Jasmine, I shall attend to this customer. You may wish to take your coffee break now.'

Jasmine nods her thanks, collects her handbag and leaves to have her break in the nearby café with a friend. I know this, for I have seen her there on many occasions. The shop bell tinkles as she closes the door. Mr Sebastian and I are alone.

He selects one of the scarves from the pole, one made of smooth saffron silk.

'Sit down,' he says, and I obey. He kneels easily before me, graceful for such a tall man. He cradles my foot on his lap as he takes the broken sandal from me, slips it back on to my bare foot, and deftly wraps the scarf around my ankle, weaving it around the leather straps of the sandal, binding it to my foot.

His touch is gentle and makes me tingle. The silk is soft and warm against my bare skin. I find myself holding my breath as the silk merchant cradles my foot against his warm leg in those linen trousers. His long fingers wrap around my ankle bone to check the binding is secure, but not too tight, before he ties a neat bow in the silk scarf.

This triggers memories of my voyeuristic enjoyment, and I try not think about them, or the sheer sensual pleasure this arouses. I want to stroke his thighs with the heel of my sandals, tease his balls through the linen of his trousers . . . my leg is trembling with the urge to do it, and with my determination to resist.

'Thank you,' I say throatily. 'I'll return the scarf tomorrow.'

I am stunned as his palm gently follows the arch of my foot, brushes admiringly against my bare toes, the nails which are painted silver-pink. He is slow to surrender his gentle grip on my ankle.

'There is really no need,' he reassures me pleasantly, 'Consider it a neighbourly gift.'

I could swear that he gently guides the spiky heel of my sandal across his crotch as he surrenders my left foot.

Before I have a chance to object he takes my other foot, replaces the right sandal, carefully buckles the leather strap, and again softly caresses the bare toes, the high arch of my foot, with reverential fingertips.

This time I surrender to the urge and let my heel dig a little into his thigh, scraping against the slight bulge in his crotch, and I see the flicker of appreciation in his eyes.

'Would you like to see the silks?' he asks softly, acknowledging my signal.

'Yes, please,' I whisper, before I have a chance to think. After all, I am in Aladdin's cave at last and I want to see just how far he is willing to go, and just how far I am willing to let him. This is, I suppose, the final temptation of all voyeurs.

I wonder how long Jasmine will spend on her tea break, and whether she will surprise us doing ... what?

'Come through to the next room,' he says, clearing his throat, betraying a hint of command. As I walk across the wooden floor, hips swinging to keep my balance in case the scarf suddenly gives way, I am conscious of Mr Sebastian watching my figure. And I glow with a reciprocal desire. It feels good to be the one being watched for a change. Maybe Mr Sebastian is tired of letting me play the voyeur, and maybe I am too.

The silk scarf feels smooth as moonstone, warm as his skin, against my ankle bone, and I already feel hot and eager for more.

The next room contains shelves with bolts of luminous silks stacked high to the ceiling. In the centre of the room is a broad, wide table for laying out the material and cutting lengths to be made up into kimonos, dresses, whatever the client desires. There are stacks of pattern books in the corner, an array of scissors and measuring rules ... and a full-length mirror, where clients hold the silks against their body, their hair, and check that the colour suits them.

I glance at myself. My legs are long, somehow glossier, with the addition of the saffron silk around my left ankle bone. My summer blouse, my linen skirt, look suddenly superfluous. All I want to wear are my sandals, and some silk. My shining eyes, my moist parted lips, betray this thought to me. I look like one of Vermeer's women, watched and waiting, hoping the worst may happen.

I glance back to the silks, guilty fantasies racing through my head, while Mr Sebastian watches me with a half-smile on his lips.

'Which silk do you like?' he asks me as I travel the shelves stroking the bolts of colour that take my eye.

I pause at a warm ginger-saffron, which almost matches the scarf he has wrapped around my ankle. Somehow it glows against my pale skin, giving it lustre, and I sense that it matches the highlights in my chestnut hair. It also feels warm, inviting, like softest eiderdown against my fingertips.

'Good choice,' he compliments me, and takes this bolt of silk down to lay on the counter, unfolding an ample length.

I smooth it with my palms and the backs of my wrists. It is so soft, so smooth, so yielding and sensual. I want to be wrapped in the gossamer lightness of its erotic cocoon.

'It is very lovely,' I whisper conspiratorially.

'It is one of our most expensive silks, handwoven in China, hand-dyed in Tibet. Here, hold it against you.'

I stand in front of the mirror while he wraps a sinuous fold of fabric around my bare shoulders.

I look like a different woman. I look like the type of woman he would desire, who would do unspeakable things in the back of a silk shop on a summer's afternoon.

I clear my throat, suddenly nervous. I do not know what to do while he looks at me with his large brown eyes, appraising me, my curves of breast and hip, made so obvious beneath the saffron fabric.

'Wait there,' he orders, and returns with a large pair of silver scissors.

With one swift, shearing motion he cuts free the fabric entwining me, and I know that he has decided, and I am glad.

I gather the silk more closely to me now.

'It feels good, doesn't it?' Mr Sebastian says. 'It feels even better against totally naked skin.'

There is a challenge in his voice, in the amber glint of his dark eyes.

I continue to look at him as I slowly undo my skirt, letting it fall. I shrug out of my blouse, and let that fall too.

Mr Sebastian clears his throat and continues watching me.

I undo my bra, and struggle out of my panties. Now I am naked except for my high-heeled sandals and his saffron silk.

'You're right,' I say briefly. 'It feels heavenly.'

There is a pause, and I wonder if I have been too forward, betrayed my need for him too easily, like I imagined the willowy blonde once did. But from the way his eyes feast on me I know he is enjoying my nakedness beneath the exclusive silk.

'I am so glad you decided to come in,' he whispers at last. 'I have often watched you going to and from your work, stopping to look in the window, and I thought you would look so beautiful, wrapped just so in saffron silk. May I touch you?'

'Yes,' I whisper.

I feel as though I am a statue, worshipped by his fingers that stroke and follow every curve of my body through the material. I am afraid to move and spoil the moment. I revel in the way his long fingers toy with my nipples, and stroke between my legs, and test the mettle of my inner thighs and my calves, and softly stroke the nape of my neck, until I am resonating to his touch like a fine-bred filly.

I gasp with surprise when finally he kneels and licks at my mound, nibbling my clitoris through the warm saffron. His tongue is gentle and precise, teasing me to full arousal, unhurried and generous in its voyage of discovery through my inner folds. My breath shortens; I take little gasps, tug at his dark hair as he begins to gently probe inside me, holding me steady with a firm grasp on my buttocks. His palms brand me through the soft delicate stuff that encases my limbs.

It seems the most natural thing in the world to let him pick me up, lay me on the counter, explore me like I was a banner of his most precious fabric. When he unzips his fly, releases his erect penis, I finger it gratefully, and its silken ridges are warm and solid. My cunt is wet for him as he slides gently in, balancing my buttocks on the edge of the counter while he stands between my spread-eagled legs.

We are by this stage both trembling, clinging to each other with strange vertigo and sensuous need, hurrying to climax before we are disturbed. My sex spasms and its innermost spot quivers to welcome him further into me. He fits so perfectly. We rock and wave against each other like silken flags in a warm breeze until the orgasm, soft and satiating as cinnamon sugar, runs its course.

We hear the shop doorbell tinkle. Jasmine has returned from her tea break.

Mr Sebastian smiles, puts a finger to his lips and reluctantly withdraws.

I dress with haste, while he tidies away the bolts. The length he cut, which we have used in our lovemaking, is still pooled on the table, and I wonder what he will do with it. Keep it as a souvenir?

When I am ready, Mr Sebastian escorts me back through the shop, nodding to Jasmine, and opens the door onto the sunny street, treating me with the same respect I have seen him show to his other clients. I am grateful that he keeps it all so calm and natural. He seems in no hurry to dismiss me. He shakes my hand politely, holds onto it a few moments longer than necessary, making me tingle.

'Well, thank you. For everything,' I say uncertainly.

'You are most welcome. So, when can you drop by my office for an appointment? Would Thursday at five p.m. suit you?'

'An appointment? In your office?' I ask, feeling a little dizzy at this sudden invitation.

'I think that the saffron would look most becoming on

you as a simple dress for the summer, but I'll need you to try it on in case I have not remembered your measurements exactly. And of course we'll need to discuss the appropriate payment.'

I stare at him a moment and he raises on eyebrow slightly, a ghost of a smile on his lips. Again there is a glint of challenge in his dark eyes.

I smile in return. After all, I have always wanted to purchase a bespoke silk dress, ever since I first paused in front of his shop window. And I have always wanted to be invited into his office, ever since I saw him there with that willowy blonde.

How easily he has read my mind.

'Thursday at five would be perfect. I look forward to it,' I reply.

'And I will enjoy seeing to your needs, as my new favourite client.'

I'll let you know how the dress turns out. I am sure it will be very beautiful and fit me perfectly.

As does Mr Sebastian, purveyor of silks.

Precipitous Passions
Michelle M Pillow

'You can't deny that you want me to fuck you.'

'Excuse me?' Hallie asked, unsure she had heard him right. She swung around from the top edge of the New York skyscraper. Her round green eyes widened in shock as her short blonde curls bounced excitedly in the wind. She immediately recognised the voice as that of her boss Peter Bartlett; he was the only one she knew with such a sharp British accent. He was also the only one she knew with keys to the rooftop door, aside from the janitor whose set she had borrowed. His perfectly formed words could give any American girl chills. But surely he would not make such a blatantly sexual remark? Theirs was a working relationship, tempered by the mix of a little humour and stoic attitudes, although they had always gotten along in the most proper of workplace senses.

Hallie peered through the soft glow of fluorescent lights that lined the edge of the building and questioned uneasily, 'Mr Bartlett?'

'Call me Peter. We're off the clock.' He flashed a quizzically boyish smile as he answered casually, 'And you cannot deny that you would miss out on this view. New York is one of the most fabulous cities in the world. I should know. I've seen most of them.'

'Oh,' Hallie said, turning her eyes to the dim sky blazing with the light fog of the bright city night. The top of the Harrison and Kenton office building was a perfect spot to see the city. The skyline was indeed beautiful – the most untamed spot in the New York. She was careful not to look down, lest her stomach lurch with unease. Standing on this part of the roof was perilous; one false step and you could fly to your death.

But Hallie liked the freedom of the roof; it was why she visited it often. It resembled a wild sense of freedom and longing within her. She was normally tame, cautious. Here, the world looked so big and alive, and she felt like ruling it all.

Hearing her boss near her, she wanted to melt into the stone in embarrassment; her cheeks flamed with the mortification at her wayward thoughts. Her only redemption was that Peter couldn't read her dirty mind. She felt him lean next to her on the railing, could feel the heat of his body as he stood close yet not quite touching. Ignoring the flush that threatened her skin, she managed to respond after some time.

'I suppose it's much more exotic when you haven't lived here forever.'

'Why does every American woman dream of Paris?' He chuckled in amusement. 'Yours wasn't the only application I had to rifle through this last week. Every girl in the office put in for the overseas job.'

'I'm not sure why,' she lied, turning to go as a strong breeze whipped sharply over her flushed skin. It ruffled the neckline of her white linen shirt, exposing her bare throat and a hint of the top of a lacy bra. His eyes caught hers in a brief grasp before they dipped lower to glance at the exposure of curved cleavage. Suddenly she wished she hadn't unbuttoned the stuffy collar. Weakly, she said, 'I should really be going. The meeting will be over soon and Mr Kenton is leaving some paperwork on my desk.'

'Always working late, aren't you, Hallie? It is nearly eleven o'clock.' Peter's words weren't really a question but a deliberate pondering. He drew his eyes away and Hallie forced herself to relax. 'Don't you ever go out for fun?'

'Are you giving me permission to call in sick tomorrow?' she asked with a sheepish smile. 'Mr Kenton will be sorely disappointed if the modified reports aren't on his desk first thing in the morning.'

'Do you always do as you're told?' His mouth barely moved as he murmured the low question. Hallie felt a chill over her skin and convinced herself it was the wind.

'Only when it's one of my bosses doing the telling,' she quipped matter-of-factly. 'I won't lie. I want that Paris job. I'm one of the hardest workers you've got down there and –'

'Hallie,' Peter broke in, giving a small shake of his head as he stopped her words with the softness of his tone. 'Save it for the interviews.'

'Sorry,' she said with an apologetic smile she didn't mean. 'Like I said, I've got to get back to work.'

She turned to go, unable to take his unfamiliar nearness. The whole of New York didn't seem big enough for the both of them, as they stood facing each other on the empty roof. Her fingers worked uneasily with a will of their own, wanting to feel where Peter's T-shirt moulded to his strong chest. She could smell his scent, purely masculine, as it drifted to her in diluted waves, filling her senses.

Taking slow steps towards the door, she forced herself not to run. The image of his unusually casual attire burned into her mind, though she had tried hard not to look at him. Peter was her boss. During the day, everything was all business with him. Never had he given the slightest impression that he was attracted to her. Hell, he never gave her the impression he even really liked her. But tonight, on the roof of their office building, things were about to change. Had she imagined it? Were the powerful night air and the dizzyingly spellbinding influence of the tall building and surrounding city playing tricks on her?

'I've seen the way you've been looking at me,' he said.

Hallie froze, her back turned to him, sure that her mind was again playing tricks on her. She had misheard him. He couldn't know what she thought of him, how she thought of him. Rotating slowly on her high heels, she said, 'I'm sorry? I didn't hear you over the wind.'

Suddenly his mood changed. His arms moved with the assurance and certainty of his perfect body. 'Don't you ever say what you want? Why do you play all these coy games?'

He smiled in devilish enjoyment. His T-shirt again sculpted to his muscled chest. It glowed eerily in the combination of moonlight and fluorescence. His short black hair ruffled defiantly in the breeze, as confident as its master as the locks pushed over his brow.

'Games?' she squeaked. Her pulsed raced. She couldn't read his face. She didn't recognise the man before her.

'You want me,' he persisted. 'Sexually. I can see that you do. I have always seen it.'

Hallie shook her head in denial, embarrassed by the truth in his words. She had wanted him from the first moment she saw him standing in the boardroom, introducing himself to the company. But the jolt of that first encounter had faded into a dull ache of vague disappointment when he returned nothing but a passing interest. Even now, she couldn't read any fondness in his face.

'Be honest,' he continued. 'For once, tell me the truth.'

'Why?'

'Let us just say I'm curious.' When she merely lifted an eyebrow, he added, 'Whoever we send to Paris needs to be bold. Mr Kenton wants to hire a man. He thinks woman are too timid to lead a company.'

'I don't want to lose my job,' she bit off tersely. Mr Kenton was an old-school chauvinist. Had he sent Peter to test her? Lifting her chin, she decided feigning irritation was better than admitting she was attracted to Peter's stiffly charming smile and hard, dark eyes.

'You won't,' he promised. 'Tell me what you think of me.'

'You exasperate me. You are domineering and cold. You never smile and are sparse with praise. If anything, I have been silently glaring at you in irritation.' Hallie took a step away from his perusing glances. His eyes raked over her form in a way she had never seen him look at her. After a long moment, his gaze took in her short black skirt.

'So you aren't attracted to me?' he questioned. The tip of his tongue darted playful over the lower line of his lip. A challenge lit on his face as his full mouth curled into a dangerous smile. His eyes dared her to lie to him.

'No,' she said. Hallie lifted her chin proudly into the air. Her heart beat in wild thumps. Yelling as the wind picked up, she hollered, 'I can't stand you.'

'I don't believe you. Your body language says otherwise.'

Hallie stood transfixed. She couldn't run. She was excited as she listened for his next words. She followed his movements, noticing his hand as it lifted from his waist to pass over his rising cock in a steady massage, drawing her gaze to the bulge to emphasise his meaning. A fire shot through her limbs. Her body jolted to life, begging her hips to gyrate in the air, crying out for her hands to tear away clothing that felt too constrictive.

'And I'd bet I could smell it on you if I were to press my nose between your legs,' Peter said.

'Is that why you followed me up here? You think I wanted you?' Hallie refused to back away from him again. His thumb deftly unbuttoned his fly. She again caught the musty scent of his cologne on the stout breeze. The rooftop dimmed all but the man before her. 'Don't think for a second that I wanted you to.'

'No?' he questioned. He cracked a smile as she shook her curly head. 'Then give me one minute of your time. If you are not crying out in passion by then, I'll leave you alone.'

Hallie frowned in disbelief. She had been caught out by the truth and was burning was a mixture of shame and arousal. As he came up to look her steadily in the eye, she shivered. She was already moist from his bold proposal. Pleasure hummed through her, running rampant in her veins, sparking her nerves to life. But it was a hateful tease on his part to get her body singing to such an extent.

'Is this a test?' she breathed, her voice raspy as she tried her best to control it. 'Are you trying to see if I will do anything to get the Paris job? I'll have you know I've more than proved myself as qualified. I'm one of the highest ranked associates in this whole city.'

'I am testing you,' he admitted. 'But not for Paris.'

'Then –'

'I'm testing your control, Hallie. How tightly do you have that body of yours reined in? How tight are the ropes of your sexuality? Let me untie them. Let me untie you. If you don't enjoy it, I'll quit my job and never bother you again,' he whispered near her ear. His heated breath tickled her skin.

'Really?' she asked, knowing full well that men will say anything to get into a woman's panties. Her breasts heaved with a heavy sigh. Her lips parted in expectation.

'I promise,' he murmured huskily. He touched her shoulder and lightly ran his hand over her shivering arm.

The idea had merit. Peter had been an aggravating pain in her ass since he took over her department three months ago. Still, she knew she shouldn't believe him; he was just a horny man trying to get laid. He had never come on to her before. Peter wasn't really attracted to her, was he?

'You're a pain in my ass,' she said. 'You are aware of that, are you not?'

At that his smile deepened. Taking the tip of his finger, he traced it boldly over the line of her nipple as it peaked under her shirt. Hallie trembled.

'I could be.' He smirked. Slowly he began to circle around her. When he reached her ass, he grabbed it and squeezed. Hallie stepped away from him. Again he came up behind her before she could turn around. This time the firm outline of his penis pressed into her soft cleft. She jolted in surprise. She never would have guessed Peter to be so well-endowed.

Belatedly, she tried to pull away but his hand shot over her stomach to stop her. Her head whirled in confusion. Peter's flat palm slid lower to hover over her sex. How was this happening? Only in her darkest dreams had she thought about this moment. And yet, here it was, pressing between the cheeks of her ass.

Peter leaned over to whisper darkly in her ear, not giving her time to think or reason. 'Why won't you admit you want me to fuck you? You want me inside of you. I can sense it. You're wet and aching through your black skirt, aren't you?' Moving to her other ear, he lightly licked the sensitive nub with a quick dash of his tongue. 'Your pussy's begging my long, hard cock to release it. Bend over for me, Hallie, feel my cock. Let me take you here and now on the side of this building. Let me ride you.'

'So what if I am aroused? It doesn't mean I want you.' Hallie made a pathetic attempt to try and pull away. The height of the building combined with his sexual advances made her dizzy. He sensed the game, and wouldn't let her go. Trying to be as bold as he, she stated, 'And I don't wish to feel your cock anywhere near me.'

Peter chuckled, disbelieving. He reached his free hand to caress her neck before dipping his callused palm into the top of her blouse. It found a home in the valley of her breasts. Pulling her body harder against him, he ground his hips slowly against the cheeks of her ass. He felt her body stir in desire. He could feel her growing heat as he stoked her inner flame, leaving a trail of goosebumps in his wake. Her heart pounded wildly against his fingertips.

'You're aroused,' he said in a breathy hush along the nape of her neck. Lightly, he began to kiss her creamy skin. 'I'm horny.'

'Your emotions are not my problem,' Hallie put forth as she ripped his hand from her shirt. She threw his fingers from her. Twisting away from him, she ignored his groan of discontentment. 'Now, Mr Bartlett, if you'll excuse me –'

'You can't escape. The door's locked,' Peter said quietly from behind her. His hands strayed to his hips. The dark orbs of his eyes glared in annoyance at her withdrawal. 'And that janitor key won't open it.'

Hallie marched to the door. She hadn't seen him come up so didn't realise he had locked her out of the building. The only other way down was over the side – a seventy-two-storey fall.

Hallie swung around to face him. By now he had taken off his T-shirt and stood proudly before her. She caught her breath at his rippling muscled form. Swallowing hard, she said, 'You can't keep me here.'

'Can't I?' he smirked.

'You have no right to take me prisoner.'

'You're not my prisoner . . . yet.'

'Mr Bartlett –' she began in stern warning. But, even as her words were hard, her eyes were aflame. They dipped over his chest, focusing on his cock.

'Didn't you say you always listened to your boss?' he questioned logically.

'Yes, I did, but –'

'If you don't listen to me, listen to your body.'

Hallie stood silent. She was terrified – terrified of the passion inside her. This was Peter. It wasn't a good idea to get involved with one's boss. No matter how badly she wanted it to happen, it could ruin her career.

'Fine, then come and get the key and unlock the door,' he said when she held silent. His words were harshly delivered but a gleam entered his wicked eyes.

'Where is it?' she stammered.

'Hidden in a very safe place,' he said. Then with a cheeky glance he motioned to his protruding trousers. 'Though you are most welcome to try and find it.'

'Don't think I won't,' Hallie said, trying to intimidate him. Inside she shivered with lust.

'I won't stop you,' he paused meaningfully. With a flick of his fingers he unzipped his blue jeans, before continuing, 'But I must insist you use your mouth.'

That stopped her. Turning from him with uncertainty, she took a deep breath. The more he spoke, the more she wanted to forget decorum and fuck his brains out. But this was Peter she had to remind herself – her irritating boss who hardly said two words to her unless it was to criticise her work.

'Why are you doing this now?' she asked.

'Why not now?' he answered.

'We have been working together for three months. You have never shown interest before.'

'I've been waiting to get you alone,' Peter answered.

'We have been alone in your office plenty.' Hallie turned around to face him, sure that she could keep her face composed. Her eyes automatically drifted to his crotch. His pants hugged at his tapered waist in a snug fit.

'I thought about it,' he admitted. 'I've thought about it a lot. Especially at night, with a raging hard-on.'

'Then?'

'There are too many distractions in the office during the day. My office door doesn't lock. Janice always walks in unannounced.' He took small steps as he spoke. Hallie stood enthralled by his low, husky voice. 'How would she like it to find you bent over my desk with my dick in your ass?'

'You could have said something.' Hallie licked her lips. 'There were other times.'

'When?' he questioned urgently. 'You always work late.'

'You could have said something.' Her resolve continued to slip. Silently, she wondered, Why not take him into her mouth? Why not control him for once? Who would know?

'Yes, I could have. I could have asked you out on a proper date, took you to a fine restaurant. But I don't want a date. I want to fuck you. I want you to suck my rock-hard cock. I want to bend you over and taste your wet pussy.' Peter stopped in front of her, letting his bold words sink in. 'I want to lean you over the side of this building and –'

'But –'

'And,' he began again with impassioned emphasis. 'I want to shove my dick in your hot and willing body.'

'Peter,' she stated with a blush fanning her cheeks. 'Who put you up to this? This is an office dare, right? Everyone is hiding behind the door, listening.'

'Would you like it if they were?' he asked. 'Would it excite you to have them watch?'

'No,' she stammered. The lie was obvious.

'Who would you like to join us? Gladys from copying? My secretary, Janice? Your secretary, Stephen?' He pulled the phone from his pocket, and smiled as he shook it at her. 'I could call them. Tell them to come up here for an emergency meeting.'

'That's preposterous,' Hallie shot in confusion.

'No, I've seen the way Stephen looks at your ass. I've seen you bend over a little extra when he is around to let him.' Peter laughed when she pinked in slight embarrassment. 'Tell me, have you had him yet?'

'Of course not.'

'Have you called him into your office? Taken off your panties and sat on your desk while making him eat you out?' Peter persisted.

'No,' Hallie said, barely able to believe the way her boss was speaking to her.

'But you want to, don't you? Between us, admit it. You want the power of being in charge. That is what really attracts you to Paris. You want complete control.' Peter eyed her lips. His words fanned over her in a low, seductive murmur. 'Be a woman – admit it.'

'Fine, I admit it. I've thought of him naked. I've thought about almost every man in the office naked. It doesn't mean I would act on it. It's human nature to be curious,' Hallie said.

'Shall I tell you what I would think about when you come into my office? Shall I tell you what I've been waiting to do to you?' Peter looked unashamedly at her breasts as they coloured with her excited breath. 'Shall I tell you how you affect me?'

Unable to stop herself, Hallie nodded.

Peter smiled that devilishly wicked grin that made her flesh tingle.

'As you would speak, rattling on about financial proposals and stock options I would stare at your mouth. I'd imagine jumping over the desk and sticking my cock in your face, making you talk around it until I came in your throat. As you spoke I would secretly masturbate under my desk, asking you questions so you wouldn't stop moving your lush, full lips. And I'd stare at your breasts, perky and round as they moved under your blouse, wondering what kind of bra you had worn for me that day.'

Peter grabbed her by the arm, and this time she didn't move. His low voice entranced her as he spoke forbidden words of passion. Gently, he raised his fingers to her blouse and undid a button, letting the breeze pull apart the material to discover her lacy white bra. His eyes narrowed, his breath deepened.

It amazed Hallie that he'd thought of her in such a

way. But she read the truth of it in his wildly fervent eyes.

Continuing, he said, 'I've often wondered . . .' He paused to press a kiss on her exposed collarbone. Licking her chest in a long hot stroke, he trailed up her neck to claim her parted lips.

'What?' she breathed in a low murmur when he almost kissed her.

Moving his lips lightly against her mouth, he said, 'Are you as hot as I want you to be?'

She pulled back. 'Now you're just teasing me. Game's over, Peter, give me the key. I've got to go. I've got a long hard day tomorrow.'

'I've got a long hard night for you here,' he shot back just as smoothly.

He took her hand and held it to his cock. She jerked away.

'Let me show it to you.'

Hallie froze, curiosity causing her to look down to his exposed black silk boxers. He pulled back his fly, groaning slightly when his dick sprung free. Hallie licked her trembling lips. Her eyes grew wide with interest. Tilting her head to the side, she stared at his protrusion, waiting for him to pull it free from its silken prison.

He stroked himself over the silk, starting deep at the base before slowly moving to the head of his shaft. Unbidden, Hallie's hand strayed to the valley between her breasts.

'Just pretend you have to work late,' Peter said. He massaged himself again with a groan. 'I'll tell Kenton I kept you late and the report won't be done until noon.'

'How late?'

'I just might keep you here all night.' Grinning, he asked, 'How many times can you orgasm?'

'Depends on how good the man is,' she said with a matching smile.

'I'm good.' Peter lifted a hand to undo another of her buttons. He growled when he laid bare her heaving chest. 'Let me taste your skin.'

He didn't wait for her to answer. Leaning over he licked the valley of her breasts. Then, trailing his caressing lips over the edge of her bra he dipped his tongue underneath the thin material to lap her pointed nipple. Hallie gasped and her knees weakened as she stumbled back. Peter smiled and caught her. She fell to press against the hard metal door.

'You're trapped,' he told her. He placed his hands on either side of her head. Looking down at her chest, he moistened his lips. 'You need a man to free you.'

'I –'

'Shhh,' Peter hushed. 'It's all right. A lot of women haven't been with a man secure enough in himself to give her real pleasure. I can feel the hesitation in your body. You're scared of me. You're scared of what I am offering you.'

'And just what are you offering?' she threw back.

'Pure –' he stopped to kiss the rapid pulse at her neck, '– pleasure without any commitments or attachments. No phone calls to make the next morning or awkward moments after. Just a good, solid fucking and no one will ever have to know unless you want them to.'

Hallie's breath deepened as his lips continued a reckless course over her tender flesh. The hard metal door pressed into her skin, holding her steady in the strong wind blowing over the skyscraper's roof. Her heart raced in excitement as she anticipated being discovered. She imagined someone listening on the other side of the thick steel.

The movement of his bold lips entranced her and his body shielded her from the harsh glow of the rooftop's fluorescent lights. Behind his head she saw the dim poke of stars as a helicopter flew in the distance. Her will slipped and she felt him taking over.

'Spread your legs, Hallie,' he commanded. 'Open them up for me.'

Hesitantly she complied. Parting her thighs under the tight black skirt, she moved her heeled shoes to the side. Peter chuckled as his hands rose from the door to touch her slender frame. He caressed her body in long, worshiping strokes. Slowly, he made his way down to her hips to kneel before her.

'Lift your skirt,' he ordered.

Hallie shivered. Following the trail he had blazed over her body, she moved to touch the hem of her skirt. Her hands trembled, unsure.

'Show yourself to me,' he growled harshly. 'Now.'

Hallie obeyed. She was so wet, so hot. Her hands grasped the fine material and slowly began to lift it.

Peter avidly watched the unveiling of her athletic thighs. Her skirt inched higher to show the rim of her white lace panties covering her mound of trimmed blonde hair.

'More!' he demanded fiercely. 'Show me your pussy. Show me how hot it is for me.'

Growing empowered by his attention, she slowly inched the skirt higher. The thin straps of her panties hugging her hips came into view. The cool night breeze caressed her skin. She felt powerful, conquering, as if she were on top of the world.

Peter grabbed her hips, his thumbs hooked under the thin straps. He sniffed delightedly in the air. Hoarsely, he said, 'Touch yourself for me. Make yourself moist with desire. I want to watch you give yourself pleasure.'

Hallie followed his instructions, unable to resist her body's longing. Her flesh swam with too many sensations not to comply. Placing a finely manicured hand on her flat stomach, she brought it down over her panties with agonising slowness. Pressing her middle finger into the lace to part her moistening lips, she moaned in delight.

'Go under,' he urged in a throaty command.

Once more she obeyed him. She raised her fingers and looped them inside the lacy barrier. His mouth moved closer to pant hotly on her thighs. His eyes bore into her, watching as she stroked herself. With a mischievous glint shining from his dark eyes, he raised his arms and pulled roughly at her blouse. The last clinging buttons caught in the wind and blew away as he ripped her shirt open. The wind hit her aching breasts and she ground her hips wantonly against her probing hand.

Peter touched her flesh in heated strokes, liking the way her heels lengthened her legs. His penis stirred in delight and strained to be free from the confines of silk. He wanted to push himself roughly into her, but held back; waiting was half the pleasure.

'Are you wet for me?' he asked.

'Mmm,' she hummed her assent.

'Are you hot for me?'

'Yes,' she answered in a tortured pant.

'Then show me,' he said grabbing her hips. 'Let me taste you.'

'OK,' she said. 'Taste me!'

With an almost inhuman growl, Peter ripped the panties down. The torn lace flew away in the wind, disappearing over the edge of the building. Her fingers kept up their agonising pace and he watched as her manicured nail rubbed the swollen nub of her clit. Her finger dipped inside her opening. Then, seeing a glint of metal, he licked his lips in playful surprise.

'You've got a piercing,' he said looking at the curved barbell hanging from the top of her arch. 'That excites me very much. I didn't think you would have been that type of girl.'

'What type is that?' she questioned in distraction. Her fingers continued to stroke, moving faster now that the panties no longer pressed into the back of her hand.

'My type,' Peter said.

He took the circular barbell into his lips, and sucked the metal ring in between his teeth. Hallie groaned in encouragement, her fingers stroking faster. Peter sucked his lips fully onto her cunt in an opened-mouth caress. Licking and lapping next to her fingers he pushed his tongue inside her moist velvet lips.

As the movements of his mouth became more pleasurable than those of her fingers, she tore her hand away and shoved them into his dark hair. Pressing at his head more insistently she thrust herself against his probing tongue. His pulled on her ring with his teeth and his tongue delved inside her, stroking keenly at her core. A rumbling growl escaped his lips, reverberating off her flesh like the fine-tuning of a vibrator.

Hallie yelled as she thrust her hips faster and faster. Peter grabbed one of her legs and threw it over his shoulder to better angle her to his searching mouth. She pressed his head into her cunt, smothering him with her slick juices.

He felt her tense in ecstasy then tasted the flow of her desire. He grabbed her hips, refusing to let her back away from his mouth as the pleasure began to shake in her body.

Hallie shouted her climax high into the night. They were surrounded by a city of millions and yet no one would hear her gratified cry. Peter pulled his mouth away with a delighted smirk. As her eyes flew down in wonder to look at him, he licked his lips. Slowly her leg fell back to the ground.

'I told you I could give you pleasure,' he said with a confident smirk.

Hallie grabbed her skirt and tugged it over her hips. She smiled back playfully. 'Thanks, I needed that. Now can I have the key?'

'Oh no,' he said. 'We're not done.'

Peter looked down at his cock, still hard and straining with a violent need.

'I already told you,' Hallie said. 'You are not my problem.'

Peter grunted his denial as he shot up to grab her about the shoulders. He pressed himself into her black skirt. 'I am, if you ever want to get off this roof.'

Hallie grinned wickedly, taking control. Feeling liberated by the delight that still coursed in her veins, she pushed him backwards. Peter grew confused.

'Are you going to push me over the side?' he asked, unconcerned.

'I've thought about it,' Hallie answered coyly.

Peter's back hit the concrete of the building's wall. He placed his arms over the side to hold himself steady. Glancing down at his crotch, he said, 'Well, get the key if you want to leave.'

Hallie pressed her body near him.

'Use your mouth,' he said in a heated whisper.

Hallie drew her face close to his. She could smell the traces of her wetness on his lips. She kissed him, licking her tongue over his teeth.

'Kiss me lower,' he urged.

Her hand found his hard cock. She freed it from its black silk prison. Peter's eyes bored into her, urging as she fondled him. His hips ground into her hand, teased by the warmth of her palm and the contrasting coolness of the night air.

Hallie's torn blouse whipped behind her in the breeze. Her free hand moved over his smooth chest, caressing the rigid folds of muscle. Behind his head was the distant pattern of countless windows, some illuminated, but most as dark as night.

'I see you work out,' she commented with a coy smile.

'Suck me, Hallie,' he said, ignoring her appraisal of his physique and growing more insistent. His used his strength to push her to her knees before him. Holding her steady, he edged his hips to her tauntingly lush lips. 'Suck it, now.'

Hallie spread her knees apart, sensually thrusting her hips in the air as she licked lightly over the taut flesh of his cockhead. Peter's stomach tensed and flexed with excruciating torment. He gripped the ledge for support.

Hallie continued her gentle licks as she grabbed his jeans. Pulling them roughly down, she exposed his balls, smiled at his vulnerable position and took them in her hands. Squeezing gently, she elicited a moan of delight. Then, after trailing her lips over the length of his erection, Hallie took the large tip into her mouth.

Peter felt the moist slickness surround his shaft like the opening of a snug, moist cunt. Her teeth grazed him lightly; her hands stayed with his balls. Gripping the wall, he grimaced in satisfaction as she blew lightly and sucked heavily in turn. Nearly gagging her with his length, he thrust deeper within her throat. Then, as an orgasm approached, he pulled her roughly off.

Hallie looked up in surprise.

'You're much better at that than I would have thought,' Peter said. 'I should have had you beneath my desk rather than on the other side of it.'

'Let me finish it,' Hallie returned huskily. Her eyes were clouded with an aroused light. Opening her mouth, she hissed, 'Give me your cock. I want to make you come.'

'I'll give it to you,' he promised, 'but I don't want your mouth.'

'Then –' she began.

'Get up here and lean over this wall. Look over the edge,' Peter said.

Hallie obeyed. Unconcerned, she teased, 'Are you going to try and push me over?'

'Oh no,' Peter said laughing. 'Not before I've had my fun.' He forcibly spun her to face the stars and her head reeled back on her shoulders. Her vision swam with the wide night sky as the wind embraced her flesh. With a gently insistent push, he urged her head down over the edge of the building. Whispering hotly into her ear, he said, 'I have much more enjoyable tasks in mind for you and this soft body of yours.'

She braced herself more deftly against the concrete, and he came up behind her. Her stomach lurched, torn between the natural fear of being so vulnerably suspended and the excitement of Peter's forbidden touch. The ground became but a black hole beneath her vision, causing the blood to rush in her veins. Only the streetlights sprinkled the ground, bringing light to the darkness by mimicking the starry heavens.

Peter yanked her skirt up then slapped her exposed cheeks before roughly grabbing her hips. His strong fingers journeyed up the small of her back to press her more firmly forwards. Her skin scraped gently over concrete and her hair dangled towards the earth as she looked over the steep, unforgiving edge.

'Where would you like me?' he asked.

She was beyond caring. 'Put it wherever you want.'

Peter chuckled. Taking himself in hand, he rubbed his cock along the crack of her ass. Then, holding her still by force of will, he placed his hand possessively on her hips. With each word he spoke, he rubbed himself against her in a teasing caress.

'Is your cunt wet and hot for me?' he asked.

'Uh-huh,' she answered. She closed her eyes to the drop below.

'Do you want me to ride you with my enormous, hard cock?'

'Yeah.'

'Do you want to be fucked rough and strong?'

'Yes, do it!' Hallie commanded. 'Do it now! Fuck me!'

Peter guided his cock to the opened lips of her moist

pussy. Instinctively knowing she had never taken it in the ass, he decided to begin simply and work his way up to it. The last thing he wanted was for her to back out.

'Hold on to the edge, baby,' he said.

'Do it!' she ordered in frantic persistence. 'Take your giant cock and stick it in me now! Fuck me! Claim me! Ride me hard!'

With stiff confidence he embedded himself deeply within her, prying her apart as he sank the whole of his thickened shaft inside her luxuriously wet passage. He had wanted her since the first moment he saw her in his boardroom, pouring coffee for some investors. And now he'd hit pay dirt.

Hallie bucked and shouted to the stars in noisy rapture before looking down the long drop of the skyscraper's outside wall. Her heart hammered at the dangerous thrill as Peter jabbed inside her, thrusting and pulling with unrestrained vigour. The heavy push of his engorged cock nudged her closer to the edge until her head was flying past the corner, only to be drawn back by the powerful strength of his hands on her hips. The rough stone of the building brushed up against the top curves of her breasts, snagging her lacy bra. The concrete kisses on her erect nipples sent chills over the aching tips to radiate through her.

Peter threw back his head in sheer ecstasy at the dominant force of his possession. His body controlled her passions, pushing her higher with every commanding plunge. Their movements became frenzied as he rode her like a wild man.

Hallie felt her body began to shake. Her stomach lurched and trembled in mounting gratification. Peter held back, taking his orgasm inside of himself so as not to lose his solid erection. He was not done with her yet.

Giving her only a moment to dwell in her pleasure, he moved his finger to the crack of her ass. He kept himself moving deeply inside of her cunt as his fingers sought reaction to his touch. Hallie tried to jerk away from him but he refused. Her body hummed with unsteady pleasure as Peter's thrust slowed by a small degree.

He controlled her completely and grew mad with the power of it. And as her trembling began to subside, he started to pump once more in his frenzied pace. Instantly, Hallie began to quiver in response to his hard persistence. She hollered in wicked delight.

In amazement, she felt her body tighten with a second orgasm. She cried out with the strength of it – the unexpected payoff for risking her life in this wild crazy moment. Her body went numb from the onslaught of pleasure. If not for his hold on her ass, she could be falling over the precipitous edge. With a grunt of approval, Peter again controlled his release, though it was hard not to spurt inside her slick, inviting warmth.

Hallie collapsed in a daze, unable to lift herself off of the building's edge. She mumbled incoherently in satisfaction. Peter slowly withdrew his still hard cock from her. A sly smile formed on his masculine lips. She was exactly where he wanted her to be. Her body was too weakened by pleasure to deny him anything. She was his to do with what he pleased. For this moment, he owned her.

'Peter,' she panted.

'I'm not done with you yet.'

'Give me a second, I can't move,' she begged, laughing. She closed her eyes, no longer concerned with falling over the edge. Her heart hammered in her chest.

'Good,' he said with a swarthy chuckle.

Peter massaged himself gently, enjoying the glide of her slick juices still on his penis. He stroked his hand between her legs until her pussy started to once again grow moist with cream at the attention. He flicked his finger over her sensitive nub until it stiffened with acceptance. Hallie protested weakly, unable to stand on her unsteady feet. Her high heels pressed firmly into the concrete.

He rubbed his cock over her flowing moisture, to ready himself it for penetration. Then, as he heard her moan, he slowly drew the tip of his shaft up her exposed cleft to spread her soft cheeks. With a primal growl he ignored her jolt of surprise as he narrowed in over her untried hole.

He took hold of himself and nudged at her, dipping the tip inside the tight opening. He grunted loudly in approval. Her ass clasped firmly around him like a squeezing vice. Hallie's eyes opened in wonder at the melee of nerves that jumped in response to his forbidden entrance. She didn't expect him to actually claim her in such a taboo way.

Unable to stop him, she tried to relax as she felt him glide a little deeper to break open her second purity. Her insides jumped with the giddiness of a virgin. His cock stretched her mercilessly and Hallie gasped in a combination of wonder and gratification. Hearing her soft pants of excitement, Peter smiled victoriously and eased inside her completely. He huffed in gratification as she tensed and squeezed her canal.

With the aid of her juices he began to move within her, slowly at first and then more insistently when she could not find the words to protest. Feeling the ultimate pleasure of domination, he began to jerk within her. He felt himself losing complete control as he took her. It had been his fantasy to have the proper, conservative Hallie for so long. He wanted to control her, to take her in a way she had never been taken before. She had been his obsession.

Hallie felt a strange, warm feeling spread over her midsection. Her entire form began to tremble in fulfilment as he pounded at her tight core. And then she exploded with a tight-lipped cry of pleasure.

It was too much for Peter, who grunted and released himself inside of her with a howl, coming in hot streaming jets. When he finished, he fell against her back, completely spent, pressing Hallie into the rough stone ledge. Their sweaty skin slid together, cooling in the wind, and Peter pulled his cock from her ass with a slow groan of contentment. Hallie shivered.

Pushing up from the ledge, she turned to him. Her eyes glittered with wicked contentment. Licking her lips as she righted her clothing, she watched him button his fly. When he looked at her it was from under lowered lashes.

'I am sure going to miss you,' Peter said with a lopsided grin. His devilishly black hair fell over his eyes.

'Miss me?' she questioned in alarm. 'Are you firing me?'

'Your promotion came through this morning. You leave for Paris in two weeks.' Peter hummed contentedly as he turned from her. With a smirk, he threw over his shoulder, 'Oh, and you're definitely getting a raise.' He pulled the roof key from his front pocket.

She watched his naked back draw farther away from her. Whistling, he unlocked the thick metal door and disappeared within the dark passageway. The door shut loudly behind him and then all was silent.

Turning back to the ledge, Hallie sighed. A smile came to her lips as she revelled in the rapture of her sated body.

'Goodbye, Peter,' she said, 'I'll miss you, too. Even though I barely got to know you.'

WICKED WORDS ANTHOLOGIES –

THE BEST IN WOMEN'S EROTIC WRITING FROM THE UK AND USA

Really do live up to their title of 'wicked' – Forum

Deliciously sexy and explicitly erotic, *Wicked Words* collections are guaranteed to excite. This immensely popular series is perfect for those who enjoy lust-filled, wildly indulgent sexy stories. The series is a showcase of writing by women at the cutting edge of the genre, pushing the boundaries of unashamed, explicit writing.

The first ten *Wicked Words* collections are now available in eye-catching illustrative covers and, as of this year, we will be publishing themed collections beginning with *Sex in the Office*. If you never got the chance to buy all the books when they were first published, you can now complete your collection and be the envy of your friends! Look out for the colourful covers – guaranteed to stand out from everything else on the erotica shelves – or alternatively order from us direct on our website at www.blacklace-books.co.uk or through cash sales – details overleaf.

Full of action and attitude, humour and hedonism, they are a wonderful contribution to any erotic book collection. Each book contains 15–20 stories. Here's a sampler of what's on offer:

Wicked Words

ISBN 0 352 33363 4
£6.99

- In an elegant, exclusive ladies club, *fin de siècle* fantasies come to life.
- In a dark, primeval forest, a mysterious young woman shapeshifts into a creature of the night.
- In a sleazy midwest motel room, a fetishistic female patrol cop gets dressed for work.

More Wicked Words

ISBN O 352 33487 8
£6.99

- Tasha's in lust with a celebrity chef – it's his temper that drives her wild.
- Reverend Billy Washburn needs salvation from Sister Julie – a teenage temptress who's set him on fire.
- Pearl doesn't want to get married; she just wants sex and blueberry smoothies on her LA poolside patio.

Wicked Words 3

ISBN O 352 33522 X
£6.99

- The seductive dentist – Nick's encounter with sexy Dr May turns into a pretty unorthodox check-up.
- The gender-playing journalist – Kat lusts after male strangers whilst cruising as a gay man.
- The submissive PA – Mandy's new job fulfils her fantasies and reveals her boss's fetish for all things leather.

Wicked Words 4

ISBN O 352 33603 X
£6.99

- Alexia has always fantasised about being Marilyn Monroe. One day a surprise package arrives with a sexy courier.
- Bridget is tired of being a chef. Maybe a little experimentation with a colleague is all she needs to get back her love of food.
- A mysterious woman prowls the back streets of New York, seeking pleasure from the sleaziest corners of the city.

Wicked Words 5

ISBN 0 352 33642 0
£6.99

- Connor the tax auditor gets a shocking surprise when he investigates a client's expenses claim for strap-on sex toys.
- Kate the sexy museum curator allows a buff young graduate to make a thorough excavation of her hidden treasures.
- Melanie the interior designer and porn fan swaps blokes with her best mate and gets up to nasty fun with the builders.

Wicked Words 6

ISBN 0 352 33690 0
£6.99

- Maxine gets turned on selling exquisite lingerie to gentlemen customers.
- Jules is stripped naked and covered in cream when she becomes the birthday cake for her brother's best mate's 30th.
- Elle wears handcuffs for an indecent liaison with a stranger in a motel room.

Wicked Words 7

ISBN 0 352 33743 5
£6.99

- An artist's model wants to be more than just painted, and things get pretty steamy in the studio.
- A bride-to-be pays a clandestine visit to the bathroom with her future father-in-law, and gets much more than she bargained for.
- An uptight MP has his mind (and something else!) blown by a charming young woman of devious intentions.

Wicked Words 8

ISBN O 352 33787 7
£6.99

- Adam the young supermarket assistant cannot believe his luck when a saucy female customer needs his help.
- Lauren's first night at a fetish club brings out the sexy show-off in her when she is required to wear an outrageously daring rubber outfit.
- Cat's fantasies about hunky construction workers come true when they start work opposite her Santa Monica beach house.

Wicked Words 9

ISBN O 352 33860 1

- Sarah gets a surprise when she and her husband go dogging in the local car park.
- The Wytchfinder interrogates a pagan wild woman and finds himself aroused to bursting point.
- Miss Charmond's charm school relies on old-fashioned discipline to keep wayward girls in line.

Wicked Words 10 – The Best of Wicked Words

- An editor's choice of the best, most original stories of the past five years.

Look out for future themed erotic short-story collections at £7.99

May 05 – Sex on Holiday

August 05 – Sex at the Sports Club

November 05 – Sex in Uniform